MW00464001

ALSO BY LEIA STONE

Gilded City

House of Ash and Shadow

House of War and Bone

Kings of Avalier

The Last Dragon King

The Broken Elf King

The Ruthless Fae King

The Forbidden Wolf King

Wolf Girl

Wolf Girl

Lost Girl

Alpha Girl

Mated Girl

Fallen Academy

Fallen Academy: Year One

Fallen Academy: Year Two

Fallen Academy: Year Three

Fallen Academy: Year Four

HOUSE OF WAR AND BONE

LEIA STONE

Bloom books

Copyright © 2024 by Leia Stone
Cover and internal design © 2024 by Sourcebooks
Cover design by Fay Lane
Cover images © vasssaa/Depositphotos, faestock/Depositphotos, Milan/
Adobe Stock, Minicel73/Adobe Stock, Olesia/Adobe Stock, fotoplot/Adobe
Stock, Na.Ko./Adobe Stock, ola-la/Depositphotos, iLexx/iStock

Sourcebooks and the colophon are registered trademarks of
Sourcebooks. Bloom Books is a trademark of Sourcebooks.

All rights reserved. No part of this book may be reproduced in any form or by
any electronic or mechanical means including information storage and retrieval
systems—except in the case of brief quotations embodied in critical articles or
reviews—without permission in writing from its publisher, Sourcebooks.

The characters and events portrayed in this book are fictitious or
are used fictitiously. Any similarity to real persons, living or dead,
is purely coincidental and not intended by the author.

All brand names and product names used in this book are trademarks,
registered trademarks, or trade names of their respective holders. Sourcebooks
is not associated with any product or vendor in this book.

Published by Bloom Books, an imprint of Sourcebooks
P.O. Box 4410, Naperville, Illinois 60567-4410
(630) 961-3900
sourcebooks.com

Originally self-published in 2023 by Leia Stone.

Cataloging-in-Publication data is on file with the Library of Congress.

Printed and bound in the United States of America.
MA 10 9 8 7 6 5 4 3 2

To my mom.
Thank you for letting me
play in the mud with the fairies
and make food for their queen.
I'm convinced you are the reason
I have this gift.

1

FALLON

"Why does the queen want to meet with me?" I asked Master Clarke as I paced his basement-level office during my private elective hour. It had been a full week since Ariyon disappeared, and I was no closer to finding him. I'd even begged Yanric to try to go to him, but my familiar assured me he could only travel to the realms of the dead if it were to find me—or if he died himself. I was working with Master Clarke and Master Hart, but I couldn't replicate whatever I'd done to transport Ariyon and myself to the Realm of Eternity. I'd been barred from going to any further classes until we figured this out. The other students would glare at me as I passed by, so I wasn't keen on going back to school either. They all knew that I had (accidentally) burned down the mansion the dance was being held at and had played a role in Ariyon's disappearance.

"I was not privy to that information, but I imagine it won't be a social call," he said as he used his power to float a piece of paper across the room until it settled before me.

Reaching out, I took it into my gloved hands. Peering down at the new class schedule, I frowned.

Fallon Bane

- *Fae Class: Healer*
- *Year: One*
- *Advisor: Master Clarke*
- *First Period: Energy Sensing (Master Hart)*
- *Second Period: Entry Level Mending (Mrs. Reebus)*
- *Third Period: Practical Applications (Student Clinic)*
- *Lunch*
- *Fourth Period: Fae History 1 (Mrs. Hilton)*
- *Fifth Period: Private Elective with Master Clarke*
- *Sixth Period: Private Elective with Master Hart*

I groaned. "Seriously? I have to go to all new classes?"

I had three classes with Eden right now, and this new schedule would cut that down to one—Fae History.

Master Clarke pinned me with a pointed look. "You traded powers with The Gilded City's most advanced healer. What do you expect me to do with that? Continue to teach you how to conjure flames? I think you have that covered."

'I don't appreciate his tone,' Yanric commented, and my gaze flicked to the side of the room where I spotted my familiar, a large black raven, just outside the window.

"But I don't want to use Ariyon's powers." I hugged my arms to my chest.

I'd majorly screwed up somehow when I'd healed Ariyon. I'd stolen—no, switched—our powers. No more fire and destruction magic for me; Ariyon seemingly had that gift. Instead, I had the Maven healing powers Ariyon was famous for. No matter how I had tried to hide them, everyone knew. These marks on the tops of my hands were a constant reminder of that.

Master Clarke crossed the space and stood before me, forcing me to meet his gaze. I didn't expect to see so much compassion there. He somehow looked older, like the past week had added years to his life. Maybe that was true for all of us. I certainly wasn't sleeping much. His hair had a bit more gray; his face was slightly more weathered in appearance. "You want him back, right? You want to figure out how to fix this?" he asked.

I bristled at his direct question. "More than anything."

"Well, then you have to learn about the new powers you carry so you can figure out how to get back to the Realm of Eternity and bring Ariyon home. In one piece. Alive. And preferably not as a Nightling."

I winced at that last part. When the queen had nearly killed my familiar and sent him to the Realm of Eternity, Yanric had seen Ariyon being arrested. I had then been informed that the only reason he would be arrested was because he now had my powers and was being transferred to the Realm of Rebirth. There, he would fight through some battles or obstacles, and only if he won would he be reborn...as a Nightling. There was zero chance I could let that happen.

"I'm afraid that if I use Ariyon's healing powers, it will take time off his life." I confessed my true reasoning for not wanting to attend the classes.

Master Clarke's lips pulled into a frown. "I see. Listen, Fallon. Maven healers know what they are signing up for when they take the oath. Ariyon knew his life would be cut short. It's the hundreds of lives he will save, the thousands of people he will heal, that give him purpose." He laid a hand on my shoulder. "Maybe you can glean purpose from that too?"

I nodded. Maybe.

'Incoming,' Yanric announced, and I straightened.

"The queen is here," I whispered to Clarke, and he nodded, crossing the room and waiting at the base of the steps.

'Okay, get lost. I'll meet up with you after,' I told my familiar.

'Fine, but I want it noted that I do so with regret. I would very much like to see Queen Soulless again,' he growled.

I covered a grin at the new nickname. *'Complaint noted.'*

The footsteps echoed off the basement walls, and I steeled myself. I had yet to have a pleasant encounter with this woman. Her two Royal Guardsmen arrived first, decked head to toe in the royal armor of The Gilded City. Then came the queen, wearing a sleek and stylish pastel-blue pantsuit. Following her was a fae I didn't recognize, but from the looks of her tattered apron and dirty shoes, she was a fellow Westie.

"It's wonderful to see you, my queen. To what do we owe the pleasure?" Master Clarke bowed deeply.

Queen Solana waved her hand, acknowledging him, and then flicked her wrist to me. "I've been meeting with my council to brainstorm a way to get my nephew back, and they've come up with a fabulous idea." She grinned at me then, and it felt like ice-cold water had been dumped into my veins.

I swallowed hard, bracing myself for whatever she was about to say or do. This woman hated me beyond words right now. All trust was lost, and I knew whatever she was about to say would not be in my favor.

"Misty is a beloved and loyal housekeeper in my palace." Queen Solana motioned to the woman with the apron, and the fae blushed, curtsying deeply. "And she is of low magical talent and therefore a prime candidate to switch powers with Fallon."

Master Clarke and I shared a confused look.

"Switch?" Master Clarke asked, and I was grateful because I felt that the less talking I did around the queen, the better.

Queen Solana nodded, pursing her cherry-red lips. "It's clear that Miss Bane has the power to steal someone's magic and replace it with her own, like she did with Ariyon, and so now she will do it with Misty. I cannot have my greatest healer be a Bane!" She roared the last part, and I flinched.

Ohhh, she wanted me to have Misty's low-grade fae powers and for Misty to be the new Maven healer.

"Umm." Master Clarke looked alarmed at the suggestion. "Not to question your council, my queen, but—"

"I listened to you and schooled the girl," she said, cutting off Master Clarke and pointing a finger at him, "instead of locking her up. Look where that got us!" She snapped a glare at him.

I had to say something. "You seriously think I know how to do that? You think I had any clue what I was doing when I switched with Ariyon?" I laughed, but it was cut short the moment the queen shot me an icy stare. "I just wanted to save his life. I have no idea about the specifics of what happened, and there is zero way I could replicate it," I assured her.

The queen's nostrils flared, and her lips thinned to a line. "Lies," she growled.

I rolled my eyes. "Really? And how many lies have you caught me in?" I removed my glove and held my hand out to her. Both guards stepped closer to me, mistaking this for a threat, but the queen just sighed.

She had used her power on me more than once in an effort to catch me in a lie but had yet to do so. And she knew that even though I had healing power now, it still hurt to be touched. I wouldn't offer this if I were hiding the truth.

"Oh, drop your hand." She waved me off and then started to pace the room. After about a minute, she stopped in front of Clarke. "This could get me dethroned! You think The Gilded City fae are going to put faith in someone who cannot even control one child? It's time to cage her."

A whimper left my throat as my stomach dropped, and I took two large steps backward. Had she built a cage that could hold me already?

'Permission to enter,' Yanric bellowed in my mind.

'Denied,' I shot back. My heart constricted, and a rush of adrenaline shot through me. The idea of being locked up for the rest of my life caused panic to flood my system, and I began to eye the exit. If I somehow got away, maybe I could hide in the outlying towns past Isariah. My childhood hometown was a three-hour walk south, and past that were many more villages and cites in the realm I could disappear in.

Clarke scoffed at the queen. "How will she learn to get Ariyon back if you cage her?"

My heart calmed slightly at that rationale.

The queen pulled a thumbnail to her mouth and began to chew. I'd never seen her so uncomposed and...frazzled. "What do you suggest?"

"Let Master Hart and me work with her on healing—"

Solana barked out a laugh and shot me a glare from across

the room. "Have you cast a spell over this entire school to see you as some deity?"

"No, your majesty. I haven't learned spells yet," I said honestly, and Master Clarke's lips curled.

The queen marched across the room and stood two feet from me, causing the breath to freeze in my throat.

Don't kill me.

'I'm coming in,' Yanric warned.

'Do that and I'll tell Eden to stop sharing snacks with you,' I shot back.

'You're evil.'

I stared at the queen eye to eye as she assessed me, no doubt dreaming up my fate. If I wanted to save myself from a lifetime of being locked up, I was going to have to think of something clever.

I cleared my throat. "Your majesty, if I may offer some suggestions?"

Her eyes narrowed. "You think you're wiser than my council?"

I shook my head. "Of course not, but I do know what it's like to be disliked and have people disapprove of the job I'm doing."

She crossed her arms. "Go on."

"If the fae people are worried about your ability to…control me, I understand that. The fire at the dance was my fault, but—"

"But you saved sixteen students and four staff members when you burned up every single Nightling in attendance," Master Clarke shot back, and I nodded.

"But I did save a lot of people that night," I told the queen. Master Clarke was quick thinking. I needed to talk up my more positive attributes.

"Get to the point, Bane. I don't have all day to chat with you," Queen Solana snapped.

"Right. I propose that I make a public declaration of allegiance to you, to the wonderful people of The Gilded City. I can acknowledge my past mistakes, those of my family, the instability of my magic, and that I'm willing to work hard at my schooling to master my magic. For the good of everyone, including myself."

She raised one well-manicured eyebrow. "And why would anyone believe a Bane would be loyal to anyone but themselves?"

I frowned, feeling desperate at the thought of being locked up forever, but then an idea came to me. "I'll do all of this under the power of your magic. So that I cannot lie."

That elicited a gasp from the queen. "You would publicly declare allegiance to me under a spell that renders you unable to lie?"

I nodded. "One hundred and ten percent. I have no desire to harm you or anyone in this city."

Her body sagged a little, and her face morphed from one of confusion to one of annoyance at my heartfelt answer. She then released a long, pent-up sigh. "Clear the room!" she announced.

Everyone stood in silence for a moment, and she peered back to look at them. "Do not make me repeat myself." Her words were so sharp, they could cut glass.

The maid was the first up the stairs, then Clarke, who cast a worried look over his shoulder, and finally her two guards.

'Permission to—'

'Shut it, Yan!' I warned. That damned overprotective bird was always listening. The queen ran her fingers through her hair, as if tired of this entire thing. "Listen, Fallon, you seem like a decent kid."

I nearly fell backward with shock. She paid me a compliment?

"But"—she held up a finger—"all Banes start out seemingly normal and good until the magic—"

"Takes them over and they become evil. Yes, I've heard this," I groaned.

She pursed her lips. "So, as much as your pledge of loyalty would mean a great deal to calm my people, I worry about when you get your powers back. What about as they grow? What assurance do I have you will still be loyal to me?"

I reached into my brain and willed an answer to come forth, but I couldn't think of anything. "Trust me" didn't seem like it would carry any weight.

I simply shrugged. "All I can do is promise to do everything in my power to bring Ariyon back and switch our powers. Then if I go dark and start doing…evil things, I give you permission to lock me up forever."

She appraised me with a raised chin. "You would go willingly into exile?"

I barked out a dry laugh. "If I start burning down buildings with my friends in them? Yes, in the name of the Light, please lock me up! Why would I want to roam free if I was doing that?"

She rubbed her hands together as if assessing everything we'd spoken about. "I'll bring this up with my council and get word to you about my decision."

I sighed in relief. "Until then, I'm free?"

She simply gave me a curt nod and strode from the room.

I backed up three feet until my back hit the wall, and then I sagged against it. I'd just bought myself some time, but it seemed like the queen had her mind set on my eventual imprisonment. Yanric poofed through the wall in a ball of black shadows and then transformed before me.

'I pray nightly that she chokes on a piece of meat and ends up in the Realm of Eternity,' he stated dramatically.

I chuckled, holding out my arm for him to land on. *'Don't pray that. Because then Ayden would become king at nineteen years old, and I don't think he's keen on that.'*

Master Clarke began to stride down the steps, and I straightened myself. Yanric moved to my shoulder, and I put my glove back on.

Master Clarke shook his head, but he was smiling.

"What?" I asked.

"That was brilliant, but I'm not sure you realize what you're getting yourself into," he said.

"I'm getting myself not locked up for life. That's all I care about."

"I'll be honest, I thought she was going to haul you out of here for a second." He ran a shaky hand through his hair, and I frowned.

"Hey, thanks for sticking up for me like that with her. I mean…seriously, you're the only adult here at school who's on my side, and I really appreciate it."

He appeared nervous at the praise for a moment but gave me a curt nod. "Of course. I'm invested in your success, Fallon. I told you from the beginning, I will not let you go dark under my tutelage."

"So, what have I not realized that I've gotten myself into?"

He winced. "You strive to distance yourself from the Bane family and their dark deeds. Publicly taking responsibility for them and pledging allegiance to the queen as a Bane heir will have every fae in The Gilded City take notice of you."

I swallowed hard.

Crap, I hadn't thought of it that way.

"Well, it's better than being locked up."

He sighed, looking tired. "True. All right, well, you'd best get to class. If you don't figure out how to get Ariyon back, you are assured to spend the rest of your life in a cell."

That was not the kind of pressure I needed, but I nodded and thanked him again, shoving my new schedule in my bag and slipping up the staircase and out the door.

It was time to switch gears. Instead of learning how to control fire and levitate objects, I needed to learn about healing and all things of the Light.

'Ironic,' Yanric observed.

'Shut it,' I told my bird. *'I can be light and good and heal people.'*

'You're going to have to. Otherwise, Ariyon is trapped forever, you end up in a cage, and I'm guessing I end up in this said cage with you.'

No pressure.

2

ARIYON

I WAS ATTRACTED TO FALLON FROM THE MOMENT I LAID EYES on her. She was like a magnet, and I'd been drawn to her from the start, no matter how much I hated it. When I found out she was the daughter of the woman who killed my parents, I loathed myself because I still wanted her. I wanted to touch her a thousand times a day—because *I* could. Me and no one else.

I wanted to know how soft her lips were, what she tasted like. Unfortunately, so did my brother: Ayden, the better half of our twin duo, compassionate and caring, rarely raising his voice or getting angry with me, no matter how much of a dick I was. So when he came home after meeting Fallon for the first time and told me it was love at first sight, I felt like I died inside. I tried to dissuade him with all the reasons I was constantly using to remind myself I shouldn't feel what I felt: she was Marissa Bane's daughter; her mother killed our parents.

I wanted to hate her. If I was being honest, the moment I

found out who she really was I wished Fallon dead. But with every moment I spent around her—seeing Blair activate her curse, watching her cry out in pain, seeing how kind she was, how hard she tried to make me laugh, how self-conscious she was about people knowing who her mother was and judging her for it—my anger transformed to something else.

I wanted to protect her. I wanted to heal her. I wanted to be the one to give her everything that had been denied to her because of her curse.

Watching Ayden date the girl I was falling in love with was one of the hardest things I'd ever had to do. But it was worth it to me if they were both happy. I didn't want them to break up, but I felt like the relationship would run its course. After all, how long could Ayden last without touching the girl he was dating? How long would Fallon be able to handle it? How long would they both last knowing I was the one who could touch her?

On the night of the dance, when Ayden came home and told me he couldn't do it anymore, I knew he had figured it out—he knew I had fallen for Fallon too.

"Go be the one who makes her happy. For both of us," he'd said.

Typical selfless Ayden. But I hadn't hesitated. I couldn't. She drove me crazy, in both good and bad ways, and all I wanted to do was finally kiss her, hold her, feel her body relax into mine like it'd found its missing other half.

I knew being with Fallon would be complicated, maybe even dangerous at times, but I didn't care. It wasn't her fault that her psychotic mother was trying to start a war and kill everyone.

A hard slap rang out across my face, and I gasped, my eyes snapping open.

The Grim.

The Grim?

"Careful, boy. You can get lost in your thoughts down here," the Grim said, eyeing me with concern.

Holy Fae!

Everything came back to me in a rush. Marissa had killed me. I had then woken up here with Fallon standing over my body with Master Healer marks on her hands.

I bolted into a standing position, pulling up my shirt to look at the spot where Marissa had embedded the ax into my chest. There was a smooth, pink puckered scar and the wild beat of my thumping heart. Something felt off, different from the time I had been down here with Fallon's father.

I reached up and grabbed my warm face, pulling at my skin. "I'm physically here?" I asked, my stomach turning sour.

He nodded casually. "Your girlfriend messed up. I told her I'd keep you alive until she could figure out how to transport you back topside."

Oh, Fallon.

How? How had she pulled my soul *and* body to the Realm of Eternity?

"All right. Thanks, I guess," I told him. Slightly awkward to be raised from the dead and yet still be in the place where the dead were laid to rest.

The Grim winced a little. "Don't thank me yet. I had to follow protocol and report you to the Realm of Rebirth. Only thing I could think of to keep you here. Otherwise, you'd start to wither away and die."

Wither away!

Wait, he said the Realm of Rebirth?

I choked on a laugh. The Realm of Rebirth was for Nightlings and whatever dark magic they did to reanimate their bodies, and…

Shock ripped through me. The only reason I would be going to the Realm of Rebirth was if I had the same type of magic that Fallon had. Slowly raising my arms, I stared at the smooth, tan skin on the top of my hands.

No marks.

No healer marks. No master marks. No Maven marks.

Fallon.

She… We…

The Grim nodded. "She switched powers with you to save your life. You're House of Ash and Shadow now for all intents and purposes."

No!

"But—I'm a healer!" I tried to argue, pulling my forearm up to my nostrils and inhaling the skin there.

My gift of scenting magic was gone. I smelled like sweat and salt. Nothing more.

"What are you saying, Grim?" I asked the fae as I took two giant steps backward.

Two male fae popped into view then, assembling their bodies from black smoke and shadows as they loomed over the Grim and stared down at me. One of them had a black mohawk and the other, a red man-bun with a matching beard and snake tattoo on his neck.

Nightlings. Fallen fae of the House of Ash and Shadow—just like I was now.

The Grim gave me a sad smile and stepped to the side as the two fae lunged forward, golden gleaming cuffs in their hands.

It hit me in that moment that I was in the same place as my parents. They died before I had any memory of them—only pictures and stories that my aunt told us—and I wanted to see them, *meet* them, really.

"Grim, let me meet my parents first. Please," I begged.

He looked sad, and I was surprised by the compassion I saw in his eyes. When I'd last seen him, we had fought to the death over Fallon's father, and he hadn't seemed quite so understanding then.

"I cannot allow that. You are no longer dead and therefore cannot exist where they are," he said.

It was like a knife to the heart, to be so close to them and yet denied even a moment together. As heartbroken as I was not to meet my parents, I had to push it aside and survive whatever this was, as the mohawked fae spun me around and the cold bite of metal pinched my wrists as the cuffs clamped in place.

"Where are you taking me?" I yanked against their hold.

One of them balled his knobby hand into a fist and punched me in the jaw, causing black dots to dance at the edges of my vision.

"Don't resist. Or we'll just kill ya," the fae with the snake tattoo on his neck snarled.

The Grim stepped forward and blocked their path. "I would like to take this moment to remind you that you *must* follow the rules set forth by the Accords, lest your realm be shut down and the souls there *disposed of*."

The fae holding me frowned, and I kicked myself for not paying more attention in class. What were the Accords?

"The Accords will be honored," the fae growled.

"Ariyon!" an unfamiliar voice called out behind me.

I spun and blanched when I saw Yanric. Fallon's familiar was lying on the grass, heaving in deep heavy breaths with his wings spread out limp beside him.

He spoke. I heard him speak.

Then he blipped out of existence before I could answer.

"Interesting," the Grim mused.

Before I could open my mouth to ask the Grim how in the fae that was possible and if it meant Fallon was hurt, the fae holding my cuffs yanked me backward, and everything went black.

I spun in the darkness as if I was rolling down an invisible hill, and then my feet slammed into solid ground, the room around me came into focus, and I was greeted by the damp smell of a basement or dungeon. The fae still held my cuffed wrists firmly as he marched me forward without a word. We had landed in a large stone room with various openings into hallways and what looked like a network of tunnels. Along the walls of the large room were shelves with skulls and crystals and other dark artifacts. A desk stood against the farthest wall with two chairs. It was like some morbid office break room.

"Are the cuffs necessary?" I asked. "I won't resist."

The truth was, other than trying to physically grapple with the fae, which was a stupid idea, I couldn't have resisted. I had no idea how to use Fallon's magic yet. Of course, my own magic was more powerful than most knew. I wasn't sure if even my aunt was fully aware of the deadly side of my power. I'd shown my abilities to her a few times, told her what I could do, but I'd hidden some of it. I didn't want to admit that I could make a grown fae's blood boil or that I could force someone's heart to stop or make their brain melt. I didn't want her to know that, although I was one of the greatest healers to have ever lived,

I could also kill a man with a single thought. It was my own dark secret to bear, and one that I feared Fallon now carried. Regardless, I couldn't control the undead even had I had my own magic, so I was at the mercy of these fae until I figured out another way to get out of here.

The redheaded fae with the tatted neck flicked me a glare. The pointed tip of his left ear had been shorn off, leaving a nubbly scarred lobe in its wake.

"Hey, Hawk, pretty boy wants the cuffs off," he told his friend, seemingly aptly named after his hairdo—or he got his hairdo because of his name, which was equally stupid.

Hawk sneered at me, and his nostrils flared. "He smells like House of Ash and Shadow, but he looks familiar." He cocked his head to the side, and my stomach knotted.

If they found out I was the heir to Solana's throne, I was dead. The sound of footsteps drew my attention to the doorway where a dark-haired female had entered the room. She wore the same black military-style uniform as the men, but hers had a golden snake pendant over the bust, signifying some type of authority.

She grinned when she laid eyes on me, and bile rose in my throat at the sight of her sharp, pointed teeth. This fae was bad news. I could feel it in my bones.

"A live one?" she crooned, nostrils flaring.

Although their bodies looked solid, they flickered every so often in some kind of soul glitch. I knew from fighting the Grim that if I reached out and touched her face it would feel real, even though it wasn't. It was one of the million things I couldn't explain about this place.

Somehow, she could tell that my body had joined the journey down here.

"Some kinda screwup," the snake-tatted fae said. "The Grim seemed protective over him. He must be important."

Crap.

I stiffened, and the woman's smile grew larger. "Well, let's identify him so we can get him booked, shall we?"

Identify him?

She strode across the room like an animal stalking prey, and I tilted my chin up to meet her gaze. I didn't care if I was powerless. I wouldn't back down from an attack.

I flinched as she reached up to my face and stroked my cheek.

My head immediately pinched with a sharp pain, and then I felt her presence slithering in my mind like a serpent. I tried to reel back, but she held me by some invisible force at her mercy. Her eyes widened in shock, and then that sadistic smile was back.

"Oh my, you've brought me a jewel beyond value," she crooned. It was like my mind was a file folder and she had sifted through it, looking at whatever she wanted.

Finally, she released me and gave my cheek a little slap.

"Welcome to the Realm of Rebirth, Prince Ariyon Madden of The Gilded City." Her voice had a musical quality to it, but her words made me sick.

The two male fae gasped.

"He's not one of us! He shouldn't be here," Hawk snarled.

She raised her fist, and the man stopped, freezing where he stood.

This woman looked familiar in a way. I couldn't place her, but something about her nagged at my mind.

"He has switched powers with Fallon Bane and therefore must be treated like a Nightling, as he carries our magic. He is now governed by our legal process and will be granted Nightling rebirth if he wins the tribunal," she declared.

I choked on my spit—she knew everything but also things I had no idea about.

Was this what happened when a member of the House of Ash and Shadow died? They were hauled off to a different place and put through a trial, then reanimated into smoke and shadow, feeding on blood and essentially living forever unless killed?

I wanted nothing to do with that. Being a Nightling was literally my *worst* nightmare.

"Legal process?" I wondered how long it would take Fallon to figure out how to get me out of here. She was smart but new to our world, our magic. I didn't even know half the stuff they were talking about, so I knew Fallon would have to dig for information.

I thought of Master Hart and a few books in the library that could help her get back down here, but to pull my body back up to The Gilded City? I wasn't sure that was possible. She broke so many rules when she dragged my mortal form down here.

The woman grinned, saliva glinting off her sharpened teeth. "Yes, Prince Madden. You are hereby entered into the Rebirth Tribunal. Winner gets to go back to their origin of birth. In your case, The Gilded City."

"He doesn't deserve that!" the snake-tatted fae growled.

The woman's smile wasn't dropping, and it was really starting to creep me out.

"And if I lose?" I swallowed hard, my mind going over a hundred scenarios. What was the tribunal? How would I fare in them without my magic? And worst, did I really have Fallon's magic? Fire magic and mental telepathy? These were things I'd envied in Ayden, and now I just wanted the familiar symbols on my hands.

The woman stepped uncomfortably close to me, and the smell of rotting flesh hit my mortal nose. "Well then, my dear, you will either get to stay here and work for me…for eternity… or I will decide to toss you into the Bottomless Pit, and you will cease to exist." She ran her pink-tinged tongue over her sharp teeth, and I shivered.

Okay, I guess I'll be winning the tribunal.

I had no idea what they did here, but from the looks of these hallways and some of the bars in the distance, I was in some type of jail. There was no way I was staying here for eternity or being thrown into the Bottomless Pit.

Since she now had my Maven healer magic, Fallon was literally the only person I knew of who could cross over into this world.

Everyone had wanted her to avoid using her magic before. Now, I would need to harness it to stay alive. And she'd need to figure out mine to get me back home.

3

FALLON

I couldn't figure out if Master Hart was reclusive and odd or just scared of me. He barely made eye contact. His hands shook when he was too close to me, and he stuttered when I asked him a question. Our elective hour was basically him fumbling over what to teach me, knowing I'd accidentally swapped powers with Ariyon and didn't know how to use his magic.

"In your energy-sensing classes, you will learn to see a person's energy field. This can clue you in to any maladies they may suffer from to better help you heal them," he said, not making eye contact.

I stared at him as if willing myself to see his energy, and a slice of terror ripped through me, causing chills to race up my arms.

What the Nightling was that? Was I picking up these feelings from him? Like Ariyon said he did when around someone.

'He's definitely afraid of you. Reclusive and odd, yes, but also terrified,' Yanric informed me, and my heart pinched with guilt.

There were only a few minutes of class left, and I didn't want every encounter with him to be like this.

"Master Hart, can I ask you something personal?"

For the first time, his gaze flicked up to meet mine. There was so much panic in his deep-brown eyes, it knocked the breath out of me. He looked like he wanted to run.

"Wh-wh-what?" he stuttered.

I folded my gloved hands over my lap and gave him the most timid-looking smile I could muster. "Did you know or ever meet my birth mother, Marissa, by any chance?"

His eyes grew wide as he took two steps backward, swallowing hard. He was the same age as Master Clarke, and for all I knew, they went to school together. "I—I, yes, I did." He kept walking backward, the distance between us growing, and a lump formed in my throat.

"Okay, well, I just wanted you to know that I'm not like her. I didn't know her. My father raised me in Isariah and—"

He held up his hand, taking in a deep breath, and then his face contorted into a painful wince. "I—I'm an empath. I feel things very deeply. When I'm near you, it brings memories b-back about M-Marissa. You look just like her. I'm sorry." Then he turned and bolted from the room, the door slamming behind him.

My hand went to cover my mouth as guilt and horror rushed through me. What had Marissa done to him? He could barely stand to be around me. It dawned on me: I looked so much like her, he must feel and remember so much when he was around me. It explained why on the first night I'd met him, the night of the school dance, he'd been so cagey around me.

'Poor thing,' Yanric said.

Anger suddenly flushed through me, fast and hot. Marissa

had left a whole host of problems in her wake, and I was the one having to deal with them.

'*Grr. Marissa and her mistakes are really starting to annoy me,*' I told Yanric.

'*You're going to be late for your library meetup with Ayden and Eden,*' he counseled.

With a sigh, I picked up my bag and sulked the entire way to the library.

I stared at the folded piece of paper with absolute trepidation.

"Are you going to open it?" Eden asked, peering at me from across the table in the school library.

It was the piece of paper Marissa had tried to hand me right before she'd buried an ax in Ariyon's chest. Eden had grabbed it before the building went down and waited until now to give it to me.

Come find me. There is much you need to learn, Marissa had said.

Was it a map to find her? Was it a list of things I didn't know that she felt I needed to?

"Did you open it?" I asked, looking at my best friend.

Eden shook her head, her red curls bouncing with the motion. "I wanted to, but then I thought it might be private… personal. Then I wanted to burn it because screw Marissa Bane and anything she touches. But it's yours to decide what to do with. I thought it might upset you so soon after what happened, so I wasn't sure when to give it to you."

I nodded, appreciating that. Reaching out, I slipped the note into my backpack. "I'm not ready. I need to focus on Ariyon. I don't care about anything else."

Eden reached out and squeezed my gloved hand. "Totally agree. How can I help today?"

Eden had become my fellow researcher. We met every day in the library whenever we had free time. Ayden came most days too, but now that he was the queen's sole living heir, he'd taken over a lot more official duties.

"I need more information on how a Maven healer transports to the Realm of Eternity. Can they do it by themselves or only by carrying a dying person's soul?"

Eden nodded, pulling piles of dusty, leather-bound tomes onto her lap and starting her research.

While she did that, I was going to look more into the magic of the House of Ash and Shadow and what being a Nightling really was all about—the rules, the powers, how they were created. I wanted to know more about this apparent series of fights that Ariyon might be going through right now.

An hour into our reading, Ayden showed up and plopped down beside me. "Sorry I'm late. How can I help?"

I handed him a book titled *Shadow Magic*, and he started reading without complaint.

More time passed before Yanric landed on the table.

'Your dad said dinner will be ready soon,' my familiar announced into my mind.

I slammed the book shut and peered out the window to see that it was getting dark.

"We should call it quits for the day. Find anything good?" I asked our little group.

Eden yawned. "Maven healers are so rare, we don't have as much info as we would like, and what we do have on the Realm of Eternity and the Grim, all deals with a person dying."

Great.

"'A Nightling must drink blood to keep their magic alive; otherwise, it withers away,'" Ayden read, pressing his fingers across the page.

I perked up. No wonder they fed on blood. It wouldn't help us get Ariyon back, but it was interesting. "Anything about Nightlings and the Realm of Rebirth?" I asked.

He shook his head and shut the book, rubbing his eyes. Our normally sunny Ayden had been reduced to a depressed shell of his former self. Without his twin, he was lost, and the guilt of that rested on me like a thousand-pound stone.

Reaching out, I placed a hand on his shoulder. "Ayden, I'm so sorry—"

"Stop, Fallon; it's not your fault. We've been over this. You saved him." Ayden looked at me with determination.

Though we'd tried not long ago to have a romantic relationship, Ayden and I had fully moved into best-friends territory. Eden, Ayden, and I hung out constantly and were there for each other in every way, but there were zero romantic feelings on my end. I was a hundred percent Team Ariyon.

"Okay. I just feel awful," I told him. Though Ayden was right—I did save his life.

He nodded. "I know, but we'll get him back."

Ayden stood, looking at Eden. "Your mom working late at Hummingbird Inn tonight?"

Eden nodded.

"Wanna grab dinner?" he asked.

A blush crept up her cheeks, and she peered at me. I gave her a grin and a subtle nod.

"Sure!" Eden smiled easily at him, and they both wished me good night and left.

Hayes, who Eden had asked to the Winter Belles Ball and who had then ditched her at the last minute, didn't deserve her. And as weird as it might have been for a minute, I really liked the idea of Eden and Ayden together, mostly because I trusted each of them not to hurt the other. Not on purpose, anyway. Sometimes, despite how much you cared for someone, you ended up hurting them.

Like I did with Ariyon.

I blew out a slow breath and then stood, putting the books back where they belonged. *'Tell Dad I'm on my way home,'* I told Yanric.

He was working on his communication magic and was able to transfer short sentences to other people's minds even though they weren't bonded like we were. It was easiest to do with my father and Eden, since he was closer to them—and it helped that they kept him filled with snacks.

I grabbed a few more books I knew Mrs. Silvers wouldn't mind me borrowing and slipped them into my bag before heading out.

The school was closed. The lights were off, and everyone had gone home. Mrs. Silvers had agreed to leave the library open for us, but the door locked behind us when we left.

I walked down the familiar pathway, toward the courtyard where Ariyon had first kissed me. The Gilded City had mild winters, but it was still chilly out, so I pulled my cloak up over my head to cover my ears. When I recognized the archway that led into the secret garden and the place that held Ariyon's art studio, I stopped.

My heart thumped wildly at the memory of finding him here drinking, of seeing the tally marks on the wall that counted the days that had been taken from his life, of the paintings. Suddenly I wanted to see them again, to feel like I was near him. An ache had formed in my chest, and I needed to try to ease it. Ducking into the garden, I walked right up to the door that led to the studio hidden among the flowers and vines.

If it was locked, I wasn't above breaking in. I wanted so badly to see the paintings again, to touch something he'd recently touched. I couldn't explain it, but ever since I'd met Ariyon, it felt like I was pulled in his direction no matter how many times I fought it. He was the only person in the realm who could touch me. It was hard not to feel like he was made for me.

I twisted the knob, and the door squeaked open. I fumbled with the switch until I could get the lights on, and then a sob formed in my throat when I glanced at the easel to my right.

It was new.

Propped on it was a painting of when Ariyon and I were in the broom closet. He'd captured the moment his thumb was pulling down my bottom lip.

I looked to the left of that painting to see another. I was holding hands with Ayden in the lunchroom, and at the back of the room, Ariyon had painted himself, hunched forward and staring at his food as if avoiding looking at us.

I felt like I was violating his privacy by being here, but I couldn't look away. There were so many stories being told here. Months of his artistic talent laid bare for me to see. I pulled off my gloves, shoving them in my pocket, and stroked the painted finger pulling down my lip. Then I peered at the other paintings.

Marissa painted beside me, our likenesses uncanny. The tower that held the queen, tipping forward as I stood beneath it with my palms raised, keeping her airborne.

He saw everything, committed it to memory, and then spent hours painting it with such pristine detail that it made tears leak from the edges of my eyes.

I riffled through a stack of paintings that leaned against the far wall and stilled on one that made my blood run cold.

It must have been done right after he met me.

It was a portrait of my face, but my eyes were black. He had depicted me as a full-blown Nightling with shadows enveloping me from all sides. Was this his greatest fear? That I would become this? And now, he was faced with it himself, something I was pretty sure he never thought possible.

"I'm sorry," I whispered to the room, to his art, to his memories.

Yanric burst through the wall then, a puff of black shadow, before solidifying at my shoulder.

"I'm coming for dinner!" I snapped, wiping at my eyes.

'Okay, sorry. I panicked when I couldn't find you,' Yanric admitted, landing on my shoulder and peering around the room.

'I think he was falling in love with you,' Yanric said as he surveyed the paintings around us, so many of them with me as the main subject.

My heart stopped beating at his words. *'Was?'*

'I didn't mean it like that. It's just that…' he trailed off.

I nodded. *Just that he isn't going to love me after my psycho mother buried an ax in his chest and I sent him to the Realm of Rebirth so that he can come back a Nightling?'*

Yanric winced, ducking his feathered head low. *'You two might have some relationship issues after that, yes.'*

I barked out a laugh. It was too depressing to even think about. *'Let's go home.'*

I exited the art studio, making sure the door was latched behind me, and then ducked out of the archway and back into the courtyard.

'Look out!' Yanric barely had time to warn me before someone reached out and grabbed my bun, yanking me backward.

Pain flared to life along my spine as my curse was activated, but then almost simultaneously, my healing power kicked in to dampen the agony.

I hit the ground hard and then looked up into Blair's face as she loomed over me.

'I can't fly. She's using her powers to freeze me here,' Yanric warned from the ground next to me.

Two others emerged from the dark shadows: Erica and Mindy, Blair's little sidekicks.

"Ariyon was mine," Blair growled between gritted teeth.

'I have the feeling we are about to get a beating.' I felt Yanric struggle, but he was pinned.

Suddenly an unseen force wrapped around my neck, and I was being lifted up off my feet.

'I don't have powers to fight,' I told Yanric as panic rushed through me, causing my heart to skip a beat.

'Guess you'll have to go old school,' Yanric said, as black shadows began to crawl at the girls' feet. Yanric was able to use some of his power at least.

'Old school, how?' I managed to think between my panic.

'Punch her in the face, pull out her hair, kick her. On my signal,' Yanric coached.

A wave of pain rushed through me from Blair's earlier touch, but the marks on my hands glowed and spun as the healing magic dissolved the discomfort. This seemed to enrage Blair.

"I'd be doing the school—no, the entire realm—a favor by… disposing of you!"

Erica and Mindy looked at Blair with shock. "Dude, we said we were going to scare her off, not kill her," Mindy said.

My arms were pinned to my sides, but my legs were free.

Blair shot me a malicious glare. "She killed Ariyon and stole his powers! She deserves death!"

'Now!' Yanric cried, and the shadows at the girls' feet raced up to their faces and wrapped around their eyes, blinding them.

I snapped out with my left foot and connected with Blair's stomach.

She grunted, keeling forward, and the power over Yanric and me dropped. I rushed her, swinging up with my fist, just like I'd learned in weapons class, and it smashed into her nose. Pain exploded between my knuckles, but the satisfying crunch of bone was worth it. Blair's shrill scream rose into the night, and then Yanric unleashed a torrent of bird pecking. He attacked her face like a crazed animal, and she flailed her arms trying to get away from him.

Erica and Mindy took one wide-eyed look at each other and then bolted, wanting nothing to do with my psychotic bird.

A chunk of Blair's blond hair fell to the ground, and I winced.

'Okay, that's enough. Let's go!' I jogged toward the courtyard exit, but Yanric kept on his attack.

'She was going to kill you! I want to disfigure her for life.' He sounded way too happy about his current position.

Blair conjured fire in her hands, and I growled at my bird.

'Let's go! She's got fire, so unless you want to become a ball of burned feathers—'

He backed off and soared through the air over the courtyard

as I took off at a run. Adrenaline rushed through me at the narrow escape, and I peered over my shoulder every few seconds, waiting for Blair to come out with a stream of fire and ignite me, but she stayed put.

I slowed when I reached the guards at the gate and smiled innocently at them. Then I broke into a run again, racing through the West Side gates and down to my street. Finally, I stood, huffing and puffing before my door.

'Holy Fae, that was…' I was at a loss for words.

Yanric stuck out his little pink tongue and licked Blair's blood off his beak. *'Amazing.'*

I shook my head. *'Horrifying, I was going to say. Blair went psycho. Do you really think she would have killed me?'*

'I don't know.' Yan sounded scared.

The door opened, and my dad stood there, frowning. "You're late."

'Not a word of this to Dad,' I warned Yan. My father would never let me leave the house again, and I needed the extra study time in the library to find Ariyon.

"Sorry, Dad. Got hung up at the library." I reached up to smooth my hair and tried to control my breathing, but my father looked suspicious. "Then I went to Ariyon's art studio. Then I ran home to try to make up for lost time."

His face relaxed then. "Any luck with Ariyon?"

I stepped in the house, throwing my book bag in the corner, and sat down to dinner. I told him what we'd learned today about Nightlings needing to feed on blood in order to stay powerful. Then I told him about the queen's threat to cage me. It wasn't something I felt I could avoid with my father, nor should I. It was a real threat that we needed to deal with together.

He chewed his sweet potato casserole slowly as he mulled over my words. "That was smart of you to offer a public apology and all of that, but if she says no? I have a plan."

I raised one eyebrow at my father. "What plan?"

He looked at the front door as if he was double-checking that we were alone. Wiping his mouth with a cloth, he inclined his head down the hallway. "Come here."

I followed him away from the dinner table and to his bedroom.

"Dad, what's…"

He lifted his mattress to reveal a storage cavity where I noticed two backpacks. Each had a bedroll attached to the bottom and empty canteens hooked to the top. "We don't spend much, so I was able to get these with my first coin payment."

A small gasp of surprise escaped me. They looked brand-new and really nice. "Are they what I think they are?"

They looked like runaway bags.

He nodded and set the mattress back over them. "Filled with a pair of clean clothes for each of us, an extra pair of gloves for you, and some cured meats that I'll switch out every month. Just fill the water canteens, put them on our backs, and walk into the woods."

My throat constricted with emotion as I thought about how much thought he'd put into this. "I like it here," I admitted. I didn't want to run away.

He nodded. "Me too. But I'm not so comfortable that I'll sit in a pot of water as it slowly boils me. If it looks like the queen is preparing to imprison you, we leave. I can find labor work anywhere. You can get a job at an apothecary shop in another town. Moonsreach is about three days' walk from here, and I hear nice things about it from travelers who have passed through Isariah."

My eyes felt like they were going to fall out of my head. "You mean we wouldn't leave here and go back to Isariah?"

His lips pulled into a frown as he gazed at me. "First place they would look, hun."

I swallowed hard and then nodded. "Okay, well, I hope it doesn't come to that."

"Me too."

We ate the rest of our dinner in companionable silence, both of us lost in our thoughts about the weight of the queen's decision and how it would affect our lives.

Later that night, I was walking through the hallway back to my room to go to bed when there was a knock at the front door.

My father and I shared a look. It was late, so a knock at this hour couldn't be good.

"Stay here," he warned.

I steeled myself, eyeing the back room where his mattress lay and the two bags he'd packed underneath it. Is this what would eventually come of my life? I'd be on the run? Out in the woods all alone?

"How can I help you?" My father's tone was clipped, and I couldn't see whom he was talking to because I stood in the doorway to my room.

Yanric poofed beside me and landed on my shoulder. *'Queen's Royal Guard is here,'* he warned.

I stepped out of the hallway then, ready to help my dad if they were here to arrest him or something.

"We have a message from Queen Solana for Fallon Bane," the guard said.

I entered the living room and met the guard's gaze. My father peered over his shoulder at me, and I could see from the way he gripped the door handle he was coiled like a snake. He may not have magic, but he would fight to the death to protect me. I knew that.

My heart hammered in my chest. Was this the moment they arrested and caged me for life?

"What is it?" my dad growled.

The guard held out a wax-sealed envelope. My father tried to take it from him, but the guard snatched it away. "I have strict orders to give this to Fallon Bane!" the guard snapped.

My father narrowed his eyes. "Well, my daughter isn't wearing her gloves, and I have strict orders to protect her from being touched. You will hand me that envelope or you will have to leave and report to your queen that you were unable to complete your job."

Whoa.

My dad never got mad, but he'd totally put the guard in his place. He was right. I was just about to go to bed and didn't wear my gloves to sleep.

The man's nostrils flared, but he handed the envelope to my dad, who in turn gently handed it to me, only grasping the edge so that we wouldn't touch.

"Is that all?" my father asked the guard.

The man nodded, and then my dad shut the door in his face.

I burst out laughing. "Dad!"

He shrugged as he locked the door. "You don't knock on a man's door this late at night and boss him around and expect to be treated like a king. What does it say?"

I peered at the red-and-gold-swirled wax seal with a flame emblem and gulped. Maybe it said I would be imprisoned tomorrow or next week.

With a shaky hand, I cracked the seal and peeled open the

envelope. Pulling out a handwritten note, I steeled myself and read it.

Fallon,

My council appreciates your desire to take responsibility for your ancestor's past mistakes and pledge your allegiance to me. I have approved this request. Before doing so in a public setting, you will sign the below agreement so that I know you are serious.

    My demands:

• You will legally change your family name from Brookshire to Bane.
• You will take up residence at Bane Manor on Raven Hill. Your father is permitted to live with you.
• You will follow a 10:00 p.m. curfew, NO MATTER WHAT, and be inside your residence each night at this hour.
• You agree to be forever locked in Bane Manor if you show ANY evidence of going dark.
• You are legally bound to this agreement upon signature. To break this contract would normally result in your death, but since I cannot do that without killing my heir, instead I will kill your father if you betray me.

Fallon Bane Signature _____

In duty to the Light,
Queen Solana Madden

P.S. Ayden insisted you have Ember so that you can get from Bane Manor to school on time. It's on loan until Ariyon comes back.

My head swam with her list of demands. Change my name? Forever be locked in Bane Manor if I go dark? It hit me then: the cage that she was building was Bane Manor.

"What does it say?" my dad asked again, peering at the paper as if he wanted to read it.

I folded it quickly and plastered on a fake smile. "She approved my request to publicly take responsibly for the Bane family and pledge my allegiance to her."

My dad frowned. "But?"

I sighed. "But she wants me to change my family name to Bane, and we will need to move into the old Bane family manor."

"The what?" My father craned his neck out as if he hadn't heard me.

Oh yeah. I don't think I ever mentioned its existence to him.

"The Bane family is royalty. Therefore, they have a fancy mansion on the East Side. The queen wants me to live there and keep a curfew."

His eyes narrowed. "Why? Why wouldn't she want us to stay here?"

I didn't want to lie to him, but I didn't want him to know I was about to move into my eventual prison and that if we didn't, she would kill him.

I shrugged. "Maybe the same reason she wants me to change my last name. If I am to take responsibly for the Banes, I need to start living like one?"

It was a feeble attempt to explain things, but we were both tired, and so he nodded.

"Well, we can figure it out. I'll leave early to make it to work in time. I imagine it's quite a walk if it's on the East Side."

'It would take him about twenty-five minutes,' Yanric said.

I frowned. *'How would you know that?'*

He didn't answer.

"Yeah, I'm getting a horse so we can figure it out," I told him. If Ayden advocated for me to have a horse, it meant he was in on this council meeting. For all I knew, he was on the queen's council all the time.

My dad let out a deep yawn. "Okay, kiddo, let's get some sleep."

I followed him back to our rooms, waving good night as he went to his own, and then shut the door. Walking over to my desk, I signed the contract, rolled it up, and handed it to Yanric. *'Can you fly this to the queen? I want to make sure she knows I'm cooperating.'*

He glared at me. *'Sure. And if I suddenly lose control of my bowels while I'm near her, oops.'*

I laughed and reached out to scratch the space under his neck as he took the paper into his beak. I opened the window for him.

'Yan?' I asked as he hopped up on the windowsill.

He looked back at me.

'How do you know how far Bane Manor is?'

Sadness crept over his features then. *'Because it's where I was born eighteen years ago and where I waited…alone until you finally came to The Gilded City.'*

My heart tore open then. I hadn't realized Yanric was born at the same time as me and that he'd waited for me alone all these years.

Yanric Bane, at your service.

I thought of his excitement at seeing me that first day at The Academy. He had been waiting for me. He was abandoned just like I was, but he didn't have a dad to adopt him like I did.

Reaching out, I grabbed him and brought him to my chest, squeezing him harder than I should have. *I'm so sorry I took so long.'*

My heart swelled with love for the little murderous creature. *'You are forgiven, Fallon Bane.'*

With that, he flew from my bedroom window and sealed my fate with the queen. I was about to admit to all the residents of The Gilded City that I was responsible for the mistakes of my ancestors. Whether that was a good idea remained unseen.

4

ARIYON

I HAD LEARNED A LOT OVER THE PAST DAY OR SO. THE TRIBUNAL was a series of fights. The House of Ash and Shadow believed that only its strongest should be allowed rebirth, and I had to prove my strength in combat. I was fighting every day, sometimes a couple times a day. From what I could gather—and this really screwed with my mind—the Realm of Rebirth was where the soul bodies of the Nightlings went when they were in shadow form up top, which was a lot of the time. Then, when they were absent here, their body was present topside in the real world. It was both horrifying and impressive, actually, to think of creatures who could transcend dimensions so easily like that. It didn't seem that they necessarily had to be in one place or the other but that they preferred it to whatever darkness awaited their soul when they were in shadow form topside. Even more terrifying was that I knew that meant the time would come when Marissa Bane would get word that I was here, and she would no doubt want to see me. I found myself wondering if I could kill her here. Permanently. Maybe they would pit us against each other in a fight. It seemed I was fighting a whole host of random Nightlings. Some came in chains, like me, and others seemed to work or live here or just be passing through before poofing topside into the real world.

In The Gilded City, you were innocent until proven guilty. Here, you were locked up until you proved yourself worthy to be let out. From what I could tell, based on the guards talking, there was a city outside the prison and some mountain ranges but little else. And they were all bound by the rules of these Accords, lest they be basically incinerated out of existence. They took laws and rules very seriously here, which was the only reason I was alive.

Snake-tatted fae with the red hair, who I'd come to learn was named Maze, walked over to my cell door with a grin.

"Pretty boy, you have a guest," he said.

I looked up from the bed where I'd been resting my broken ribs and, for the hundredth time, wished I had my healing powers. Was this what it felt like to be Ayden, Fallon, any of them? It sucked. Ongoing pain, without any relief in sight, sucked.

He waved me over. I sat up, wincing at the sharp stab in my side. I needed to learn Fallon's powers ASAP, or I was a dead man. They were toying with me at this point, laughing as they punched or kicked me, but I knew they had powers and they would start to use them. I'd lost my last two fights to forfeiture, and I had no idea what that meant for my overall score.

It wasn't good.

As he led me somewhere, I walked with a bit of a limp but tried to cover it.

Maze grinned. "You're weaker than I thought."

I growled but said nothing. If I had my powers, I'd liquify his insides and make him crap them out.

We turned a corner, and I stopped dead when I saw her sitting in a chair. Long, glossy black hair over one shoulder, startling green eyes. Not a day over nineteen. She looked so much like Fallon, my stomach knotted up, and an ache formed in my chest.

"Hello, Marissa." I played it cool. She couldn't kill me here. I was under some weird accord the Light and the Grim had with these evil bastards.

She raised one eyebrow and smiled. I was shocked to find that her eyes were green here, not black. "So it's true." Her gaze slowly raked down my body, and shivers ran the length of my spine. When her yellow-spotted snake familiar popped out of her shirt and coiled loosely at her throat like a necklace, my jaw clenched.

"You know I heard snake meat tastes really good battered and fried." I was going to say all the things I wanted to say to her, and she wasn't going to do anything about it.

The snake hissed, and Marissa's nostrils flared. "I heard you're losing," she shot back.

I shrugged. "Or waiting to unleash my dark powers and kill everyone."

She grinned. "You know, in another lifetime, I could have liked you."

"Gross." I made a fake retching motion.

Marissa stood, walked over to me, and peered at the tops of my hands. She looked pleased and nodded to her snake as if they were sharing some unsaid conversation. "I'm delighted to see Fallon is growing in her power, even without a decent tutor."

She was excited to see that Fallon had dragged me down here

and switched our magic? Of course she was. Because it *did* show power. But what did she care?

"She'll never fight for you," I told her.

Fallon was a good person; she would always do the right thing.

Marissa nodded. "I don't need her to."

That caused a frown to pull at my lips. What *did* she need from her daughter? Nothing, I hoped.

She turned on her heel then and walked over to the female fae with the serrated teeth. Her name was Amethyst, and I still couldn't figure out why she looked familiar. Again, I wished I'd paid better attention in school. She was no doubt in my history lessons. Amethyst was in charge down here but didn't frequent the cells or the fights. From what I could tell, she wasn't a Nightling in the sense that she didn't poof into her shadow form and go back to earth. Some of them just stayed here, never having been given the power to be reborn, or not wanting to.

"Is it true he has Fallon's power?" Marissa asked Amethyst loudly enough that I could clearly hear.

The serrated-toothed fae nodded. "You smelled it on him, I'm sure."

She could smell magic? That was interesting.

Marissa flicked her gaze to me and then peered back at the female fae. "I smell his mortal body, which shouldn't be here. So what happens to my daughter if he dies down here in one of the fights?"

Maybe that's why they were going easy on me—they weren't sure what would happen if they killed me. Neither did I. Would I go to the Realm of Eternity? Or would I end up back here? Or, worse, would I cease to exist? There was no protocol for mortals entering the realms of the dead.

Amethyst clicked her tongue. "Theoretically, Fallon's power would flow back to her upon his death."

Marissa raised one eyebrow. "Theoretically? Mother, I must be sure."

Mother. It was like I'd been punched in the gut. The psycho with the serrated teeth was Marissa's mom. Fallon's grandmother! That's why she looked familiar. Bile rose up my throat as I fought for composure.

Amethyst gave Marissa a stern look. "Have you ever switched powers with another?"

Marissa swallowed hard, lowering her head. "No."

Amethyst nodded. "I have. Dozens of times in my life. When the host dies, the powers return to the master. Though it's never been done when the host is in the Realm of Rebirth and the master is topside."

Host. Master. Those words made my skin crawl. As if Fallon were some parasite feeding on my magic.

Marissa nodded. "Very well. Let's kill him already so my daughter can get her magic back. I need her at full strength."

Amethyst nodded, reaching out to stroke Marissa's cheek. "Yes, dear."

Chills rushed up my arms at how casually they spoke of killing me. I didn't like the way Marissa had spoken about Fallon and needing her at full strength.

Before I could tell Marissa to stay the hell away from Fallon, the dreaded fighting bell rang throughout the halls. Cheers and whoops of excitement filled the stone hallway. My fellow prisoners loved watching the fights. They loved seeing me get my butt whooped.

With a sigh, I allowed Maze to escort me to the main hall.

I was kept away from the other prisoners, and all meals were brought to my room since I was the only one down here who needed to eat. Light knew where they were getting food from, but I'd gathered that they had to keep me alive unless I was killed during one of the tribunal fights.

Deep chants started as I stepped into the wide-open room. The ceiling and floor were made of stone, and the room was surrounded by iron bars at the sides, behind which were cells, each with a prisoner inside. In the center was the roped-off fighting ring. They'd pick random inmates to fight me. It was typical boxing-style rules: if you didn't get up for a ten-second count, you were considered the loser, or you could tap out. But you could also "die" and fail, something they'd spoken about, but I wasn't sure how that worked. How would one of these fae die if they were already dead? I had yet to kill one and find out. These rules all seemed to be within the Accords, something I prayed nightly I could get my hands on.

Marissa entered the fighting ring with Amethyst, and I swallowed hard, thinking about what she'd just said, how she wanted to kill me quickly so that Fallon could have her power back. I peered down at my palms and willed the purple Undying Fire to reveal itself, but there was nothing. When a giant fae, who stood a head taller than me and was much wider, stepped into the ring, I sighed. I'd come to terms with my eventual early death when I was five years old. As morbid as that sounded, it was true. Mavens died early. It was a curse we carried, the price to pay for saving so many lives. I was okay if today was my day to die, but I was not okay with being stuck here in this crap hole for eternity. I prayed to the Light that if my soul's flame were to go out today, I would end up in the

Realm of Eternity with my parents. But I would not go quietly; it wasn't the Madden way.

Rolling out my neck, I gave myself a little pep talk.

I am the son of Arkin Madden, nephew of a reigning queen. If anyone can survive this, it's me.

I shook out my palms, dipping under the ropes and praying to the Light that the most destructive of Fallon's magic would empower me now. My aunt had said that Fallon turned a guard's fae blade to ash. I needed that so I could use it on this guy's head.

Marissa walked up to the edge of the ring and grinned at the giant fae before me. She gave him a nod, and the fight bell rang again, this time signaling the beginning of our match. I was told I had to fight for up to forty days before being granted the honor of rebirth. I was on day four or five. With multiple fights a day and sleeping at weird hours, I had lost count.

The giant beast of a fae rushed toward me, and I used my smaller stature and speed to duck and sidestep him. Despite me pivoting to the side, he used his long reach and crashed his fist into my jaw.

Pain exploded in my cheek and rage washed over me. I couldn't take in a deep breath because of the aching in my ribs, and now I wasn't going to be able to chew. Assuming I survived this.

"Kill him!" Marissa snapped at the fae.

I'd gotten the impression that, the past few days, they'd been toying with me, keeping me alive until they could reach a consensus on what to do with me. Maybe they had been waiting for Marissa to come or to find out what would happen to Fallon's powers if I died. The conversation I'd heard earlier had clearly been them agreeing on a path forward, which meant me dying.

When the giant fae swung again and hit me square in the ribs, I cried out in pain, the agony threatening to make me pass out. I wasn't used to prolonged pain. Anytime I got hurt, I just healed myself. If I took on someone else's pain in a healing, it was a short-lived thing. This was awful, days on end of throbbing, stinging, and aching. Being punched in my already-broken ribs was too much to bear. I had to make that bastard pay.

I snapped out with my foot, kicking him in the balls and dropping him to the ground. I wasn't above fighting dirty. The crowd went wild at my cheap shot. They loved it—of course they did. I growled as I tried to suck in a breath but was met with more pain.

The fae looked up at me with murder in his eyes, and black shadows, like two ropes, extended from his palms as he stood— and that's when true fear that I might die ran through me.

Oh fae.

I was really starting to get pissed off about my circumstances. I knew Fallon's power worked off anger. I'd seen her go crazy at the dance after Marissa had tried to kill me. I worked my whole life to contain my anger at the world—for having to grow up without parents, for having to die young, for being born into a duty and crown I never asked for. There was so much to be angry about. To be honest, I was scared to succumb to that rage, but I knew if I wanted to ignite Fallon's powers and survive this, I'd have to let the beast out of its cage. No more alcohol to numb the pain, no more losing myself in my art—I had to finally allow myself to feel in order to embrace this dark magic. I could sense it, just under my skin, like the hum of the Gilded City gates. A live wire waiting to be touched.

As the fae before me cracked the black, whiplike ropes, my gaze flicked to Marissa.

"Marissa!" I bellowed. "*I* will be the one to kill you one day," I vowed, and unleashed every homicidal thought I'd had for the woman since I was five years old and was told about my parents' death. My aunt Solana had pointed to the portrait of my mom and dad holding Ayden and me, smiling down at us with pure joy. We were the light of their life, she had said. But someone took them early. Someone hateful and sick and jealous. Someone named Marissa Bane.

Marissa tipped her head back and laughed as if I were a small child having a tantrum just as the fae flicked his wrists in my direction, and that's when I opened the floodgates.

Unbridled rage like I'd never felt before filled my body from head to toe like a searing fire, and I reached out and caught the tips of the black ropes before they could wrap about my neck. The pain barely registered, a dull ache on my palms, before an invisible power spread out of my fingertips and flared to life along the ropes, consuming them and turning them to ash.

The fae who held the black cords paled as the destructive magic came for him. He shook his palms, trying to dislodge the dark magic he'd conjured, but it was of no use. I watched partly fascinated, partly horrified as the all-consuming magic began to eat at his fingertips.

"No!" a female fae with dark-blue hair and yellow eyes screamed as she rushed forward, but Marissa held her back. I flicked my gaze to the woman who had given birth to Fallon. Her head was cocked to the side, and she wore a slight grin. She was looking at me with…pride? I had just ashed a guy, sending him Light knows where, and she was proud? Of course she was—this was Fallon's magic. She must take some kind of credit for this.

The ash had crawled up the fae's entire body and was now

about to cover his face. He screamed, a horrible, garbled sound, and then he was just a pile of dust. Vomit lurched up my throat, and I turned my head and spewed over the side of the ropes as the crowd cheered and laughed.

Oh Light, what had I done?

5

FALLON

EDEN WAS WAITING FOR ME THE NEXT MORNING WITH HER backpack slung loosely over her shoulder. On our walk to school, I filled her in on everything that had happened since we'd parted ways the previous night. I started with my meeting with the queen and then launched into my fight with Blair.

"That bitch!" she roared when I told her about Blair and her friends attacking me. Actual smoke wafted from her nostrils, and I skidded to a stop.

"I'm okay." I placed a gloved hand on each of her shoulders. The moment I touched her, even with gloves on, a massive headache slammed into me, and I winced. Yanking my hands back, I grabbed my skull, but then the ache disappeared.

"What was that?" she asked, concern etched across her features.

I frowned. "Nothing. I just had a massive headache for a second." Eden's mouth popped open, and she took a step back from me. Her surprise shifted to a grin. "Holy Fae, Fallon, I've had a headache all morning. I think you…picked up on it."

I stared at my gloved hands. "I did?"

It hit me then—this was what happened to Ariyon when he was near sick people. He'd said he had a compulsion to heal them because he could *feel* their pain.

A lump formed in my throat. I needed to find him. Things weren't moving fast enough, and I worried about what they were doing to him down there.

"I guess I'm figuring out the healing powers."

Eden nodded. "Which brings us one step closer to finding Ariyon. Listen, did Yanric remove Blair's nose? That's all I need to know." Her hands balled to fists.

I chuckled. "No, but I'm pretty sure I broke it, and she's missing some hair because of him."

And half an eyebrow,' Yanric confessed as he landed on Eden's shoulder.

She heard that too because she grinned and gave him a fist bump. "Well done."

"So…there's one final thing I need to tell you," I said, hesitating.

Students passed by us on their way to The Academy as we lingered. Yanric flew for a nearby tree, no doubt giving me a semblance of privacy but still listening in.

Eden's freckled face peered at me with concern. "What's up?"

I chewed on my bottom lip. "The queen got back to me last night and approved my idea to give a public apology and pledge my allegiance to her."

Eden's face brightened. "Awesome. That will keep her happy and you out of a cage, right?"

I pursed my lips. "Yeah…"

Eden's brows knotted. "But?"

I blew air through my lips and swallowed hard. "But it came with some rules."

I rattled off all the rules, including the one where if I was going dark, I would be imprisoned in Bane Manor forever, and the threat to my dad. I had to tell someone; it was eating me alive.

"We won't be neighbors anymore?" Actual tears lined Eden's eyes, and my heart sank into my stomach.

"I know."

"The queen needs to get this stick out of her butt. You saved her life at the midterm exams!" Eden roared.

I had saved her. It was one of the scenes Ariyon had painted of me. When Nightlings had taken over the cannons at the midterm exam. Instead of using the cardboard our teachers had fired at us to test our skills, they'd filled the cannons with metal discs. I had been able to hover the tower as it fell with the queen in it, saving her, though not the guard who had been with her, unfortunately.

A few passersby glanced our way, and I gave a bark of nervous laughter.

"E, listen. It sounds like she's making this cage for me whether I comply or not. Following her rules will keep me in her good graces and keep those I love safe. I gotta do it."

She reached out and grasped my hand. "You're right."

The headache slammed into me again, and I winced, but this time, I envisioned the well of magic inside me, Ariyon's magic, flowing toward the source of the pain in my head and taking it away.

My hands heated inside my gloves, no doubt those wheels spinning, and the headache vanished.

Eden gave a sigh of relief. "Hey, thanks for that."

I dipped my chin in response. "I just wish I knew if I was pulling days off my life or Ariyon's when I heal people."

That topic put an even bigger damper on the mood, and we walked the rest of the way to class in silence.

Energy sensing with Master Hart was awkward. I sat at the back of the class and avoided him at all costs. I made a mental note to try to find out what Marissa had done to him because at this rate, I wasn't going to learn anything from him. He still couldn't even make eye contact with me.

My next hour was with Mrs. Reebus. She was a stout woman with curly red hair and a large bust. Other than casting me a few nervous glances when I entered, she didn't seem bothered by my presence, so I was taking that as a win.

There were only four other students in my class, and when I inquired about the low number, I was told that healers were so rare that there weren't enough to fill a regular class. It made me feel even more guilty that Ariyon was gone. They needed him and his healing, and instead they were stuck with me. They were teaching a newbie healer from scratch, even though I had advanced healing marks on my hands.

"Depending on your manifested healing ability, you might want to heal a cut, bruise, or headache differently than a fellow student would. Some might infuse their magic into a tincture, while others might want to try a direct hands-on healing approach. Learning your magic's ability and what it is capable of will be of the most use to the school and The Gilded City at large," Mrs. Reebus said.

Interesting. Kind of like how Avis infused her powers into tinctures and salves but Ariyon and Hayes went for a direct hands-on healing approach.

I jotted that down in my notebook.

"In Practical Applications, you will get the chance to try out what feels most natural. If you are a hands-on healer, you will receive marks on the tops of your hands." She indicated one male student with black hair, who waved shyly. Sure enough, there were two circles on the backs of his hands with one tiny symbol in the center.

"If you are more inclined to infuse your magic, like I am," she continued, gesturing to a desk full of dried herbs and jars, "you do not get the visible marks."

Another interesting thing to note that explained why Avis didn't have healer marks.

A girl with short cropped blond hair and black-rimmed glasses shot her hand into the air.

Mrs. Reebus nodded. "Azalea?"

"Is it true the queen only takes you on her healing staff if you can hands-on heal?"

The teacher nodded. "That's true, but she purchases hundreds of healing remedies from a long list of local apothecaries for her staff and Royal Guard each month, so there is a strong possibility you will still be in service to her."

That reminded me of when Queen Solana ordered all those tinctures that day she came into Avis's shop.

The girl, Azalea, looked relieved at that.

Mrs. Reebus spent the rest of the class teaching the basics of mending swelling through both infusing and a hands-on approach. It all felt like a foreign language to me at this point, but I was hoping something would pop out that would help me get Ariyon back.

In Practical Applications, I was surprised to see that Hayes was in charge of the student-run clinic. I hadn't forgiven the bastard for ditching Eden before the dance, and he still blamed me for Ariyon's disappearance, so this was going to be an interesting hour.

It got even more interesting when Blair walked in with two black eyes and a crooked nose and, sure enough, missing half of an eyebrow.

It took every ounce of willpower I had not to grin when she made eye contact with me. I didn't relish hurting someone, but she had been trying to kill me, so I had zero regrets about breaking her nose.

"Whoa, what happened to you?" Hayes walked right up to her, and she glared at me.

I stared back, willing her to tell everyone I attacked her so I could tell them that she'd threatened to kill me.

"I fell. Can you fix it?" she growled.

"Yeah, come on back." Hayes guided her to a bed in the back, and the rest of the students, seven of us in all, stood around as Hayes healed her. He was a good teacher, I had to admit. He described each thing he did in order. Inflammation first. Then blood vessels. Then tissue damage. Then bone.

"The eyebrow hair is going to have to grow back on its own," he informed her. "All this from a fall?"

She looked horrified at that but nodded.

After she left, we waited around, but no one else came.

"So, you wait around all day hoping for sick people to come in to train on?" I asked.

Hayes nodded. "Most people on the East Side have tinctures at home, so it's rare we get cases that aren't just other students."

I frowned. "The clinic on the West Side is overflowing with sick people."

Hayes shrugged. "I didn't make the rules."

"But you sure know how to follow them," I spat.

I didn't care if he was Ariyon's best friend. Hayes dumped Eden an hour before the dance. He was dead to me.

He just rolled his eyes and gave me his back.

Jerk.

By the time lunch rolled around, I was super excited to see my bestie. After grabbing a salad from the cafeteria, I met her on the lawn. The second she saw me, she waved a piece of paper in my face and squealed. Yanric sat atop her shoulder, eating crumbs she fed him.

"What?" I tried to peer at the paper, but she was shaking it like crazy.

She handed it to me, heaving in and out, hyperventilating.

Eden Westcourt,

It is with great honor that Queen Solana invites you to be a member of the Junior Royal Brigade next year. She was impressed with your abilities at the midterms, and it is her hope that one day you will serve in her personal Royal Guard.

Secretary to Her Royal Highness,
Maxwell Bishop

I smiled at my friend and handed her back the note. "Congrats!" I'd forgotten that the students who were unable to showcase their skills had already made up their midterm, and the queen was sending out invites to her top choices for Junior Royal Brigade.

Eden took the paper from me, but then the grin was wiped off her face. "Wait, crap. I'm totally excited about serving under the psycho that wants to imprison you. I should say no."

I waved her off. "Nah, honestly, Solana isn't that bad. She's just trying to do what's best for her people."

It was true. Although she'd been pretty awful to me, she had reason to be. My mother had killed her brother and sister-in-law, and I'd gotten her heir and nephew stuck in the Realm of Rebirth. She was doing the best she could. I understood that.

Eden opened her mouth to respond when her gaze drew upward, to someone who stood behind me.

She gasped, and I spun to see a member of the Royal Guard. He held a note out to me with my name scrawled on the front.

I plucked it from him with my gloved hand and willed my heart to chill the fae out. It was frantically beating in my chest as I peered at the queen's wax seal, identical to the one from last night's letter.

"Fallon, only those invited to the brigade are getting envelopes today," Eden whispered.

There was no way. She wouldn't. I didn't even have my own powers.

My mouth went bone dry as the guard walked away, and I ripped open the note. People were staring, no doubt wondering—as I was—if there had been some mistake.

Fallon Bane,

The queen and her council were delighted to receive your signed contract last night, although the bird feces stuck to the paper was not appreciated. It has been discussed and agreed that if you are able to restore Ariyon Madden to his former self, with his Maven healing powers intact, and you have your own magic back, there will be a spot on the Junior Royal Brigade waiting for you.

Secretary to Her Royal Highness,
Maxwell Bishop

'Bird feces!'

Yanric cackled maniacally in my head, and I shot my familiar a glare.

"Holy Fae!" Eden read over my shoulder. "We're going to be in the brigade together!"

"*If* I get Ariyon back," I hedged, guilt worming its way through me. I wanted to be excited about the invite into the brigade. It meant that I was a powerful warrior and had impressed the queen at the midterms, which I would have hoped, considering I saved her life. But it also meant she might be starting to trust me, to see me as a normal Gilded City citizen. In the meantime, though, I'd still lost her nephew—the love of my life—to the Realm of Rebirth.

"You will. I got Master Hart to get us approval to look in the rare editions library in the basement. We have to have a chaperone, but Master Clarke said he would do it after school today while he's grading papers. We're bound to find something there."

Rare editions? That sounded promising. I peered around the courtyard and couldn't help but see that Ariyon was missing. He should be here eating with us right now.

"Okay. Yeah." It felt wrong to just go on with life and eat my lunch like Ariyon wasn't fighting for his life right now in the Realm of Rebirth.

If he became a Nightling, he was never going to forgive me. Which meant I was totally going to die with my purity.

"Hello?" Eden waved her hand in front of my face. "Fallon." I shook myself. "Sorry, what?"

She was grinning. "Have you seen Blair today? She looks like she got trampled by a horse."

Yanric snickered in my head.

I grinned a little at that. "She came to Hayes for healing, but he couldn't make her eyebrow grow back."

Yanric's snicker turned into a full-on evil cackle. *'She will think twice before coming after us again.'*

He must have said that to Eden too because her smile faltered. "Or her hatred will grow and, with it, a deep-seated desire for revenge. Just be careful, okay?"

I nodded.

'Next time I'll take her tongue. Try to grow that back,' Yanric sneered.

'Okay, calm down, murder bird.' I shot Yanric a look that said to chill, and he ruffled his feathers and flew off.

The rest of the day passed quickly, and soon I was heading to Avis Apothecary. I was still working off my debt from when I'd broken in and stolen tinctures to try to heal my father and again when she'd given me help when he'd been injured at work. There wasn't much to pay back now, and she had agreed to hire me permanently three days a week until I graduated. I'd been upgraded from cleaning and dusting to actually helping her dry and bottle herbs.

"Hey, Avis," I chimed as I stepped into the shop.

She was speaking with someone at the counter, and when they turned around, I frowned. It was Hayes.

What is he doing here?

Avis muttered something to him, and he left.

As he passed me, neither of us said a word to the other.

"What was he doing here?" I growled as I walked up to the counter.

Avis had her long brown hair, streaked through with a few grays, tied into a side braid and draped over one shoulder. She'd been grinding herbs of some sort, the pestle lying abandoned to the side, as she leaned in to speak in a low voice.

"Seems someone put a bug in his ear today about the overflow of people from the clinic on the West Side needing healers."

I scowled at the door. What did Hayes care about the West Side? Though I'd hoped The Gilded City would have been more enlightened when I'd arrived here a few months ago, I'd found out that there was a strict line between the West Side and the East Side: one had money and powerful magic and even royal blood in some cases, and the other did not. Even though I had "Bane blood" and was "royal," my father and I had been living on the West Side, so I knew how little they had access to medicine and other things that the East Side was used to. It was one of the many reasons why I wasn't thrilled to move to Bane Manor on the East Side.

"Hayes wants to heal Westies?" I asked her, my brows knotted in confusion.

She nodded. "If he and I can convince Master Hart to allow it, it would be a great training opportunity for the students, and the people of the West Side would benefit as well. I've been dreaming up a way to make it happen ever since your father was injured."

She'd been amazing that night, accompanying me to help with his injury but also bringing all sorts of healing potions and tinctures and more to the clinic to help the other West Siders who were sick and injured that night. We talked about wanting to do more and open an apothecary shop on the West Side, but there was too much stacked against it.

I frowned. "Wait, what are you saying? I thought that was illegal."

She grinned. "I'm saying that I've thought long and hard about this. We should open an ice cream shop on the West Side."

Wait, what? Ice cream?

"I love you Avis, but have you been drinking? You're not making sense."

She tipped her head back and laughed long and hard at that. "Oh, Fallon. Thank you, I haven't laughed like that in a long time."

"What is going on? We're opening an ice cream shop with healing students from The Academy?" I looked at her, perplexed.

Avis shrugged. "Well, it's illegal to open an apothecary shop, isn't it?"

A light bulb went off in my head, and now I was wearing a matching grin to hers. "You evil genius!"

Avis nodded. "We will sell ice cream for a *very low* fee, and as a free gift with purchase, patients, er, I mean, customers can choose a tincture or hands-on healing to go with it."

Excitement thrummed through me. Was she serious? Was Hayes serious?

"Wait, how do you know Hayes?"

Avis beamed at me. "Every year for one semester, I take on an apprentice from The Academy. I mentored Hayes his first year. He's a good kid."

I scoffed. "He dumped my best friend an hour before the dance."

Avis nodded as if she knew. "He's a good kid," she pressed, and gave me a look. A look that said not to judge him by this one mistake.

Ugh, I hated that she was probably right. I didn't want to be judged for the fact that I burned down the student dance. It was an accident. And if Hayes really was trying to open a clinic on the West Side, maybe he was a decent person.

Maybe.

As I helped pour chopped rosemary into little glass bottles, I told Avis about the fact that I had agreed to take responsibility for the Bane family and that had somehow turned into the queen wanting me to move into Bane Manor. I left out the fact that I thought the house was actually a cage.

"Interesting," Avis mused. "It's like she's reinstating your family's royal lineage before you pledge your allegiance. Very smart, likely thought up by her council."

"You think it's okay that I'm doing that?" I hedged. My dad didn't really know anything about the magic world, so he wasn't the best to give advice on these matters, and Master Clarke had seemed a little doubtful.

Avis walked around the counter and stood before me. "I think you make Solana nervous. She doesn't know what to do with you, and so the more you can do to make her feel like she's in control, the better."

I relaxed then. If Avis thought it was a good idea, then I too was feeling better about things.

"Oh, before your shift is over, I have a book for you. It may have some information that could help get Ariyon back. Remind me, and I'll give it to you," she added.

Everyone knew about our late-night study sessions to find anything that might help me fix what I'd done to Ariyon. The queen's council, scholars, and anyone with any knowledge of healing or Bane powers was working overtime to try to figure out how to return their prince.

"Thanks," I told her, and then got busy mopping the floors. By the time I was done, the shop was sparkling, and I had a new book in my bag: *Miraculous Tales of Healing: True Stories*.

"Good luck!" Avis called out, and I thanked her and headed for The Academy.

Yanric flew toward me with something large hanging from a string that he held in his beak.

'Whoa.' I grabbed the cloth-wrapped parcel. '*You flew with this heavy thing?*'

I opened the cloth and smiled when I saw one of my dad's pulled-pork sandwiches. There was a note attached.

Luv

-Dad

The handwriting was akin to a primary schooler, and I stroked my fingers over it, grateful for my dad who was always taking care of me. He couldn't read or write much, but I'd taught him how to sign his name and to write a few other phrases like *hello*, *thank you*, *goodbye*, and *I love you*.

'*Your dad said to be home by curfew. Also, that you have to share the food with me since I carried it over here like a dumb pigeon.'*

'Hey, pigeons aren't dumb.'

Yanric gave me a look that said not to mess with him, and I just grinned. I was hungry. It was nearly dinnertime, and with all the time we'd been spending at the library, it was easy to accidentally skip meals. Ripping off a chunk of the bread, I held it out to him and then started on my half of the sandwich.

'See you later?' I asked Yanric after he took his portion.

'I'll be around,' he confirmed with a mouthful of bread, and then flew off.

I passed Royal Row, aptly named by Eden, which was a street—full of giant tidy mansions, of course—that was easy to cut through on the way to school from work. Ariyon and Ayden's house was at the end of this street, and I was pretty sure most of the popular kids from school lived here. I turned the corner and stopped immediately when I heard yelling.

"You will do as I ask or there will be consequences!" a man shouted.

I shrank into the hedge that lined the front yard of the house where the yelling was coming from so that I wouldn't be seen, and I peered through the bushes.

A young man stood, shoulders slumped forward, as an older man, who I assumed to be his father, berated him for something. The kid turned, and my heart spiked when I recognized him.

Hayes?

"But I'm a healer, Father. I don't want to take three hours of private sword lessons a day," Hayes complained.

"How my magic skipped over you, I'll never know. Maybe your mother laid with a healer because—"

"Don't talk about her like that!" Hayes spat.

His father reached out blindingly fast and slapped him across the face.

I gasped.

"I'll talk about my wife however I want. You will *not* be weak. This family has a reputation to uphold."

Hayes cupped his cheek, and the wheels on the backs of his hands spun as he seemingly healed himself.

"Yes, Father," he muttered, and then his dad stormed off into the house.

My stomach lurched as my last meal attempted to travel upward. Hayes's dad was a nightmare. My father would never speak or talk to me like that. I pulled myself from the bushes, but in the effort, my ankle caught on a branch, and I went down.

A yelp tore from my throat as I fell, my hands splayed out to catch myself.

The sound of scrambling footsteps could be heard, and then Hayes was looming over me.

"Fallon?"

Crap.

He looked so vulnerable, as if he was praying I hadn't just heard and seen what I most definitely had heard and seen. Avis, who could see the energy of a soul, had told me he was a good kid. He was hurting too, missing Ariyon like we all were. It felt like I should give him a chance to at least explain why he'd canceled on taking Eden to the dance.

"Hey." I stood, brushing off my pants. "I was just coming to ask you something," I lied.

He frowned, smoothing back his hair. "You were?"

I nodded. "I'm still pissed about you ditching Eden before the dance—"

"My father made me. I didn't want to," he growled. "And for the record, I'm still pissed about you losing my best friend in the Realm of Eternity."

Technically, he was in the Realm of Rebirth now, but this wasn't the time to argue specifics.

A day ago, his excuse might have sounded lame, but after seeing how his father treated him, I believed him.

"I saved Ariyon's life," I shot back.

Hayes waved me off. "What did you want to ask?"

I was hoping Eden was going to be okay with this, but after seeing how his father treated him, I wanted to give him a second chance.

"Eden, Ayden, and I have been meeting after school in the library to try to find any information we can about how to get Ariyon back. Tonight, we're going into the rare editions section with Master Clarke. We could really use some help. I'm on my way there right now."

He peered up at his house where his father had just stormed off and rubbed his cheek again.

"Doesn't the queen have her people looking into this?" he asked.

I nodded. "And so far, nothing. We aren't waiting around."

His lips pressed into a thin line. "Meet you at the library in ten."

He turned to leave, but I caught his elbow with my gloved hand. He peered at me, and I held his gaze. "I haven't been a healer for that long, but I can assure you they are *anything* but weak. You're amazing. Don't ever let anyone tell you any different."

His chin quivered as his eyes filled with tears. I wasn't sure if his dad treated him that way often. If he did, then I wanted to make sure someone was talking him back up after being cut down like that.

With a nod, he spun and walked away, wiping at his eyes.

Dammit, Avis was right. Hayes was a decent guy who seemed to have been put in a bad position the night of the dance.

This was going to complicate things at our library study group, but I hoped Eden would understand.

6

FALLON

"No way!" Eden growled, crossing her arms to glare at
me. I had pulled her aside in the library. Ayden wasn't here yet,
and Hayes was on his way. I hadn't told her the full story yet, and
she was acting as I expected.

"E, listen. I stumbled across his dad reaming him out and…"
I paused. It was private—what I saw was not something to gossip
about—but I really wanted Eden to understand that I didn't think
we were judging Hayes fairly. When he'd dumped Eden before
the dance to take Blair at his father's request, we'd assumed he
was just making an excuse or trying to please his parents. But this
felt bigger. Like maybe his dad hit him often and Hayes went to
the dance with Blair to avoid getting a beating that night.

I lowered my voice, leaning into her. "If I tell you something,
will you take it to the grave? Tell no one?"

Her eyes widened and her face went slack. She nodded.

"I just saw his dad hit him, E. He's a total monster. If his dad told him to break it off with you and take Blair to the dance instead, then I think Hayes did it to avoid his father's temper."

Eden gasped, her hand flying up to cover her mouth. Her eyes glistened with unshed tears. "That motherf—"

"I know. But don't say anything, okay? We all agree Ariyon needs us to work together. Let's focus on that," I told her.

She nodded, but I could see in her eyes she'd forgiven him. It was a good lesson for the both of us. No one knew what someone was dealing with in private.

Master Clarke showed up then carrying a stack of papers, and Ayden and Hayes were not too far behind. Clarke led us down to a locked room that turned out to be a temperature-controlled basement with two large tables and aisles upon aisles of books. After reading the rules posted on the far wall, we got to work. We all had to wear gloves so that we wouldn't get oil from our skin on the pages, which wasn't a problem for me, since I was already wearing gloves.

We split up into two groups. Ayden and Hayes took the task of trying to find out more about my powers, what I might be capable of, and how I could have switched abilities with Ariyon. Eden and I tried to find out more about Maven healers and their abilities.

"Holy Fae," Hayes breathed an hour later.

I'd been so deep into my own book, I'd forgotten the world around me and was actually startled at his voice.

"What?" Eden asked. Other than a shy "Hey," they hadn't spoken to each other.

Hayes peered at me with wide eyes. "Not relevant to our task, but with training, a Bane royal could be able to control someone's will, bending it to their liking. This book talks all about how they do it and a bunch of other stuff about them going dark." He traced his finger along the page.

I swallowed hard, chills racing up my arms. Master Clarke stopped grading his papers and stood. Walking over to Hayes, he peered over his shoulder, reading the line.

"I'll take that and look for anything else that might help. I'm sick of grading papers anyway." He snatched the book out of Hayes's hands and then went back to his seat.

Hayes frowned, clearly not done reading, and I chewed on my bottom lip.

"I would never do that," I told the group, shifting uncomfortably in my seat.

"We know that." Eden rubbed my shoulder encouragingly.

Control someone against their will? It was a horrifying thought. One that would probably get me killed if Solana found out that I could do it. Assuming I even could.

I looked up to see Master Clarke casually slip the book into his bag and wink at me.

It seemed he was thinking the same thing and was trying to protect me.

"I got something!" Ayden shouted so loudly we all jumped. "Sorry," he muttered, seeing our reaction.

He stood and started to pace the room as he read.

"A Bane royal taps into an ancient power, magic that accumulates over every generation. It's built upon for eons, so every Bane who comes after is more and more powerful and has access to their predecessors' magic."

"Oh," I said as my stomach dropped. I carried the same magic that my mother used to kill over a hundred people? The thought was petrifying.

"I think it's badass. In a cool but terrifying way," Ayden commented, and then went back to reading. "Then there is some type of lineage with a list of their powers. Devious Bane, born 1506, master of shadows. Known for his ability to mutate into shadows, blah blah. Bellacourt Bane, born 1609, queen of the Undying Fire. Known for her power over fire, blah blah." He looked up at us with a grin. "It lists every Bane family member for generations and what they add to the mix."

I looked up at him, "Please tell me one of my ancestors had this freaky ability to swap powers and that explains what happened," I said, hope starting to beat in my chest.

He spun the book in my direction and held it open to my face. "Amethyst Bane, born 1967, lady of the switch. Known before her death to have mastered the ability to switch powers with another and switch them back again."

Amethyst Bane. Holy Fae, she would have been my...grandmother? Maybe.

Eden held out her hand to Ayden, and they high fived.

We had a name.

"Well done," Master Clarke said. "I'll try to find anything I can on Amethyst Bane and her powers."

"This means that whatever power Fallon's ancestors mastered, she now carries that magic?" Eden asked, looking fascinated.

Ayden nodded. "If Amethyst Bane had mastered switching magic with another, then it means Fallon can do it too, and swap powers back with Ariyon."

"Once we figure out how to get to him," Hayes added.

Excitement and hope began to build up inside me. Reaching into my bag, I finally pulled out the book that Avis had loaned me, *Miraculous Tales of Healing: True Stories.*

It only took two minutes to learn that whoever had owned this book before had made copious amounts of notes in the

71

margins. A messy chicken scratch was scrawled on nearly every page. I'd also learned that it was a firsthand account of miraculous healings from the patients' points of view. A pretty cool and unique book.

Tarini Goodlock
The girl who fell.

I was twelve at the time. I'd fallen out of a tree and heard my leg snap. The bone popped out of my shin, and I almost fainted from the sight. The pain was so bad, I wanted to die. My mother was told by the clinic that they would have to amputate my leg, but then a master healer from the palace walked in. My mother told him I was a runner and to be bound to a chair for the rest of my life would kill me. He nodded and asked the other healers to step aside. He laid his hands over the bone, and the markings on top of them began to spin. My unbearable pain was suddenly numbed, and then he told my mother to have me bite down on something. He asked me to look away, and I did.

There was a snapping noise and a sharp slice of pain, but it was manageable. When I looked back, the bone was back in my leg, but there was a horrible, open, bloody gash. I watched in wonder as he magically stitched it up, the skin lacing together like tying a shoe. A month later, I was running again, and I never forgot the master healer who saved my leg.

My heart pinched at the beautiful story, and I peered across the room at Hayes and the marks that adorned his hands. I truly felt that being a healer was the most important of all the powers one could acquire, especially after reading this. To be able to take someone's pain, to restore their health, there was truly nothing more valuable. Even though I wasn't a healer, I did have Ariyon's gift for a short time, and I was honored to carry something so vital.

I quickly became engrossed in the book, reading story after story until I found one that made my breath stop. This one was different. This story was told by the patient, but the notes I glanced at in the margins appeared to be from the healer's point of view, as if the healer had gone back, read the story, and told his side of things. What had me most excited was the mention of a Maven healer.

Addie Strong
The woman who died and came back.

I had chest pains so sharp that it took my breath away. It felt like a horse was lying on me. We lived on the West Side, and the clinic was full, but my husband convinced a student from The Academy, where he worked as a janitor, to help me.

One second, I was sitting in the student-run clinic trying to catch my breath, and the next, I was in the Realm of Eternity staring up at the Grim! This student healer was standing over me, glowing marks on his hands spinning like crazy. I sat up and looked around, scared to death, when I saw that the Grim had come to claim me. What happened next was nothing short of a miracle. The healer, who I later learned was a Maven, was still learning. He'd not only hitched a ride with me, but he'd brought my entire body to the realm. Something that was forbidden. Now confronted with the Grim, he was arguing how I should be let back up!

My heart leaped into my throat. This was exactly what happened with Ariyon and me. I had to control my breathing as I read the notes in the margins from the healer's point of view.

I had no idea she was that near death. I was so new to healing at that serious of a level that I'd attached my magic to her body and soul instead of just the latter.

Of course! When Ariyon healed my dad, his body never went anywhere. Ariyon had followed my father's soul down to the Realm of Eternity, but this healer was new, like me, and had accidentally brought his patient's entire body down there as well as his own. Just like I had done with Ariyon.

I launched back into reading with renewed hope.

I watched in awe as they started to battle. The Maven healer fought the Grim for the right to restore me and allow me more life. But the Grim kept saying he'd broken a rule by bringing my body down there, that it wasn't allowed, and that there would be consequences. I was paralyzed on the ground as their power rained down around me, and then all of a sudden, I was snatched up into the light and I woke up at the school, my husband hovering over me.

But the healer was gone.

Chills raced down the length of my spine. It was almost the exact same as what happened with Ariyon and me, except in reverse.

I desperately scanned the margins, looking for the healer's notes.

I didn't know there would have to be a sacrifice. I chose myself rather than her. She was a mother, a wife; I had no one and would die young anyway.

I closed my eyes, my fingers shaking as I stroked the page. My heart welled up with love for this young healer. He made the ultimate sacrifice. It was one of the things I loved most about Maven healers—their easy ability to put others before themselves. Opening my eyes, I looked at the last scribbled note. The healer obviously survived. He came back somehow and wrote these notes.

Little did I know, fate had other plans, and the Light is merciful.

"No!" I screamed, and everyone jumped. "Sorry," I said with a wince.

He didn't say how he came back.

No.

No.

No.

I was so close.

"What did you find?" Hayes moved beside me, and I handed him the book, unable to help the heavy weight of depression that settled over me. Hayes read it to everyone, catching on that there was a healer point of view in the margins, and read that too. I watched in sadness as everyone sat up straighter, eyes alight, smiles on, hope filled. And then when he got to the final part, they had the same reaction I did.

"Why couldn't he have said a bit more!" Eden growled.

Even Master Clarke was scowling. "That's just pointless. That doesn't help anyone."

Hayes dropped the book back in my lap, and I felt exhaustion settle into my bones.

Yanric poofed through the door then, flying low and landing on my shoulder.

'It's late,' he announced, and as if on cue, I let out a yawn that traveled around the room.

"Let's meet here again tomorrow night," I told our little crew. "We made more progress today than we have all week."

Master Clarke nodded. "I'll meet you here again. Make sure you disgruntled youth don't steal any old books."

We all chuckled at that and packed up. I slipped the book Avis had given me back into my bag and promised myself I'd stay up late reading it until I'd weeded out any more Maven healing stories.

When we left the room, it was not lost on me that Master Clarke was the one who still had a book in his bag—the one that said I could possibly one day control others against their will.

For a split second, I wondered if he was going to show it to Queen Solana, but then I scolded myself. Master Clarke was always trying to protect and help me. He wouldn't turn on me.

Right?

7

ARIYON

I'd always wondered how the people in the House of Ash and Shadow actually went dark. Was the magic like an evil spirit that possessed them? Or was it more of a sickness that leached in until it ate away at their mind? Now that I held such magic, I thought it was the latter.

After using Fallon's awesome and terrible powers a few times now, I realized I was willingly feeding a beast. There was an enraged monster inside me, Fallon's dark magic, who, if rewarded with enough anger, would do what I wanted. And it was making me sick. Mentally speaking. My thoughts had started to turn dark. I wanted to go home, but I feared Fallon and everyone else had given up on me. Maybe they'd never figure out how to come back, and in order to stay alive, I'd have to keep ashing people or lighting them on fire, and my prize would be my worst nightmare: to be a Nightling.

Marissa hadn't been back since that day she watched my fight, but everyone was treating me with a lot more respect, and it was revolting. I was among a pack of rabid wolves with no option but to become a wolf myself to survive.

"Fallon," I whispered to the dark room as I lay on the cot in my cell. "Yanric."

Maybe the bird might reach me. He'd traveled through dimensions before. I'd just won another fight. I was bruised, bloody, and exhausted and felt like the edges of my mind were fraying. How long had I been here? Seven nights? Eight? Two weeks? There were up to three fights a day now. I was losing track. So much death. All at my hands. I was good with a sword back home and had no problem defending myself or those I loved, but to be pitted against others for sport…it made me sick. And yet I was doing it. I was doing whatever they wanted, just to stay alive.

"Grim," I whimpered. "Help."

I was a healer. This went against everything I believed in. Killing people. Burning people. Ashing people. Sleep pulled at my limbs, and I welcomed it. At this point, I wanted to enter the blackness of slumber and never wake up.

I was immediately pulled into a dream.

I sat in a large room, on a pillow with my legs crossed underneath me. Before me sat an old fae with white hair and a kind smile.

"Hello, son," he said.

I frowned, looking around the room to try to figure out where I was, but it was bare.

"Who are you?"

He placed his hand over his chest and dipped his head in respect. "I'm Emmeric, an Ealdor Fae."

Whoa. Ealdor Fae were badass.

"Why am I here?" I was lucid dreaming, so I had control over what I said. I'd never done it before, and it was pretty cool.

The man sighed. "You need help out of your situation, do you not?"

Chills ran down my arms, even in the dream. How did he know about my situation?

"I do," I hedged.

The man nodded. "Then, when you see Fallon, tell her to find me."

I frowned. "Okay, when I see Fallon," I said sarcastically. Like I'd see her at lunch or something.

The man opened his mouth to speak again when a painful slap ripped across my cheek, and...

I was jolted awake.

My eyes snapped open to see Maze hovering over me. "Get up, pretty boy. You got another fight, and this time I bet a week of cleaning duty on you, so you have to win."

I frowned. "I'm tempted to lose just so you will have to mop the floors."

Another hard slap against my cheek, and I wondered if this was allowed in the Accords, beating me for no reason. I wanted to hit him back, to grind his face into the stone wall beside me, but I did my best to rein in the anger and the power that surged within me, begging to be unleashed.

My mind raced, trying to remember the dream. It had felt so important, I didn't want to forget. Emmeric, the Ealdor Fae, saying something about Fallon.

I wondered what she was doing right now. Looking for me? Or maybe just moving on with her life? I wouldn't blame her if she did, but I would miss those green eyes. One look from her and it felt like I'd been pulled up for air. Like I'd been drowning my entire life without her. I was drowning now, and I needed Fallon to breathe life back into me before I succumbed.

8

FALLON

THE NEXT MORNING, YANRIC HAD TO PECK ME AWAKE. I'D stayed up nearly all night reading that book. It was full of amazing healing stories, but no more that involved a Maven. I still had one chapter left though, and I was holding out hope. Whoever was writing in the margins was the same person throughout, the Maven healer. When he commented on other healings, he surmised what the healer had done and how they could have done things differently. A critique of sorts. It was a great book, one I thought Ariyon would want to read one day.

If I ever got him back.

"You're going to be late, hon!" my dad called from the kitchen.

What do you do all night when I sleep? I looked at Yanric, who preened his feathers on my nightstand. He was always gone, in and out, but here by morning to fly to school with Eden and me.

He peered up at me. *I watch you sleep and fly overhead to assess threats.*

'Seriously?' That was one dedicated guardian. Did he not need sleep himself?

He cackled. *'No, I'm not serious. I need at least six hours of beauty sleep. When you sleep, I sleep, but I'm ready to fight if woken up.'*

He flexed his wings for good measure, and I snickered.

I got ready quickly. There was a knock at the front door just as I pulled on my second glove.

"I'll get it!" I told my dad, knowing he'd be in the kitchen cooking up breakfast.

Throwing the door wide, I stiffened when I saw the Royal Guard. He held two envelopes in his white-gloved hands.

This couldn't be good. Another note from Queen Solana or her council? Maybe she was taking back her invite for me to join the brigade.

I pulled the envelopes from his hand and thanked him before shutting the door.

"What now?" My father came into the room holding out two steaming hand pies. My mouth watered at the sight, and I tore the first envelope open and read it aloud.

Citizen of The Gilded City,

You are hereby invited to a special Winter Solstice Ball at Queen Solana's palace. There will be dancing and dinner followed by a unique commitment ceremony from guest of Honor Fallon Bane, the sole surviving Bane family heir.

I stopped reading and looked up at my father who was mid-bite into one of the pies, steam flowing out of his mouth, making him look like some mythical dragon.

"Wow," my dad said between blowing on the food, "she went for it."

"She sure did." I gave a nervous laugh and then peered at the day and time.

Only a few days away! That was quick, but it was smart to couple it with an event that was already happening. The Winter Solstice was a huge deal in The Gilded City, from what I'd heard. Street vendors made delicious food at their carts and sold sparklers and gave women flowers. It sounded magical. And it was always followed up by a light show in the sky that I'd longed to see up close since I was a little girl.

But could I really enjoy it with Ariyon missing?

I knew my allegiance vow to the queen would be public, but I hadn't expected it to be *that* public.

"Avis thinks it's a smart move too, doing whatever I have to in order to make the queen feel comfortable."

My dad gave me a slow nod. "Well, let's just remember we have a backup plan if things get uncomfortable around here." He jerked his head to his room, where the packs were hiding under his bed. I nodded. Never hurt to have a backup plan.

"What's the other one say?" he asked, and I started to tear it open.

"I'm afraid to look," I admitted, but read it anyway.

Fallon,

I am so pleased you are willing to make things easier on me. I have set up for you to be my guest of honor and pledge your allegiance to my reign at the Winter Solstice. I have movers coming today while you are at school and your father is at

work moving all your things to Bane Manor. Ember will be
waiting for you at the school stables, and I have procured a
bike for your father. An appropriate outfit will be delivered to
your new home before the ball, and I will see you at the party.

Queen Solana

It was actually a reasonable letter. I gathered that my showing up in The Gilded City must have stressed her out because she was actually seeming to relax now that I was willing to do whatever to make life easier on her. I peered down at my clothes and chuckled at her term *appropriate outfit*. What was wrong with my clothes? Probably was going to send me some ridiculous ball gown or something. But I would wear it if it kept me out of jail.

"Umm, we are moving to Bane Manor today. The queen got movers to take our stuff," I said with a wince. This furniture wasn't even ours, but I suspected after over a hundred years of being left alone, Bane Manor didn't have any furniture worth saving. Maybe Solana bought all of this from Mable.

My dad's eyebrows shot up. "Okay…"

'I wonder if they've cleaned it. It was in quite the state when I last saw it mere months ago,' Yanric said.

I forgot he'd said he was born there and had spent seventeen years waiting for me there. I had broken down and told him what was in the other letter, the one where Queen Solana implied turning Bane Manor into a prison for my eventual darkness.

'I'm sure it will be fine.'

My dad handed me the second pie and disappeared into the back bedroom. When he reappeared, he was carrying the two runaway backpacks over his shoulders. "I'm going to have Mable hold on to these, and I'll move them over tomorrow myself. Don't want the queen's men finding them and asking questions."

"Good idea." Best to not let the queen know we have an escape plan—of course, that was assuming I wouldn't be stuck in this Bane Manor house forever if things ever did go sideways.

My dad wished me a good day and then sped across the street to Mable's while I met up with Eden. She had dark bags under her eyes and looked like she'd slept about as well as I had. I pulled my cloak tighter over me to cover my skin against the chilly morning air.

"Were you out all night partying without me?"

She yanked the hand pie from my gloved fingers and took a bite before giving it back. Then she pulled a small hunk of potato out of her mouth and fed it to Yanric, who perched on my shoulder.

"Up all night reading. I found out some pretty scary stuff, and then I was too frightened to go back to sleep."

I wanted to hug her; she was such a good friend to help me like this. "I was up all night reading too. Nothing scary, though. What did you find out?" I asked.

"Nothing much," she said quickly, and then gave me a forced smile.

"Eden Westcourt. You're a horrible liar."

She groaned, kicking her feet across the cobblestones as she passed the streets of the West Side.

"Fine. I know why Master Hart stutters around you and looks generally terrified."

I skidded to a stop, my whole body turning toward her in anticipation. I wanted to know, but I also didn't because I knew it would be bad.

"What did Marissa do?"

Eden nodded.

"Hart was there the night she burned the school down. She… used that dark power Ayden read about, the one where you can take over someone's will. She forced Hart to…" Eden's bottom lip shook, and her eyes filled with tears.

My heart fell into my stomach like a boulder. I didn't know if I could take this anymore. I wanted to kill Marissa for all these things she had done. I don't care what your childhood was like or how hard it was to carry dark magic, there is no excuse for the terror she rained down on these people. I'd rather die than do the things she did.

"Tell me." My voice was barely a whisper, and Eden dipped her chin.

"She forced him to bar the doors so the students and teachers couldn't get out. So that they would…burn."

A whimper ripped from my throat, and I stumbled backward. "She's so evil."

'Come find me,' a female voice whispered, and I spun around, my eyes darting to the trees, the bushes, the buildings.

"What's wrong?" Eden asked, her brow furrowing.

Terror gripped my soul in that moment. I was hearing voices—one of the symptoms of going dark.

"Nothing. I'm… I'm just shocked at what Marissa made Hart do." I lied. Maybe I didn't really hear that; maybe in my shock, I imagined the voice.

Eden nodded. "It's awful."

We resumed our walking, and I swallowed hard, peering sideways at Yanric. He was still as a statue on my shoulder.

'I heard it too.' He sounded scared, as scared as I felt.

So I hadn't imagined it. I didn't know if that was better or worse.

'It will be okay,' I assured him. But would it?

The only measure of relief I felt in that moment was that my ability to go dark and lose my mind had not transferred to Ariyon as well.

I felt numb the rest of the day at school. My mind was spinning with too many things. How many days Ariyon had been missing? What was he doing right now? How could I get him back? Then I thought about going dark, the female voice I'd had heard that morning. But mostly, what consumed my thoughts were poor Master Hart and the way his hands shook when he was near me. It killed me that he feared that, at any moment, I might take his very will from him. Yet I understood his fear of me. I was starting to fear me, what I was capable of, the great power my ancestors held—which meant that I held it too.

"Once you learn to read people's energy signatures, your healing gift will accelerate naturally," Mrs. Reebus said, pulling me from my thoughts. "Now, this is a bit advanced, but I would like to speak about curses next because it will be on your final exam at the end of the year."

I chuffed. Curses—something I knew all too much about.

She began to write on the board, speaking as she did. "There are two types of curses, everlasting and transient. The everlasting curse is permanent and can never be healed." Her gaze flicked briefly to me, and I wanted to shrink into a tiny ball and hide. "The transient curse is attached to the person or object via some type of energy signature. Once you unravel that, you can break down the curse, essentially starving it out," she added.

I took notes on what she was saying, but I was hoping I wasn't a healer long enough to take the final. I needed to get Ariyon back before then. In reality, though, I was starting to feel quite sure he could be dead by then or have become a Nightling. And the thought caused panic to rise up inside me and dig its claws into my chest.

No.

I had to stay positive. For Ariyon. Straightening myself, I focused back on the lesson at hand.

"Now let's practice sensing energy signatures like you've done with Master Hart. That will be a good segue into my next lesson. Partner up!" She clapped her hands, and I groaned. I hadn't done that in Master Hart's class. We were sensing energy of plants right now. Whoever was about to sense *my* energy signature was about to see my curse. That was going to be mortifying. I could almost see it play out in my head.

Mrs. Reebus, what's that disgusting black blob sucking the life from Fallon?

She approached my desk, and I stiffened.

"Fallon, you can be my partner." Mrs. Reebus gave me a small smile, and I was eternally grateful. She must have known. She probably saw it on me the first day.

I stood, following her to the front of the class, where she stepped across from me, staying at some distance away from me.

She spoke to the class. "Now, as you can see, I am about six to ten feet away from my partner. It's best when doing this, for the first few times, to keep a distance so you don't confuse your own energy signature with your patient."

I took a deep breath, feeling my palms start to sweat inside my gloves. How did I get here? A few months ago, I hadn't known I had magic at all. My entire life, I'd known I was cursed but hadn't known why. Now, I knew it was due to my evil ancestors and the scary power I carried within, which I had been trying to learn to control through battle classes and learning how to wield the Undying Fire. Now, I was trying to heal and learn how to control Maven-level magic that wasn't mine. It was such a stark contrast, and yet if I was being honest, I liked this better. As someone who had suffered so much pain in my life, this type of work appealed to me much more. But we couldn't choose the way we were made, so there was no sense in complaining about it.

"Every healer from the House of Light and Ether has the ability to sense someone's energy signature, some more than others," the teacher said.

I immediately thought of Avis and how she could not only sense someone's life force energy but also see it.

"Take a deep breath in, centering yourself, and then allow your vision to go a bit hazy, almost as if you are lost in a stare after a long day," she continued.

I inhaled, staring at Mrs. Reebus, and then tried to allow my eyes to relax. My mind kept wanting to see something, but there was nothing but clear air around her.

Then I gasped, as did a few others in class, the slightest subtle, pink glow coming off her appearing to me.

"I see it!" another student said.

"My partner is green!" another said.

Mrs. Reebus smiled and opened her mouth to speak when the sound of a blaring siren filled the space.

Her eyes widened, and she stood frozen for a moment as

I reached up to cover my ears. There had never been a siren before.

"Everyone, follow me!" Mrs. Reebus shouted, seeming to jolt out of her trance as she beelined toward the door.

We all shared confused and frantic looks as we rushed to the doorway, causing a bottleneck. I stumbled backward, away from the crowd, to avoid getting touched, and then followed at the very back. We walked into the hallway with hundreds of other students, and I hissed as someone bumped up against me, but luckily no skin touched. Hugging the walls, I watched as hundreds of students and their teachers funneled into a door at the end of the hall.

"Fallon!" Eden screamed, and I spun to see my bestie bounding toward me. She was covered in soot and wearing battle gear, no doubt in the middle of a lesson on how to fight with her fire magic.

"What's going on?" I asked.

She looked behind her as if checking for a teacher and swallowed hard. "I heard it's a Nightling alarm."

There are Nightlings on campus?

Rage washed over me, causing a heady rush to pulse between my temples. The thought of seeing Marissa again after she attempted to kill Ariyon actually excited me. I didn't care if I was without my powers. I would kill her with my bare hands.

Eden must have seen the anger rising up inside me because she shook her head and grabbed my gloved hand. "We hide in the basement. That's new protocol."

"How do you know this?"

"I'm House of War and Bone. It's my job to know how to protect." She looked proud at that.

And now I was a healer out of the loop, I guess.

"Fallon!" Ayden's panicked voice filled the space, and I turned to see him rushing toward me, wearing full battle armor and holding a sword.

"What's going on?" I asked him, hoping he had more information.

"Get in the basement, both of you!" he hissed, and shepherded us that way.

It was amazing how efficient everyone was. The entire building had calmly rushed into the basement, Eden, Ayden, and I the last to go in. Ayden all but pushed us into the open doorway, and when I realized he wasn't coming, my heart dropped in my stomach.

"Ayden. Is it Nightlings? Is it Marissa?" I asked as he stood in the doorway, peering down at me with the same face as the man I missed so much it hurt.

He swallowed hard and gave me a curt nod.

I pushed forward. "Then I'm coming too! She's here for me. If anything happens to anyone—"

He gripped both of my covered arms harder than was polite and shoved me back through the doorway.

"Fallon, you have no powers to fight anymore. Stay down here. If anything happened to you…" A wild look crossed his face, like he might do anything to force me to stay put, and then his gaze fell to my lips.

What the…?

He released me and then slammed the door shut. A loud clicking noise signaled that we were now locked inside.

9

FALLON

I banged a fist against the locked door and then spun to face Eden. The subtle glow of the crystal light sconces on the wall cast shadows on her frown.

"What's wrong?" I asked her.

She shook her head. "He still likes you."

My stomach sank. "No. No, I think he's totally into you now." It felt like a lie the second it left my lips. They'd gone to dinner a few times after studying, but Eden said nothing had happened and it seemed he was holding back. When his gaze had dropped to my mouth just now, I'd wondered, but I'd hoped she hadn't seen.

She looked at the wall behind me, as if lost in thought. "I think he tried to be into me, to get over you, but...he's not."

No. No. No.

If anything came between Eden's and my friendship, I would never forgive myself.

"E, I'm over him. I swear on my father's life," I growled.

She slipped her hand in mine and squeezed, giving me a sad smile. "Fallon, it's okay. I'm fine. We're young. I'll have plenty of potential boyfriends to choose from my whole life, right?" She gave me a wink, but I could see the pain behind her eyes.

I really, really wanted her and Ayden to work out. Maybe partially to make me feel better for moving on with Ariyon so fast, but also so that Eden would have someone after Hayes broke her heart. Ayden felt like a brother to me now, and any chance of romance was gone—and not just because he couldn't touch me without activating my curse.

I opened my mouth to speak when Mrs. Reebus called up the stairs to us.

"All students must be present for roll call!" she shrilled, and we descended the steps.

'Yan?' I called for my familiar as I stepped into the basement fortress, and he poofed through the wall, solidifying onto my shoulder in a second.

I wrinkled my nose. *'You smell like burnt feathers.'*

'I just flew through a war zone,' he shot back, and I stiffened.

'What? How bad is it out there?'

'There are hundreds of Nightlings out there, Fallon.' He looked serious. *'Half the town was being attacked when I flew from—'*

"My father," I croaked.

'I flew here after making sure he was okay. He's barred himself and Mable in the cellar. They're fine.'

"Students, gather around!" Mr. Whitlock announced, and I was jolted from my momentary panic. Would my father be fine with Mable in the cellar? Nightlings could penetrate walls. They could turn to shadow like Yanric and pass through any solid mass.

Madame Mondpoint, one of the professors who I knew

worked with energy crystals and had a special kind of magic, walked over to the far basement wall. She began to throw blue glowing light at it, and when the light hit the walls, it splashed out, spreading and creating some kind of shield.

Some of the students, me included, gasped in awe as she covered every single wall of the basement as well as the floor and ceiling. We were now standing in a glowing blue box. Madame Mondpoint was covered with sweat, sitting in the corner, panting.

"This should keep the Nightlings out if they try to penetrate the walls," she said.

Should. They didn't know for sure.

Hayes walked over to Madame Mondpoint and mumbled something to her. She looked up at him, utter exhaustion lining her features, and nodded. Hayes put his hands on her back, and the marks on top of them began to glow and move.

I pushed the fear for my father to the side and stepped over to where Hayes was. "Is she okay?" I whispered.

Madame Mondpoint had her eyes closed and was slumped against the wall now with Hayes siphoning energy into her.

He nodded. "Just a lot of output in a small amount of time. She's a Dynokinetic. She can manipulate great amounts of energy, but it takes a toll on her in the short term."

The teacher mumbled as if agreeing but didn't bother to open her eyes.

I swallowed hard. "Can I help?"

Hayes looked at me then, and the seriousness of his gaze caught me a bit off guard. "Gather all the healer students in one corner. I'll be there in a bit. We need to prepare to go out in teams once they let us out so that we can help with the aftermath."

I gasped at his wording. "Aftermath?"

Again, he held my gaze. "The Nightlings are waging war on us, Fallon. There will be casualties, there will be injured. The queen's healers are the best in the realm, but they might be... compromised as well. We just...need to prepare for the worst."

Oh Light. How was this happening? I needed to get up there. Ayden! I should be fighting by his side or, at the very least, begging Marissa to stop this.

Why was she doing this? Before I'd shown up, most people in The Gilded City had thought she was dead. After so long, her appearance here had to be because of me. Ever since I had shown up here, Marissa had launched an attack almost monthly.

'Nightlings need to feed, or they wither away,' Yanric shared, and I peered over at him.

'What do you mean? I mean, why are you sharing that now?' I remembered reading about the Nightlings need to feed, but—

'Maybe they are doing a big feeding, beefing up on all their powers so that they can be strong for something bigger.'

Chills ran down my arms at Yanric's guess.

"Fallon," Hayes called, pulling my attention back to the task at hand, and I shook myself.

"Sorry. I'll go gather the others."

We would have to figure out the reason for the attack later. I turned away from Hayes, squinting in the dim blue glowing light, and glanced around at the over two hundred students and staff huddled in the large open concrete gymnasium-esque space. There was no furniture, just a few milk crates and boxes in the corner.

As I looked at the gathered crowd, I realized not many teachers were down here. They were probably up there, fighting.

Master Clarke. Master Hart. They weren't here. Dread tightened my gut, but I pushed it down and cleared my throat.

"House of Light and Ether healing students, with me!" I barked, and walked to a corner of the space that was less crowded.

Mrs. Reebus perked up and looked over at me, taking a few long strides my way.

I lowered my voice as she neared. "Hayes said we should prepare for...the aftermath. To help."

The color drained from her face, making her look sickly in this light, but she nodded.

"Come on!" She clapped twice, and one by one, the healing students broke away from the groups they were with and moved to our corner of the room.

Master Knight, the lead Pyrotechnics instructor who had shown me how to use the Undying Fire, was gone too, which made me feel a little better because it meant she was fighting on Ayden's side, hopefully keeping him safe. But Mr. Whitlock, the telekinesis teacher, was down here, and he seemed to notice what we were doing.

"House of War and Bone! Line up in rows of ten!" he barked like a drill sergeant. The students fell into line, seemingly liking that there was something to do. Then Mr. Whitlock came over to Mrs. Reebus and me.

"We should prepare for the worst," he said. "The tele students can levitate bodies and get them to the healing tents."

Mrs. Reebus nodded. "That will work." She kept her voice calm, but I could *feel* the fear emanating off her.

For the first time since I found out I had dark powers, I actually wanted them. I wanted to send a wave of purple fire into every single Nightling out there. But no. I was stuck with powers to heal, not harm.

I stroked the tops of my hands through my gloves, where

Ariyon's marks were, and my heart pinched, causing a giant cavern of grief to open inside my chest as I feared it would swallow me whole. It had been too long, and I was beginning to lose any hope of getting him back.

Forgive me, I thought, and then Yanric nuzzled against my neck.

"I want to be up there helping," I told Mrs. Reebus as Mr. Whitlock walked away and began to give his students orders.

She frowned as she stared at me, sadness in her eyes. "You're a healer now, Fallon. You'll have your chance to help, but only after the fighting has stopped."

I hated this. I hated feeling so helpless.

Hayes joined us then, and the three of us split the meager number of healers we had into three teams. It was nothing like the hundreds of warriors we had training at this school. There were almost twenty warriors for every healer, and it didn't seem fair. Now that we were preparing to go heal the wounded, it was clear how many would have to wait for relief with so few of us able to help.

"Now gather around," Mrs. Reebus whispered.

The students pressed in but were respectful of my space so that I wasn't touched.

Suddenly a scream and then a thud came from above us, and a first year next to me whimpered. Mrs. Reebus swallowed hard, ignoring the noise. "We must prepare for the fact that there will be more wounded than the queen's healers can tend to, and in that case, we will be needed."

Everyone stood a little taller then, pride showing on their faces. It felt better to patch up a man after he was injured than cut him down. I felt in my soul that being a healer was something I would love to do long-term, but I knew it was only temporary—and truthfully, I would miss being able to fight.

"Nightlings drain their victims of blood to the point of death, and if not, they drink from them until their victim is very weak. No healer can regenerate a person's blood, but we can put them in an energetic stasis until they generate it themselves," Mrs. Reebus said. "If you feel you are equipped to do this, stand over here." She pointed to her right.

Hayes and a handful of third and fourth years moved to her right.

Then she addressed the rest of us. "Nightlings can also inflict severe burns, cause wounds from weapons or shock waves, and even create mental torment." She glanced at me quickly, and I looked away, ashamed.

Mental torment?

'Don't look away from her. You haven't done anything wrong, and we aren't Nightlings yet!' Yanric snapped, giving her a glare as smoke lifted off from his wings.

'Calm down. You're so emotional,' I snapped at him, but his words made me feel better. I had nothing to be ashamed of. I wasn't mentally tormenting anyone.

"If you feel you can help stop a bleeding wound or help heal a burn, please step over here." She pointed to her left, and nearly all the rest of the students including me walked to that side. She caught my covered upper arm as I started to walk away and pulled me back to her side.

Then she looked at the two terrified students who were left. "You two can shadow Fallon and me, who will be taking the worst cases. Anyone near death should be reported to us immediately."

My mouth popped open a little as she turned to me.

"You have Ariyon's power. Your knowledge is new, but your magic is not. I need you with me for any serious cases."

I nodded enthusiastically. I wanted to help in any way I could.

Another muffled shriek came from above, and my anxiety ratcheted up a notch.

'Yan, I want to get out there.' I started to rock on my heels, feeling utterly helpless.

'I know, but you can't. Ariyon's protective magic only works against the living.'

I knew this because I'd fought next to him during one attack and also because he'd used it on me the day he and I had met, when I'd pulled a knife on him and it felt like he'd liquefied my brain out my nose. Oh, how I wished I could liquify Marissa's brain.

The blue wards that Madame Mondpoint had erected shook and stretched as black shadows attempted to infiltrate them. It looked like a creature was trying to erupt through a plastic bag, bending and pulling it as they tried to push through.

The entire basement erupted into pandemonium, first years screaming and backing away from the walls.

Mr. Whitlock called out to his warrior students. "Put the healers in the center and protect the perimeter. Grab your weapons from the trapdoor in the floor."

We, the healers, were shuffled to the center of the room, and I held my breath a few times when two people bumped into me, but luckily I was fully covered.

The blue shield distorted and wobbled as shadows attempted to enter and Yanric burst from my shoulder and flew to Eden's.

'I still have fighting magic,' he told us both, and Eden nodded.

Mr. Whitlock looked at Yanric on Eden's shoulder and frowned.

"He's with me. He can fight," Eden said, and he gave her a curt nod.

There were two trapdoors in the floor that seemed to open to giant storage chests full of weapons—swords, crossbows, bolt shooters, the works. My palms itched to get into the action, to grab a sword and cut a Nightling to pieces with it.

Madame Mondpoint had recovered from her weakness and went around the room again, reinforcing the shields as the Nightlings attempted to batter them.

"If those wards fall—" Mr. Whitlock yelled to the surrounding students.

"They won't fall!" Madame Mondpoint barked, tossing sheets of blue glowing light at wall after wall.

Mr. Whitlock pulled his sword, an orange flame erupting from it. "If they do, we give those bloodsuckers everything we've got! For our queen and our city!" he cried, and a cacophony of students' screams resounded at his call.

A man's face suddenly pushed its way through the barrier, and a few students yelped, but Madame Mondpoint walked right up to him and tossed her magic directly in his face, causing him to shriek and disappear. She fell to one knee then, panting as she swayed, seemingly trying to keep upright.

"Let me through!" I shouted, feeling my hands heat up as I knew the healing marks were already spinning. One by one the crowd parted, and I ran to Madame Mondpoint's side and laid a gloved hand on her back. I couldn't touch her skin, but I knew from Ariyon that that wasn't needed to heal her.

She swayed again, almost losing balance, and then held her hands up. They shook as she pushed more and more energy into the blue wall. I furrowed my brow, letting my sight lose focus, and then her energy signature was revealed. It was like a golden halo of buttery-yellow light that grew three feet from her body, but it was very dim and there were black, shadowy gaps.

Reaching out, I touched one of the black holes in the halo, and golden light shot from my own palm and filled it.

"There you go," Mrs. Reebus coached from beside me.

I startled a little at her voice. "Do you see that? The golden energy?" I asked her.

She nodded. "Keep filling the holes. I envy your power, Fallon. I usually need a patient to ingest herbs and oils to carry out a healing like that."

I waved my gloved hand over the holes in her energy and, one by one, filled them up. All the while Madame Mondpoint continued to strengthen the wards.

"I'm...not sure how much longer—" Madame Mondpoint said.

"It's okay, Glenda. Let go if you must." Mrs. Reebus took her hand in hers and tried to encourage her to come to terms with the fact that the shield might not hold.

"No," Mondpoint growled, and a huge burst of blue light shot from both of her palms, coating the walls. Her energy signature flickered then, like a light going off and on again. Her eyes crossed, and she collapsed into Mrs. Reebus's waiting arms.

"Oh dear. Help me get her into the center of the circle?" Mrs. Reebus asked me.

I hooked my gloved hands under her armpits and dragged her backward as Mrs. Reebus gripped her ankles. When we got her to the center of the circle, a sudden chill rushed down my arms.

'Where are you, daughter?' The voice of Marissa Bane was inside my head, and my eyes went wide. I flicked my gaze to Yanric, who looked just as terrified.

He heard it too.

The blue wards started to shake then, like something—or someone—was pulsing them with electric power. They vibrated and wobbled, and I stepped out of the circle and stood before the warriors. If Marissa was going to burst through the wards and into here, I wanted her to get to me first. No more of my friends were getting hurt on her account.

'What do you want?' I growled in my head, projecting it outward and hoping it reached her.

Was I hearing voices, or was she actually talking to me? Could Yanric hear it too? Was Marissa even here?

The blue glow on the walls dimmed before growing a sickly dark gray.

"Get ready!" Mr. Whitlock cried out.

"Fallon, get back!" Eden barked.

'What do you want, Marissa!?' I shouted it inside my head again, feeling like an insane person.

I felt her then, like a piece of clothing slithering over my body with her awareness. *'I want my heir, and then I want the throne. Both of which are mine by birthright.'*

The throne? The Gilded City throne? She was insane.

With a cracking sound, the ward shattered into a million burning embers, as if it had been lit on fire from the inside.

I steeled myself, waiting for black shadows to bleed through the walls, and screamed when Yanric turned to smoke and disappeared through the concrete to the outside.

'They have to go through me first,' my familiar said.

I rushed forward, unsure what I intended to do, when an energy shock wave blew into the room from the wall and slammed right into me, knocking me into the air and causing me to fly backward ten feet before landing on my butt, right at Eden's feet. That shock wave was bright light, yellow, warm, like the sun.

'Yan?' I asked, panicked.

'I'm fine. Queen Solana just ran off fifty Nightlings, Marissa included.'

The sunlight shock wave was her?

"Queen Solana protects us," Mr. Whitlock said, clasping his hands together. He must have recognized that was her magic.

'Oh no. She's hurt. Fallon, get out here,' Yanric called.

My heart leaped into my throat as I bolted away from the students and bound up the steps. "The queen is hurt!" I cried behind me.

When I reached the top, I pounded on the door. We were locked in here, so how the fae was I supposed to get out?

"Hang on! There's an override button," Mrs. Reebus yelled, running up behind me. She bent down to push a small metal button on the bottom of the kickplate.

There was a clicking sound, and then I spun the handle and burst into the hallway. Taking a right, I headed outside into the little garden between the buildings and skidded to a stop.

"Where is she? Are you sur—" The words died in Mrs. Reebus's throat when she stepped outside.

Oh Light.

My bottom lip shook as I took in the carnage before me and tried to process it all. Dead bodies were strewn across the lawn like discarded trash. Limbs and heads were bent at odd angles.

"Ayden!" I suddenly screamed in terror, spinning around to see smoke and burning trees.

This was a war zone, something I'd never experienced before in my life.

"Ayden!"

'Fallon, the queen needs you. I'll find Ayden and check on your father, but the queen.' I followed the sound of Yanric's voice and found Solana collapsed on the ground, a dozen guards scattered around her, all dead.

Her blond hair was spread out on the grass almost in an artistic way, and Yanric perched on her chest, looking down at her.

"Where are the palace healers?" Mrs. Reebus shrilled as she ran with me to the queen's collapsed form.

"Master Hart?" Mrs. Reebus yelled, peering around the space.

No bodies moved; no sounds were made. It was as if we were in a corner of the world where we were the only living things.

Shock and horror ripped through me as I tried to process the massacre.

The queen's chest rose and fell slightly, Yanric moving up and down with it, but I couldn't tell exactly what was wrong with her since there was no blood or external injury at first glance.

'Go check on Ayden and my father,' I told Yanric, and I swallowed hard as I peered at Mrs. Reebus.

"Tell me what to do," I ordered her.

The rest of the students from the basement funneled out into the courtyard and stopped when they saw the gruesome scene before them.

Mr. Whitlock appeared shocked for one second and then spotted me hovering over the queen and pulled his sword.

"Circle the queen and stand guard until reinforcements can come!" he barked.

Eden ran, wide-eyed, to help form a circle around us.

I looked up at the sweet healing teacher to see tears in her eyes. She peered at me with fear. "I…I don't know, Fallon. This is beyond me. Her life force is weak, but I can't tell why."

I took in a cleansing breath, trying not to let the panic overtake me because it sure was trying to.

My father is fine.

Mable is fine.

Ayden is fine.

Ariyon is fine.

Everything is going to be fine.

My hands were so hot, they felt like they were on fire, and I wanted to dip them in cool water. It was as if my healing gift knew it was needed and was charging up, getting ready.

You know what to do, I told the magic within me. We had a trusting relationship. I was a total newbie, and the magic knew that, so it was going to have to take the lead.

"Master Hart is here!" someone cried out.

Relief rushed through me as the master healer stumbled into our circle, but the relief was short-lived when I saw the state he was in. He looked like he'd been mauled by an animal. Bloody gashes were carved all over his body. His color was pale, and his hands shook.

"I…I… The queen," he muttered.

"Help me save her!" I snapped.

He looked shell-shocked, staring at me, then at Queen Solana, and then at me again.

"I'm not my mother!" I yelled at him. "You have to help me!"

He scanned her body with his gaze. "In…ternal bleeding. The Grim…" he mumbled, and then he teetered backward and passed out cold into a waiting fourth year's arms.

Internal bleeding. The Grim!

Crap.

Screw this. I wasn't waiting for step-by-step instructions.

What would Ariyon do? What did he do with my father?

"You can't have her," I growled, imagining the Grim hovering over her body in the Realm of Eternity.

Then I grabbed her exposed upper arms with my bare hands.

Screw my curse, I needed to touch her. I instinctively knew that, and so I had peeled off my gloves. This was bad, and my magic needed to physically enter her body through touch.

The second my skin connected with hers, I cried out in pain but held on.

"D-d-don't take her body down…like you did Ariyon," Master Hart's weak voice came to my right.

Good. He was awake.

Golden light flooded from my palms, and I felt a tug.

"I feel a tug! Something is pulling me," I screamed.

"Go with it but detach your energy f-f-from her body without letting g-g-go," he stuttered.

Detach my energy from her body? I didn't even know my energy was attached to her body.

Mrs. Reebus knelt beside me then. "You're physically holding her, right?" she asked.

Pain rolled through me as my curse continued activating, but at the same time, my healing powers were working to dull it, or I'd have passed out by now.

I nodded.

"Look. See her energy? It's faint, but it's there. Attach to that and follow the pull," she coached.

"Y-yes exactly," Master Hart wheezed.

My muscles were twitching. My skin felt like it was on fire, but I tried to calm myself and relax my vision so I could see the queen's energy.

As I stared, a faint glow rose off her body about two inches, very small and very weak, and little wispy cords from my hands floated over the top of her energy like tentacles.

"I see something weird. Like strings from my hands," I said.

"Yes! Hook in! Hook those into her energy and follow the pull. Save her," Mrs. Reebus coached.

I whimpered as another rush of pain washed over me, and then suddenly, I felt the cool balm of healing I normally felt with Ariyon.

I whipped my head around to see Hayes with his hands hovering over my shoulder blades. "I got you," he said firmly. He couldn't save the queen, but he could help me save her, and for that I was extremely grateful.

Feeling stronger, I looked back at the queen and willed the little energy tentacles to hook into her soul but not her body. The tug was so strong, I yelped.

My eyes slammed shut, and then the tug at my navel was so forceful, I was spinning. One second, I was in the school garden, and the next, I stood before the Grim himself.

Oh fae.

10

ARIYON

I LIMPED DOWN THE HALLWAY WITH MAZE PRODDING ME IN the back every few minutes. I'd just gotten beaten up pretty badly, but I'd held my own and ended up winning by forfeit. As I passed the main break room where all the guards hung out, I overheard a familiar voice.

Marissa.

That woman spent way more time here than I liked. I wanted to get away from her as fast as I could, but when I heard Fallon's name on her lips, I went rigid and skidded to a stop.

"Fallon wasn't there. Well, she was. I felt her, but I couldn't get to her," Marissa growled.

Amethyst tsked. "You need the girl. She's the key to you getting the crown. Otherwise, you can't give our people the permanent bodies we deserve."

What *the fae* did she just say? My entire body flushed with adrenaline.

Maze kicked the back of my knee, and I fell forward, splaying out my hands to catch my fall. I'd injured my wrist in the fight, so I hissed when I landed on it, fresh pain igniting there.

"Get up," Maze growled.

"Bastard," I shot back at him.

"I know that, but—" Marissa snarled.

"Don't tell me Solana stopped you again," Amethyst interjected.

My heart pounded wildly in my chest as I strained to hear her next words, taking my time to rise from the ground.

Marissa laughed shrilly. "No, I finally killed her. She's with the Grim now and out of my way."

I made a strangled sound, and Maze hooked his arm under my elbow. I couldn't stand, swaying on my feet as I thought of my aunt, dead at Marissa's hand—she'd been the closest thing I had to a mother after Marissa killed my actual mom.

Maze dragged me forward before I could hear any more. My mind went wild with dark scenarios. Marissa attacked The Gilded City again? She killed Queen Solana? I was the heir, but now that I was dead for all intents and purposes, it meant Ayden would rule. Was he ready for that?

I barely registered Maze unhooking my cuffs and tossing me in my cell.

I'd grown up without a mother and father. Solana was the only parental figure in my life. She'd raised us with a nanny, sure, but she'd always treated us as her own children. I knew that she'd be there for me if I ever needed her. She bought us our first swords and taught us how to be men. I couldn't believe she was gone. It felt like my anchor to the world had just been cut away, and now I was floating without an aim or purpose.

"My aunt is dead," I rasped to the empty cell, the loneliness crushing me under it like a stone. And what the fae did Marissa want with my girlfriend?

I hadn't technically asked Fallon to be my girlfriend, but I was pretty sure if I did, she would say yes, so I was giving her the title anyway.

I'd never wanted to kill someone as much as I wanted to take Marissa's life right now. She was lost to darkness and murder, bent on revenge. And for what? The innocent citizens of The Gilded City hadn't done anything to her. My family hadn't done anything to her.

I slumped into the pathetic excuse for a mattress, feeling a sickening depression swallow me up. I wasn't sure I wanted to fight anymore. I wasn't sure I wanted to go on living in this cruel world. Marissa killed my aunt. She'd go after Ayden next and then me. And, of course, Fallon. Did I want to live in a world where all my loved ones were gone? I had prepared my entire life to die young, to be the first to go. I couldn't conceive of a world where I had to bury Aunt Solana or even Ayden. The very thought tore my heart in two. If I had my paints and a canvas, I would draw this feeling inside me right now. I'd paint the entire thing black and edge the painting with teeth and blood. That's what this felt like, like I'd been eaten alive, and now I was in the belly of a beast with no way out.

11

FALLON

The queen lay semiconscious before the Grim on a bed of grass.

"You would dare let me die?" she asked him, clutching her stomach. "My people need me."

The Grim shrugged beneath his cloak. "Death doesn't care about royal lineage."

"By the power I carry as a temporary Maven healer, you *will not* take her!" I screamed, and stalked in front of the queen, making myself a shield.

I peered back to see that Solana's head craned in my direction and her eyes grew wide. I had a few regrets in life, but my biggest one right now was not asking my dad more about what it was like when Ariyon saved him. I had zero clue what I was doing.

Focusing back on the Grim, I watched as he cocked his head toward me. "Hello, Nightling."

"I'm not a Nightling!" I snapped. "Not yet. And I asked you to keep Ariyon safe, and instead he got arrested."

The Grim walked over to a large boulder and reached his hand inside. The boulder wavered, going translucent, and he pulled out two swords.

What the...?

"I *did* keep him safe. He's still alive, isn't he?" he commented.

"Ariyon?" Solana perked up at that, and hope unfurled in my chest at the mention of his name.

Why was he grabbing weapons? I peered around for anything I could use to defend myself. There was a small rock, but it would do nothing against two swords. I was suddenly reminded of Ariyon's body being bruised and cut as he fought the Grim for my father.

No matter what happens, if I pass out, wake me. He'd said that. Why? If I died down here, would I die for good?

The Grim walked toward me and tossed one of the swords up into the air. I reached up instinctively and grabbed it.

"It is true that you currently carry the power of a Maven, so I am permitted to honor your request to return this soul back to her body." He pointed to Solana.

"Oh, thank the Light," Solana said weakly from behind me.

The Grim then pulled off his hood, dropping it to the floor and showcasing his entire face and bare chest. Once again, I was struck by his handsomeness. Dark-brown skin, ice-blue eyes, chest riddled with hundreds of puckered scars; his looks were spellbinding. He clenched his chiseled jaw, dipped his chin, and grinned sadistically at me. "If you can fight me for her, that is," he added.

Panic seized me. Sword fighting was not exactly my strong

suit. The one thing I had going for myself was that I was kind of a badass with the Undying Fire. Hefting heavy swords was something I had yet to master.

"But...you healed Ariyon without fighting me for it."

He nodded. "A leniency I will never again allow another soul."

I wondered for a fleeting moment why he was so forgiving in this one instance but then decided I didn't care so long as Ariyon was safe.

A puff of black smoke materialized before my face and turned into Yanric. He hovered between the Grim and me, and the Grim nodded. "I'll allow your familiar to assist."

Thank the Light.

Fighting for Queen Solana's life was one of the most stressful things I could think of. If I lost, she died, and now I wondered if I would die too.

"Strike three blows to any part of my body, and you win your prize—her soul. If I am the first to strike three blows, she is *mine*."

He growled the last words.

I'd thought Ariyon practiced his swordsmanship just to be able to fight without magic. Now I knew the real reason why and was kicking myself for not paying more attention in weapons class.

'Simply strike him?' Yanric laughed. *'I've got this.'*

The Grim took in a deep breath, and Queen Solana cleared her throat. I looked back at her soul body to see it blip from physical to a more spectral form, and she held my gaze. "How do I know you will truly fight for me and not just appear to and let me die?" she asked.

This woman had serious trust issues with me.

"Because I've known for weeks that Avis is your sister, and

I haven't told a soul," I said, and her eyes went wide. "I will give this everything I have," I promised her.

She nodded. "Well, please try not to screw this up."

She said please, so I was going to take that as a win.

"Begin!" the Grim shouted. I spun in his direction, and a gasp ripped from my throat. His sword came down on my arm, slicing right through it. My physical form flickered for a moment, showcasing my spectral spirit, and then a deep throbbing pain appeared at the wound. I instinctively knew that wherever my body was, a painful gash had just appeared on my arm.

'Holy Nightling poop, he's fast!' Yanric flew up and out of the way as I spun to escape another swing by the Grim as well.

His speed wasn't just fast—it was otherworldly. He moved like lightning.

"I'm going to die," Solana moaned from behind me.

"Shut up!" I snapped at her, sensing Yanric's next move and trying to keep the Grim's attention. My bird and I were getting good with mental communication, and in this moment, I could sense what he was about to do.

I rushed at the Grim with a battle cry on my lips and held my sword high. He moved forward to meet me just as Yanric dropped from the sky and crashed into his neck, coming away with a small piece of flesh that instantly healed before my eyes.

The Grim smiled. "It seems we are at a tie. One to one."

He appeared to be enjoying this.

With lightning speed, he used his proximity to kick out with his boot. It landed on my chest, sending me backward.

I crashed into the ground, and even in my not-fully-physically-here state, it hurt.

Solana held her stomach and moaned as she looked over at me. "You have no idea what we are up against, Fallon. I need to return to take care of my people. A Nightling war is coming!"

"I'm doing my best!" I growled at her.

Yanric tried another dive from the sky, but the Grim twisted out of his way. As I was getting up, I felt a small rock under my palm and grabbed it.

He said I only needed to strike him, right? I was a decent throw, probably better at it than wielding a sword.

As the Grim rushed forward to attack me again, I reeled my hand back and chucked the rock right at his chest. It slammed into the meat under his neck, and he skidded to a stop, giving me a slow grin. He looked impressed.

"I'll allow it," he mused.

I couldn't get past that this seemed like it was some form of entertainment for him.

"Once more, Fallon! Come on!" Queen Solana begged, and I wanted to tie something over her mouth to shut her up. The pressure she was putting on me was too much.

Yanric flew into a mad frenzy then, trying to attack left and right, which caused the Grim to zigzag in the meadow to avoid him. I used this opportunity to creep closer. Yanric melted into shadows, swirling around the Grim like a funnel of black smoke and forcing him to freeze lest he be touched.

I met his gaze and grinned.

Gotcha.

Thrusting into the funnel of shadows, careful not to strike the black and accidentally kill my familiar, I slammed the tip of the sword into the Grim's rib cage.

He winced, and I retracted the blade, watching in fascination as the wound I'd created sealed up as if it were never there, leaving only a fine scar in its wake.

Yanric solidified back into a feathered bird and landed on my shoulder.

"I went easy on you." The Grim winked.

Relief spread through my chest. We did it—we saved the queen.

Yanric scoffed. *'We won fair and square.'*

"Thank you," I managed.

"Something's happening!" Solana screamed, and I turned around to see her body flickering wildly and then fading away, turning to dust as her spirit was carried up into the air.

I turned back to face the Grim with a panicked expression.

"She has returned to her body as promised," he said, looking bored as he pulled his cloak back on and up to cover his face. My body sagged with relief, and all the tension I'd been holding fled my system. I'd never have forgiven myself had I not saved the leader of The Gilded City. Ariyon and Ayden's aunt. Even though we had a complicated relationship, she was a good queen who loved her people, and I respected that.

I was relieved to hear I had saved the queen, but I couldn't help but think of Ariyon. I peered at the rolling hills behind the Grim. Was Ariyon somewhere out there?

"You said you'd keep him safe," I said again, this time filled with so much sadness that my voice broke.

The Grim sighed. "There are rules here, Nightling. You brought his mortal body here, to the resting place of souls. It is an unforgivable offense that takes great sacrifice to undo. Had you brought his soul, I would have bargained with you. His arrest and transport to the Realm of Rebirth was the only way I was allowed to keep him alive."

"What sacrifice? Ask anything of me and I will give it." I opened my hands and held them out to him.

He placed a hand over his heart and closed his eyes for a moment, as if reliving a memory. When he opened them again, he looked at me in a way that felt like he was looking into the depths of my very soul. Literally.

"I'm an old fae, Nightling. I've seen countless souls come through my weigh station. Never before have I met one so selfless."

His assessment of me was surprising. I wasn't selfless. I just wanted to right my wrong.

"It's my fault Ariyon died, and it's my fault his body was brought here."

The Grim frowned. "Yes, it is your fault his body was brought here, but the reason he died?" He pointed to a large, flat rock, and a scene suddenly burst to life across it as if playing on one of those movie projectors my dear friend Sorrel had read to me about. It played the scene of the dance.

Me standing before Marissa and then her embedding the ax in Ariyon's chest. He collapsed, and the scene dissolved.

I squirmed. "Okay. I didn't kill him, but...I...love him."

I hadn't wanted to admit it to myself. The only person in the realm who could touch me? Of course I loved him. What choice did I have? But it was more than that. I was drawn to him—his eyes, the way he tried to fight off smiling, the way he threw himself into saving people, easing their pain, even though he was so aware of what it did to his own life.

He nodded. "Do you know why he can touch you when no one else can?"

I stood up straight, startled he had read my mind but also

that he seemed to have an actual answer, and I held my breath as I waited for him to continue.

"Because the world requires balance. A curse to make you feel pain when touched needed at least one person to give you pleasure. Balance. Ariyon is your balance. That you found him in your lifetime is incredible."

My throat constricted with emotion. "Please let me have him back. I'll fight you for him."

I raised my sword, and Yanric jumped off my shoulder and into the air where he spread his wings, ready for an attack.

The Grim appeared sad, frowning at me. "If it were allowed, I would. But a blood payment cannot bring a physical body back from the land of souls. And it cannot transfer someone from the Realm of Rebirth."

Desperation filled my chest, sitting so heavily on me that I fell to my knees. "Please. Do something. Give me something! I can't stand not knowing if he's hurt or if he will ever come back. I study all day and night trying to find a way to bring him home. It consumes me!" I cried.

The Grim stared at me for a full minute and then looked over his shoulder as if to make sure no one was there. Walking over to the rock, he set down his sword and grabbed his sickle. In two strides, he'd moved over to a small flat rock on the ground, one that looked worn.

"You have only a few minutes," he said, and then slammed the staff of his sickle down on the rock.

I yelped as something tugged at my navel again and I was transported elsewhere. One second, I was standing in the meadow, and the next…

"Ariyon!" His name was a mixture of a garbled cry and a scream.

I was standing in a jail cell of some sort, and Ariyon was crumpled in the corner, lying on a mat. His bottom lip was split, he sported a black eye, and his arms were littered with bruises. He looked different, toughened, the muscles in his arms and back bigger somehow. But he was alive! Thank the Light, he was alive.

He was sleeping deeply, his chest rising and falling, so I stumbled forward, falling to my knees before him.

"Ariyon?" I reached out and shook him. Though my body was made of the flickering translucent spirit form, I still felt him. Somehow, my body felt fully materialized here. His warm skin under my fingertips caused a whimper to form in my throat. He shook awake at my touch.

His eyes flew open, and he put his fists up as if to fight me.

When his gaze landed on my face, his hands relaxed, and his mouth dropped open. But it only took him a moment to process it, as he lunged forward, pulled me to him, crushing me to his chest as he wrapped his arms around me.

"Fallon." My name was like a love letter on his lips. One word and it was filled with so much affection, reverence, and relief.

"Are you okay?" He pulled back and ran his gaze over my body.

I barked out a laugh. "Me? Ariyon, are *you* okay? We've been so worried. I screwed up. I switched our powers and accidentally brought your body down here. I didn't know how to save you, and now you're stuck here, and Hayes, Ayden, and Eden have been meeting me in the library to try to find a way to get you back, and—"

He leaned up and pressed his lips to mine, a zap of heat rushing through my body. When he pulled back, his eyes were glittering silver. "You saved my life," he said firmly.

I swallowed hard. "Marissa killed you because—"

"You saved my life, Fallon," he said again. "Thank you."

I felt a sobbing breakdown in my future but held it together for Ariyon. I didn't know how much time we had left together, and I wouldn't waste it.

"We don't have much time. I just came down here with Solana."

He gasped, and I put a hand on his chest to assure him.

"She's okay. I fought the Grim for her."

I pulled my hands up to show him the marks on the backs. His marks.

He swallowed hard and nodded, his body sagging in relief as he looked up at the ceiling as if sending a silent prayer to the Light.

"How do I get you out of here?" I asked, turning to look past the cell door behind me. But there was nothing to see, just a long hallway.

Ariyon blew out a deep breath. "I have no idea. Does Master Hart?"

I tried not to let desperation fill me at his words but shook my head. "He's hard to work with because Marissa traumatized him, and he can barely talk to me."

Ariyon nodded in understanding. "Fallon, because I have your powers, I've been given the opportunity to be…rebirthed. As a Nightling."

Even though I already knew all this information, I still winced. "I'm so sorry." I couldn't help the tears that lined my eyes.

He reached out and cupped my face. "It's okay. You can undo it, right? Whatever you switched, you can switch us back?"

I nodded. "I'm still trying to figure it out, but I need to get you back first. You can't become a Nightling."

He looked down the hall with determination. "I've lost track of time down here. I don't know how many days I have left until the tribunal is over. If I win, I'm granted permission to be reborn. Fallon, you have to get me out of here."

Panic seized me. Were days here the same as they were for me? What if it was less? What if I couldn't figure out how to bring him back?

Ariyon peered behind me, down the hall again, and then lowered his voice. "I overheard some of them talking. This place is full of House of Ash and Shadow descendants. Some of the ones who don't survive the tribunal stay down here forever, but they still speak to those up top. When a Nightling is in shadow form in the land of the living, their soul body is down here, Fallon. It's crazy. I don't fully understand it."

A shudder ran through me at his words. It seemed impossible, but it also made sense.

"Have you seen…" I couldn't bear to finish the sentence, but he nodded, knowing who I meant.

"Marissa is active down here. Her mother, Amethyst Bane, runs the place."

Amethyst Bane. The one I read about who mastered switching powers.

"What do you hear them saying?" I matched his whisper.

His face went ashen, and he collapsed back on his pillow, taking my hands into his. "Things that don't make sense. Things I need to ask my aunt about. That the Nightlings seek permanent bodies. Ones they will get if Marissa rises to power as queen. That she needs *you* to do it."

I frowned, shaking my head to clear it. "What? That doesn't make sense. Even if Marissa became queen, how would that give Nightlings permanent bodies?" And how did that involve me?

Nightlings fed on the blood of the living to stabilize their form and were otherwise mostly shadows. But Marissa being queen couldn't happen. It would be a nightmare come to life!

I felt a familiar tug at my navel, and I thrust myself forward in panic, clinging to Ariyon. My bare hands on his arms combined with my emotions immediately fired up my healing power, and I watched in delight as Ariyon's bruises and cuts mended before my eyes. He sighed in relief, looking more like the Ariyon I remembered.

"Ariyon, I'm being pulled back, but I won't let you get turned into a Nightling. I promise," I whispered against his neck.

He held me tightly against his chest, and I was so glad to hear his heart beating. He was alive—he was okay.

The pull on my navel was stronger now. When I pushed myself up to look at him, there was a look of confusion on his face.

"What's wrong?" I asked, as the tug at my navel grew more powerful.

"I wonder if Emmeric was real," he muttered.

"Who?" I asked, panic tinging my voice as the pull strengthened.

"I dreamed of him. He's an Ealdor Fae. Find him and—" His voice cut off as I was ripped from his arms.

I screamed and scrabbled at his arms, trying to stay with him, but the pull was too strong. It felt like I'd been sucked into a wind tunnel. Before I knew it, I was on my hands and knees, panting on the grass in front of the school. Queen Solana sat beside me, watching me with wide eyes.

I peered over at her. "I saw Ariyon," I said before I'd even gotten my breathing back under control. "He's okay!"

She looked shocked at that news. Her Royal Guard rushed around us, barking orders and pulling blades as they tried to coax her onto a healing stretcher.

"I'm okay!" she snapped at them, still looking at me. "Fallon saved my life." Her lips pursed as if she didn't want to admit it.

"Fallon!" I heard Ayden's voice from across the courtyard and craned my neck to see him running toward us, sword aloft. He was covered in blood and ash but looked unharmed.

Eden broke away from where she'd been protecting us and stepped into his line of sight.

"E!" He crashed into her as he reached her first. They embraced and pulled away smiling. I pulled on my gloves and stood, helping the queen up.

She wouldn't stop looking at me with a quizzical gaze, as if I was some puzzle she was trying to solve.

Ayden reached me then, and I gave him both hands to squeeze, so grateful he wasn't hurt.

"Is Master Clarke okay?" I asked him.

He nodded. "That old bastard is unkillable. Ripped two Nightlings apart with his mind."

I swallowed hard at that. "I thought Nightlings were nearly impossible to kill."

His face faltered, looking more serious than ever before. I found myself studying his face, marred with ash and sweat. "In their shadow form, only the Undying Fire can do that. But if you catch them in their physical form, they can be put down."

Good to know.

"My queen, please come back to the castle where it is safe," a guard said to Solana, but she waved him off.

"How many people did we lose? Are the healers tending to the injured? Have we doubled the guards at the gates? What else can we do to help?" She snapped rapid-fire questions at him, and for the first time, I saw her perfectly in her role as queen. She cared about her people, and she was a quick strategic thinker.

"Death count is still rising, unfortunately, your highness. Healers are tending to the injured, but there aren't enough. Guards are at the gates with horns ready to blow if there is another attack. It would help me if you were to head back to the castle and remain safe." He ended the last line with a slight growl, and she rolled her eyes.

"We have healers who can help," Hayes piped up, and Master Hart, who stood beside him, nodded.

"My students are still training, but it's better than nothing," Master Hart said, and I noticed that he was able to speak normally in my presence for the first time. Probably because he'd forgotten I was here. There was so much going on.

Solana nodded, smoothing her hair, and then met my gaze. "Fallon, I would like a word alone, and then you may help the other healers."

Nervousness bloomed in my stomach, but I nodded as the rest of the crowd began to break away into groups. Other than half a dozen guards who now flanked Queen Solana, we were alone.

"Ariyon is okay. He's surviving, and although I don't have an exact way to get him out, I have a good lead," I said, hoping it wasn't a lie. I had no idea who this Emmeric person was who Ariyon had spoken about before I was pulled away, but I was hoping I could find him and that it would be a game changer.

"You saved my life. Twice now." She crossed her arms and looked at me with suspicion.

"Umm, yeah?" Was it a question?

She sighed, chuckling to herself. "You're going to make a fool of me, aren't you?" she mumbled.

"Huh?"

She waved me off. "You're either playing some long-term game to gain my trust before you steal my kingdom out from beneath me…"

My head reeled back at that accusation.

"Or you're genuinely a good kid. That would be the sadder of the two because then when you go dark, it will break my heart." Her voice caught, and my fists clenched.

I was sick of everyone assuming I was going to lose my mind. How could I get through this if no one believed in me?

"And what if I don't go dark?" I took a step closer to her, causing her Royal Guard to draw their blades and glare at me. I stepped backward. "What if I spend my entire life protecting yours and those of the people of this city, and on the day you finally go meet the Grim and have to account for how you've treated people, you will look back and see how *you* have tormented *me*? Not the other way around."

Her face went slack, and her head reeled back as if I'd slapped her. She took a long moment to compose herself and nodded. "I think it's time you saw something, Fallon. When you come to the Winter Solstice party tomorrow, please arrive an hour early."

Dread filled me, creeping over my skin like a sickness. What did she want to show me? I hated the anticipation, but I nodded.

"So we're still doing the ceremony?" I asked.

She looked around at the dead bodies on the ground and the

burning trees. "Now more than ever, my people need to know where your allegiance lies. But I will cut down on the revelry. It will be a somber dedication to the fallen."

My people. Not our people. She didn't see me as one of them.

She smoothed her dress and then turned from me, barking orders at her guard to be taken to the wounded.

That wasn't exactly how I'd expected that to go. With a sigh, I wasted no time in finding Hayes and Master Hart and the rest of the healing students. They had set up a makeshift clinic, and I got right to work, doing everything I could to help patch up the bleeding and broken. It proved to be the hardest day in my short time as a healer. I tended to people in pain, and I *felt* it all. Stomach lacerations, burns, lost limbs. Witnessing the gore firsthand and feeling the pain over and over was so awful that I threw up twice. Now I knew why Ariyon was compelled to help everyone, even though it took time off his life.

As the hour grew late, Yanric brought word of my father and Mable being safe. The sky had darkened. It was long past dinner, and yet I couldn't leave, not while there were people to be healed. Avis had gotten word of the attack and had brought tinctures to help people recuperate. She was outside handing them out.

"You're exhausted." Ayden growled from beside me as I hovered my hands above a guardswoman whose skin was bubbled with painful burns. I felt them on my own skin, similar to the searing agony of my curse.

"I'm fine," I growled, watching the bubbles retreat and fresh pink skin replace them.

"And what if you're taking time off your life?" Ayden pressed.

Eden was asleep in a cot in the corner. She had passed out a few hours ago. She'd been assisting me, handing me gauze and salves, bringing me water. Only Hayes, Mrs. Reebus, Master Hart, and I were still going. And just barely. Hayes slumped forward on a patient's cot and appeared to fall asleep right before me.

I swayed on my feet. "Then so be it."

Ayden swam into view and got right up in my face, close enough that I backed up a little so a stray hair wouldn't touch him.

"And what if you're taking days off Ariyon's life?" he asked, and I yanked my hands away from the patient.

My throat constricted with emotion, and I peered around the tent. The casualties had already passed on; those who remained would live, maybe in pain, maybe scarred, but they would live. Ariyon might not.

I wish I knew more about switching powers and how it all worked because if it was just my life I was affecting, I wouldn't hesitate. The black wall in Ariyon's studio with the white marks loomed in my mind, and I nodded, folding my gloved hands into my chest.

Ayden reached out and rubbed small circles on my back. "You saved my aunt's life today, Fallon. That's a win for the whole realm."

He was right. It felt good to save a life, even the life of a woman who didn't like me. Having this great power to heal and take pain felt like a waste when it wasn't used.

"I think I'm understanding Ariyon a lot more now," I shared.

Ayden nodded. "When we were younger, he tried to describe what it felt like to be around people and constantly feel their pain. It made me sad, so he stopped talking about it."

That sounded familiar—like what I did with my own father when describing my curse.

I sighed, walking over to a makeshift handwashing station and peeling off my sweaty gloves. "I saw him, you know? When I saved the queen."

Ayden nodded. "I heard from Eden. Is he...okay?"

I pursed my lips. "He's alive. Seems like a rough place to be. I've got a lead on someone who might be able to help us figure out how to get him out. Want to take off school tomorrow and go searching for him with me?"

Ayden chuckled. "Tomorrow is the Winter Solstice. You can't miss that. My aunt is very much looking forward to you bowing before her."

Right. That whole thing I was doing to keep from being imprisoned.

"The day after, then. Ariyon said he was an Ealdor Fae? Emmeric."

"An Ealdor?" His brows drew together. It was painful to notice how handsome he was. Falling in love with someone and then looking at their identical copy was a confusing experience.

"You know where he might be?"

"Well, yes, but—"

Hope bloomed in my chest. "Awesome. You know where he lives? I'm guessing the West Side?"

Ayden shoved his hands into his pockets. "He's an Ealdor Fae, Fallon. They live in a secluded realm past Isariah. An entire day's travel on horseback, and you can't go there unless invited. My aunt sent them a letter once and didn't get a reply until a month later. They do as they please."

"Ariyon might not have a month!" I protested.

"I'll ask my aunt if we can get permission to see him. It's a formal process. You don't sneak up on Ealdoria unannounced and live to tell about it."

Chills raced up my spine at this information. "Okay, thanks. If not, I might have a backup plan." My so-called plan had to do with breaking into Ealdoria, so I hoped he could get us an invite.

The edges of his eyes crinkled. "You always have something brewing in that brilliant mind of yours, don't you?"

My heart pinched—the look he was giving me right now was one of adoration, maybe even love. Eden couldn't have been right about what she'd said earlier, could she? Ayden didn't still like me as more than a friend, right?

His eyes fell to my lips, and I frowned. "Ayden," I said gently. "I can't—"

"I know," he sighed and took a step backward, reaching up to rub his face as if needing to shake himself from a trance. When he pulled his fingers away, he glanced over at the beautiful sleeping form of my best friend. When he peered back at me, there was so much pain in his eyes, I wanted to pull him into a hug.

"I know what would be best for everyone. I tried…and you and Ariyon make sense. It's like the Light created him just for you, but… I can't help how I feel." He looked down at my feet, and I had to swallow a whimper as my heart broke for him.

This was exactly how I felt about Ariyon. I had tried to make it work with Ayden, but my heart wanted his brother.

"I'm so sorry." I reached for his hand and then stopped short, realizing I wasn't wearing my gloves.

We both looked at our hands, two inches apart, and chuckled. The curse would keep us apart no matter what.

Ayden waved me off. "If you and my brother are happy, how could I be sad? I love you both." Then he picked up his blood-crusted sword and waved to me. "See you tomorrow, Fallon."

"Yeah." I waved back, but it was hard to lift my spirits after that. Ayden was the poster boy for kindness, and I felt that we were all blessed to have him in our lives in whatever capacity, but what just transpired still sucked.

Yanric flew into the tent and perched on my shoulder.

'Your dad wants you to come home and get some rest. He's heading there now. He just finished helping the guards reinforce the gates.'

I nodded, walking over to rouse Eden. She blearily followed me outside into the darkness, where I said goodbye to Avis. The apothecary was still handing out tinctures and doing her best with Mrs. Reebus to make custom remedies on site. It seemed the Nightlings nearly pillaged the entire city before coming to the school, and now The Academy was a triage center of sorts for people to seek healing. Walking among the sick and injured was the queen, dutifully making her rounds and speaking to every single person as over two dozen guards followed her. She'd gained my respect tonight. My view of her had changed. She was like a mother bear protecting her cubs. The entire Gilded City was her children, and she saw me as a threat. I couldn't argue with that. I could only try to change her view of me.

I waved to Master Clarke, who was helping train a contingent of guards who were sparsely placed around the school. After dropping Eden off at her house and seeing that she got home safely, Yanric and I walked to my house.

'What a day,' I told him.

He yawned. *'I'm ready for bed.'*

Yanric slept with me now. I couldn't stand the thought of him out in the rain or cold.

When I stepped up to our door, I paused. My dad was standing frozen in the open doorway, staring inside.

"Dad?" I glanced past him and was confused to see all the furniture was gone. The apartment had been completely cleared out.

What the fae?

"Have we been robbed?" my father asked as he walked deeper into the apartment.

I was tired and my mind felt foggy, so it took me a second to figure out what was going on.

"Oh, we were supposed to move into Bane Manor," I said.

His posture relaxed. "Oh, right." Walking over to the kitchen counter, he pulled a note off the top. It was directions to Bane Manor. My father looked at me bleary-eyed. "I'm too tired to trek to the East Side right now. Are you too pampered to sleep on the floor?"

I grinned. "Never."

With that, he walked back over the street to Mable's to borrow some blankets, and we made two bedrolls on the floor, just like in Isariah.

"I'm glad you're okay, kiddo. I was worried today," he said, peering at me from across the living room floor.

I let out a big yawn as Yanric snuggled deeper into my blanket. "You too, Dad."

The words barely left my mouth before I drifted to sleep.

12

ARIYON

IT HAD BEEN A FEW DAYS SINCE I'D SEEN FALLON. BUT DOING so had given me renewed hope. She was looking for me; I should have known she wouldn't stop. I grinned at the memory of holding her against my chest in this very cell. She'd brought me the best news when she told me that my aunt was safe and not dead. I was going to do whatever it took to get back to Fallon, my aunt, my brother, and The Gilded City. So far, I was winning my tribunal, and they were throwing everything at me, three to four fights a day. Marissa was also back, watching from the corner of the room like a psycho. I think she liked seeing what her daughter's power could do. Watching me was like watching Fallon in some weird way. I couldn't help but get a creeped-out vibe that Marissa was obsessed with Fallon and her power, and I wanted to know why. What she'd said the other day, about needing Fallon in order to be queen and getting the Nightlings bodies, was so beyond disturbing. It didn't make sense. Even if she succeeded in finally assassinating my aunt, she couldn't be queen. Right?

I decided the next time I saw Marissa, I'd ask her about it. Worst case, I pissed her off and she slapped me. But she couldn't kill me. Not according to the Accords, which I still longed to have a copy of. From what I gathered, I was a prisoner, so I could be roughed up and forced into fights, but I couldn't be killed unless it was during a fight. They had to treat me like one of their own until my tribunal was over. I feared what would happen to me if I lost my tribunal. You were allowed to forfeit the fights, but it was frowned upon. Would I just live here in my bodily form forever? Become a guard and just… No, I couldn't allow myself to think like that. Or about the Bottomless Pit that Amethyst had threatened me with. I had to stay positive.

Footsteps sounded outside the cell, and I sat up, clutching my rib cage. Fallon had healed me, which had been amazing, but then I'd been put in another fight.

I peered down the hallway to see a young, lanky fae with light-brown skin and tattoos covering 75 percent of his visible body. He was being dragged down the hall by Maze.

"Eat shit and die!" the teenage fae spat in Maze's face, and my head reeled back in surprise.

Maze froze, turning his face in the dude's direction, and came up with an upper cut so hard, the dude was lights out on impact. His body went limp in Maze's arms, and the fae guard had to now hook him under the armpits and drag him to his cell, which was right next to mine. There was a small window between our cells, and I could see that he was still breathing when Maze laid him in his bed haphazardly.

"Brat!" Maze returned the spit, hocking a big loogie onto the dude's face.

I met the guard's gaze but said nothing, praying he wouldn't take me out for another fight today. I was still nursing my wounds from the last one. When he passed my cell without a word, I sighed in relief and went back to the window to watch the other fae. My gaze ran along his tatted neck and arms. A raven, a snake eating a rat, roses, the crest from House of Ash and Shadow. He was covered in artwork, really well done too.

I watched him for an embarrassing amount of time, but I was bored out of my mind in here and he was the best entertainment that I'd seen since I got here. I also hoped he was okay since he'd been passed out a while. Finally he roused, and I backed up, not looking so eagerly through the window. I hadn't had a normal interaction with another fae in a long time. I missed my brother and Hayes and having a friend.

"Hey, man, you okay?" I called to him.

He groaned, looked over at me, and sat up, taking full stock of the cell before zeroing in on my face. Reaching up, he rubbed his jaw.

"I'll live. You been here long? You look like shit." He got up and moved closer, eyes running over my wounds.

I chuckled. He reminded me of Hayes. No nonsense.

"I lost count. A couple weeks. Maybe forty fights."

"Geez. They make us work hard for rebirth, don't they?" He shook his head. "As if we want a chance to be a bloodsucker, anyway. Sick."

My interest was piqued at that comment. "I know. It's gross. But it seems like we're stuck in some type of legal system."

He nodded. "The Accords."

I sat up straighter. "You know about them?"

He snorted. "I'm House of Ash, bro. I read the Accords when I was like seven years old. Didn't you?"

So he'd recently died. How was that possible unless there were more House of Ash living out in the realm than we previously had thought? I swallowed hard. This fae seemed nice enough, but would his friendliness wear off if he knew who I really was? I needed to hide it, get more information out of him—that would be the smart move. But the worst thing would be to not tell him the truth when I had the chance and have him hear from one of the guards and lose trust in me.

"No... I'm not House of Ash, actually. It's a long story."

His eyebrows shot up, and he came over to lean against the window causally. At this close distance, I judged he was about twenty years old, black hair and hazel eyes. He had a sharp chin and beaky nose. The tattoos and small scattering of scars across his chin and eyebrow let me know he was a badass and not to be double-crossed.

"Long story, huh. I seem to have a lot of time on my hands," he said, looking at me expectantly.

I chuckled, took in a deep breath, and told him my story. I was careful to leave out anything that I wouldn't want Marissa to know in case this guy was a plant of some sort, but I started with meeting Fallon, and by the time I got to the part where Fallon switched powers with me and dragged my body down here on accident, the dude was wide-eyed.

"That's incredible. This chick sounds powerful! I mean, obviously, she's Marissa's daughter," he said.

I nodded. "I'm Ariyon, by the way. So, what's your story?"

He bowed lightly to me. "I'm Pax Weathers, humble fae from the Outer Stretch."

My eyebrows rose. The Outer Stretch was a deserted wasteland full of cliffs and oppressive heat. The cave dwellers there had struggled to find enough water or food. "I thought the people in the Outer Stretch died off a long time ago."

He grinned. "That's what we want you to think so you won't come looking for us and tax us into eternity."

That caused me to chuckle. I liked this guy. "What did you do there?"

Pax shrugged. "I acquired hard-to-find things, black-market-type stuff."

Illegal things, it sounded like. "And you were living there recently? I mean you…just died?" I didn't think there were any House of Ash and Shadow fae left living.

He nodded, a frown pulling at his lips. "Double-crossed a fae I shouldn't have. Woke up here. Was promptly arrested. Nice welcoming party."

He was murdered. *Damn.*

"Can you tell me about that? The Accords and all that."

He nodded. "In the beginning, the Light created everything, including the two houses, House of War and House of Light."

I frowned. "Three houses. The Light created the House of Ash and Shadow as well."

Pax frowned. "No, the early royal fae leaders of the House of War became obsessed with power in an innocent attempt to protect all fae, but they went too far," he said. "They are the ones who created the House of Ash."

I stayed quiet, trying to school my facial expressions because his story had already veered off-course from the one we were taught growing up in The Gilded City.

Pax went on. "They voted and decided that a few of the less-than-desirable House of War families should be experimented on to see if they could create even more powerful magic."

I held up my hand at this point. "Wait, what? This is nowhere close to what I've known my whole life."

Pax shrugged. "We have tons of books about it in the Outer Stretch."

I swallowed hard. "Go on."

"So the Banes, the Wixes, and the Yearwoods were the unlucky recipients of some pretty grotesque dark magic. Stuff that required ritual living sacrifice and blood magic. Dark stuff, bro." He gave me a look, but I couldn't respond. I was frozen in place, my hands shaking slightly as I was held captive by this story. I didn't want to believe it; I wanted to tell him it was total crap, but somewhere deep down inside, I felt that Pax was speaking the truth.

Pax sighed. "They were enticed into the experiments by being told they would be made powerful royal families and given mansions and riches beyond their wildest dreams. But once they started going dark and losing their minds to the magic, the royals in House of War realized they made a mistake they couldn't undo. So the House of War royals distanced themselves from them, segregated anyone with that dark magic into their own house, House of Ash and Shadow. This was all in the hope that they wouldn't be blamed if House of Ash killed everyone or burned them in their sleep."

I could barely breathe. I hung on his every word.

"What does this have to do with the Accords?" I managed to ask.

He nodded. "A century or so later, House of Ash had spread quickly, building up a nice little population of a couple hundred fae. When the House of War decided they couldn't control House of Ash anymore, they killed them off. Nearly all of them in one fell swoop. The Realm of Eternity was suddenly filled with a bunch of angry fae whose magic no longer came from the Light. Then the Grim dealt them the hardest blow. Since they had been changed from their original creation, they were not permitted to enter the Realm of Eternity. They had to go to another place where their previous fallen ancestors had already been sent, separate from the other fae who had passed on, for fear that they would infect Eternity itself with their darkness."

I felt like I was on the verge of tears, which was so stupid. It was just a story, probably not even true. But also…what if it was? What if Fallon and her ancestors were experimented on and made to be evil?

"The House of Ash families were shuffled into this shithole," he continued, gesturing around the cell, "and told that all of them would be given one chance at new life, reborn as magicless fae. A penance for their years of dark magic."

"Okay now, this just sounds fake," I told him.

"So," he went on, "they were given the opportunity to be reborn but must remain magicless. If you were reborn, remained magicless, and died, you would get to rejoin the fae in the Realm of Eternity, but only if you proved your worthiness of such a place. Proved that you could let go of the temptation of the dark powers. But if you were reborn and were drawn again to dark magic, all you would need to do would be to feed on the blood of a fae with magic to restore your House of Ash powers."

"You're saying that Nightlings are reborn magicless at first?" I couldn't believe what I was hearing.

He nodded. "Yes, in a fully functioning fae body, but there is a catch. If you feed upon blood and become a Nightling with your dark powers restored, then you must constantly feed to be corporeal in the world, lest you be turned to shadows."

Holy Fae. If what he was saying was true, it explained

everything—why the Nightlings fed on blood, why they turned into shadows, how when they were in shadow form, their souls came here…

I swallowed hard. "So, if you kill a Nightling in the real world…" I wanted to know what would happen if I tried to kill Marissa Bane. Would she just keep coming back here?

Pax looked somber. "They are thrown into the Bottomless Pit, disappearing forever."

That part was good news at least, but the rest was…crazy. I slumped in on myself. I didn't know why the story affected me so much, but it did. Pax hadn't specifically said that the Madden royal family did these experiments, but it was implied that all the royal families of House of War were guilty, which included mine.

"So"—Pax gestured—"the Accords were drawn up as a rule book for handling souls from the House of Ash that cross over. How they must all be given a tribunal, a chance to be reborn. No one having a family feud can just deny you the right to rebirth or throw you on the hot coals of the Bottomless Pit for no reason. There is order, and if a Nightling dies topside, then there are protocols that force them to the Pit."

I sat up straighter at that. "So the Bottomless Pit is…the erasure of your soul?"

Pax's face grew serious. "Yes. If you lose the tribunal or if you decide not to be reborn and you piss someone off down here, your soul is thrown into the Bottomless Pit, where it is eaten up and disappears forever."

I frowned. "So, if I win and get reborn, I won't be a Nightling."

Pax nodded. "You'll be magicless."

I was ashamed to say I wasn't sure which I felt would be worse.

13

FALLON

CLASSES HAD BEEN CANCELED FOR THE REST OF THE WEEK.
Today was the day of Winter Solstice, and word had spread
throughout town that I would be making some kind of statement. After the attack last night, every Gilded Citizen was acting
differently. They stared at my father and me as I rode through
town on Ember. My dad walked beside the horse, carrying our
runaway bags he'd retrieved from Mable's. Regular shopkeepers
now had swords and maces on their belts. Guards were stationed
at every block, and we'd been questioned about our credentials
twice. My father now had an ID badge that would get him in and
out of the West Side at any hour.

"The queen said she would get you a bike so you don't have
to walk to Mable's inn," I told him. A second horse was probably out of the question, and I didn't want to push the queen's
kindness.

"I like walking. It's good for health," was all he said.

He'd been quiet this morning, and I couldn't help but feel bad that I'd displaced him so much.

"I miss Isariah," I told him as we followed the map past the palace and into the countryside full of homes and hilltops.

My father smiled. "Floating down Dead Snake River in the summer while eating wild huckleberries."

"Running through the village during the flower festival." I beamed, closing my eyes. I could almost smell the roses.

"There are nice things about this city as well," he said, and I nodded.

"Like Eden and Mable."

He gave me a wry smile. "Yes, and flushing toilets."

We both laughed at that.

It's up ahead.' Yanric flew from my shoulder and arced through the air, heading between two weeping willows to a skinny dirt road.

Ember trotted along the lane at a slow pace so that my dad could keep up, and I peered up at the mansion on the hill. A little gasp escaped me at the sight of it. It was almost as large as the main school building at The Academy. It stood four stories high, and the structure looked like it had been carved of black stone. Sunlight hit the building, and it sparkled with a sleek onyx shine. Two black raven statues perched on pillars flanking the gate. In the center of the metal gate was a snake curved into an infinity symbol.

"How do you suppose we open i—" The gate suddenly opened as we approached, and Yanric flew overhead.

'It opens for a Bane, or if you use the lever, which the guard standing at the top can.'

I followed Yanric's line of sight, and sure enough, there was a Gilded City guard standing by the front garden, which was unkempt and overrun with weeds.

"It's huge," my dad commented.

I nodded. "Could probably house the entire village of Isariah."

"At least half of them, yeah," my father agreed.

'This was once used as a dormitory where all House of Ash and Shadow fae lived to remain safe. They were hunted many centuries ago.'

Holy Fae. Hunted? That didn't sound right.

We wound up the driveway, and my gaze went to the overgrowth of weeds and wildflowers that ran the length of it. It looked like someone had to recently cut back growth just to be able to use the road. The queen's guards, I assumed, and whomever else she had working here at my prison. It was hard to look at this giant manor and see a home and not its other intention, which was to cage me if I went dark.

The guard nodded to me as we approached, and I dismounted Ember.

He kept his posture stiff and looked straight. "This post will be guarded at all times. You are to make yourself seen before coming or going so we can catalog your whereabouts," he stated.

"In her own home?" my father growled, and I placed a hand on his shoulder. He didn't know the extent of my agreement with the queen. She clearly wanted to keep an eye on me to make sure I was keeping my curfew, and I was okay with that.

"Okay," I told the guard, and gave my dad a look that said *don't press it.* If Solana wanted to waste resources babysitting my whereabouts, then so be it.

"Is there a stable for my horse?" I asked him.

The guard nodded once. "Around back."

My dad took the reins and tied Ember to a post with a bat carving on top. "We can stable her after. I want to look inside."

I nodded. I was eager too. Would there be frog legs hanging from the ceiling and bat wings as dinner plates?

Yanric laughed in my head at that thought, and I glared at him. *'You're not far off, but only in some rooms,'* he stated.

Walking up to the door, I wrapped my hand around the serpent-head carved handle and pulled it open.

I expected to be met with decades' worth of dust but, instead, was pleasantly surprised. Stepping up into the foyer, I appraised the entry room.

It was light and bright and unlike the outside. It also smelled of fresh paint and lemon-and-vinegar cleaning spray. The walls were light gray and the floors, a white marble stone. A huge double staircase with black velvet carpet led to a second floor, but my eyes were glued to a tiny letter that was propped up on an entry table.

Walking over to it, I tore it open and read it aloud for my father.

Ms. Bane,

Due to the neglected state your family manor was in, the queen had to send her household staff to ready the home for your arrival. You will see that not all the rooms could be prepared for you, as it was not a feasible use of time and resources.

Since your heir status has been officially reinstated, you are entitled to three household staff members paid for by the crown: one butler, one maid, and one stable hand. They will arrive daily from morning to night. You are expected

*to observe the rules laid out in your previous arrangement
with the queen.*

*She hopes you will be settled and arrive early for the
ceremony tonight.*

*Secretary to Her Royal Highness,
Maxwell Bishop*

"What rules?" my dad asked.

I waved him off casually and stuck the note in my pocket.
"Curfew and stuff."

He nodded and then pointed to the letter. "I'm not forcing
some servant to open the door for me and clean my dishes."

I chuckled. "We can tell the maid and butler they are not
needed, but I think the stable hand would be good to keep. I don't
know anything about horses."

My dad frowned. "On second thought, what if the maid and
butler are depending on this coin to feed their families?"

My gut tightened with dread. "I hadn't thought of that. We
can keep them all but tell them they don't need to fuss over us?"

My dad nodded as if that made him feel better.

We then set about exploring. I lost count of how many rooms
there were. Two of the bedrooms had been freshly painted and
cleaned and held our furniture from the West Side. The rest of
the bedrooms were drowning in cobwebs, with a musty odor and
furniture full of moth holes and thick dust.

I quickly learned the top three floors were all bedrooms
with attached bathrooms. There were over thirty of them, which
all held two bunk beds apiece, which meant this manor once

housed over a hundred people. The main floor was where the giant kitchen, sitting room, dining hall, office, and a colossal library were. Covering all the books were thick canvas sheets that I longed to rip down, but I still had to explore the mysterious basement level.

"Going to the basement with Yanric!" I told my dad as he stepped outside to take Ember to the stables and get her some water and shade.

"All right," he said.

I took the stairs two at a time, reminded of the dark entrance to Master Clarke's office, and then flicked on the light at the base of the stairs. The little crystal inside the sconce glowed a lilac hue.

"Whoa." I peered around at the giant open space. It was like a museum. Rows and rows of glass-top display stands filled the area. Most of them looked as though they'd been cleaned recently.

'Dark artifacts room. Queen probably had her people go through it first to take anything out she didn't want you to have access to,' Yanric explained.

I peered in one of the cases, and sure enough, there was a red velvet pad covered in dust with a missing item in the shape of a dagger. I moved to the next case and saw a bunch of crystals. *'Does she know what it all is?'*

He laughed. *'Does she know? That dumb—'*

I cut him a glare. We were working on being nicer to the queen. She was the reason we were still alive and not in a tiny cell with bars.

He cleared his throat. *'I doubt it.'*

I looked over all the stuff and then finally saw a small basket at the back of the room. A red velvet blanket was stuffed in it with black feathers poking out. Next to it was a map of the realm.

My heart pinched. "Is this where you…?" I looked at Yanric.

He flew over to the basket and peered at me. *'Yes. And I searched for you in every village and town within a two-hour walking distance either way.'*

I was three hours' walking distance away. Kneeling and reaching out, I held up my hand and he perched on it.

'I'm sorry for how I treated you when I first met you,' I told him.

Here he was living in a musty basement and searching for me every day for seventeen years, and the first time I saw him, I strangled him.

'Forgiven.' He bowed slightly.

"Boo!" Eden jumped into the open room with her hands out, and I startled a little and then laughed.

"Hey, you made it!" I stood, and Yanric flew from my hand as I moved closer to greet my bestie. With no school today, Eden had promised to come by before the Winter Solstice ceremony and see to it that we were settled in.

"Whoa, what is all this stuff?" She ran her fingers over the glass cages.

"Old, dark artifacts. The queen went through and took some but left a bunch behind."

She looked up at me in disbelief. "Girl, you own a mansion. This place is crazy big."

I chuckled. "It comes with a maid and butler. Oh, and a stable hand."

Eden crossed her arms, sulking. "Lucky."

Laughter pealed out of me but quickly cut off in my throat when I heard a muffled voice.

I froze.

"What the fae was that?" Eden looked at me wide-eyed.

Oh good, she heard it too.

Yanric soared overhead, flying circles around the room, and I heard it again—a muffled, possibly male voice.

Chills raced up my arms as Eden scooted closer to me. "If we find a dead body or a ghost down here, I'm never coming back. Sorry, girl."

I nodded in agreement. "Neither will I." I'd rather live in the woods.

Yanric landed on a glass-top case that was covered in dust. His little feet made claw prints on top as he cocked his head and peered into the glass.

That voice came again, and Yanric looked up at me. *'Someone is speaking in there.'*

What the...?

I stepped forward, a little less worried since I knew a whole person couldn't fit in the display case. Yanric hopped onto my shoulder as I flipped the latch and opened the case.

Dust fell around me as I coughed and peered into the display. There was a single black onyx crystal in the shape of a seashell— and unintelligible voices were coming out of it.

Voices I didn't recognize.

I swallowed hard and placed a finger to my lips, looking at Eden to be sure she knew to keep quiet. She nodded, and I hesitantly picked up the shell and held it to my ear.

"We should do a two-on-one fight next. Winning team gets to go topside. I'd like to see the pretty boy try to survive that," a raspy male voice said, and confusion swirled around me.

"We can't do that. We have to follow the rules, Maze. You've been working the Rebirth Tribunal long enough to know that," another softer voice spoke, and chills ran the length of my arms.

This couldn't be. I pulled the shell away from my ear and studied it to make sure I wasn't imagining things. It glowed with a faint blue hue inside as if it were possessed by magic.

Were they talking about what I think they were talking about?

I put it back to my ear.

"If the prince lives through this and gets to become a Nightling, I'm going to be pissed," the deeper voice growled. "Others would kill for that spot. Literally. And he's not even technically dead!"

My heart hammered in my chest. They were talking about Ariyon. Somehow, this crystal was linked to somewhere in the Realm of Rebirth, and I was privy to a conversation about Ariyon.

"Well, he carries the magic of the House of Ash and Shadow, so we gotta put him through the tribunal, same as the others," the man spoke.

"He's a Madden. He's not worthy. He won't survive," the growly one said. "I'll make sure of it."

Dread sank in my gut as I realized what we were truly up against.

"Just follow the Accords. We don't need the Grim pulling the rule book on us and sending us all into the Bottomless Pit."

The other man grumbled, and then I heard footsteps and a door slam. After a few more moments of silence, I pulled the shell from my ear with a shaky hand. Bile crept up my throat as I thought of Ariyon.

"What's wrong?" Eden looked at me with wide eyes, and I

tried to think of the words to formulate an explanation of what had just happened.

I placed the crystal back into the case and latched it before dragging Eden into the stairwell with Yanric. Once the basement door was closed, I looked her in the eyes.

"I think that crystal was linked to another in the Realm of Rebirth where Ariyon is. They were talking about him."

"What!" she shrieked.

I gave her and Yanric a quick rundown of what I had heard, and Eden began to pace the hallway, climbing up four steps and down another four.

"We need to get Ariyon out of there, E," I begged her. "The queen thinks I portaled Ariyon to the Realm of Eternity. Maybe we can research how to make portals. I mean, that's your specialty, right?"

That's all Eden was learning to do with her fire magic. It would take years, but eventually she would be able to create a ring of fire that led to anywhere in the realm…and beyond.

She finally stopped pacing and sighed. "Here's the thing. You may have portaled him into the Realm of Eternity, but I don't think you can just take him out that way. A mortal body in the land of the dead is a grievous offense. Besides, it would take months for me to catch you up on all the knowledge I have of portal magic."

I growled, fisting my hands and feeling like the edges of my sanity were unraveling.

"You said this Emmeric guy might know how to help Ariyon, right?" Eden said.

I nodded. "But Ayden said the Ealdors are hard to get an audience with."

Eden nodded curtly, tipping her chin high. "You leave that to me. I'll see you at the ceremony."

I frowned. "What are you going to do?"

She looked determined and pursed her lips. "If the queen really wants her nephew back, she's going to get us an audience with the Ealdor Fae. But *first,* you have to get through this ceremony. Gaining Queen Solana's trust is your number-one priority."

It wasn't, though. Saving Ariyon was.

I rubbed my face. "There's too much going on."

Eden reached out and grasped my shoulders. "It's okay. You've got this."

I nodded, giving her a half-hearted smile. "You're the best friend ever."

"You're not too bad yourself," she said and grinned.

14

FALLON

THE QUEEN HAD A BLACK BRIGADE SUIT MADE FOR ME. EVEN though I was only invited to the brigade on the condition that I got my powers back from Ariyon, I think she wanted the entire city to see me bow to her and pledge my allegiance wearing the uniform that signaled loyalty to her in and of itself. I didn't care. I just wanted to be done with this charade and then to be on my way to getting Ariyon back.

My father didn't have any super-nice clothes, but he wore pants without holes in them and a button-up shirt. His hair was slicked back, and he said he was going to get Eden and Mable and then meet me at the Gilded City castle for the festivities.

I shoved my pants into my boots so that my skin wouldn't touch Ember and then headed out for my early meeting with the queen. On the way, my stomach tied into knots over everything. The queen had said it was time to show me something. That felt ominous. If I stopped to think about all that had happened since my short time in this city, it was hard not to feel like I was a harbinger of bad things. I show up here after seventeen years, and Marissa and the Nightlings start attacking? It couldn't be a coincidence. I just wish I knew more about what they wanted. Ariyon said they wanted permanent bodies, but that didn't make sense or even seem possible. I was hoping for some answers now. I'd been patient. I'd agreed to publicly say whatever the queen desired. Now I just wanted to get it over with and find Ariyon.

A memory of him running his thumb over my lip caused warmth to travel down my spine, and I longed to get him back now more than ever before. He'd saved my father's life, and even though I saved his life, it felt like I'd repaid him by trapping him in the Realm of Rebirth.

Way to go, Fallon.

Before I knew it, I had arrived at the Gilded City castle. A stable hand took Ember from me, and a guard walked me through the palace. I gazed past the extravagant gardens where people were already lining up and filing out onto the great lawn. We walked by dozens of open doors, and even though I tried not to peer inside, my curiosity won. Bedrooms, libraries, offices… This place was five times the size of Bane Manor.

We finally reached a set of double doors, and the guard knocked three times rapidly and then twice slower.

"Enter," the queen's familiar voice called out.

The guard opened the door and escorted me inside.

"Wow," I said as I took in the large office. It was circular, filled from floor to ceiling with shelves. On the shelves were all kinds of things—books, crystals, daggers, artwork, framed letters. It was like a museum. Sitting in the middle of the room was the queen. She perched behind a sturdy, dark wood desk. Beside her were a sofa and two chairs, and she gestured there for me to take a seat. I did, my gaze flitting around the space in awe. There was a golden-looking egg that had a slight illumination to it. I wanted to ask what it was but thought better of it; now probably wasn't the time.

After I sat, the queen looked to the guard.

"You may wait outside," she directed him.

"But—" he began to interject.

"You question your queen's decision-making?" she snapped.

"No, your highness." He bowed and left, shutting the door behind him.

I folded my hands in my lap as the queen came to stand over me. "I have to admit, Fallon, I like you better without your dark powers."

I looked up at her to find her smirking. Was she teasing me? The queen teased?

I chuckled. "I like your office. All this stuff is really cool."

She nodded. "Relics from past monarchs. Precious artwork, powerful objects, books that hold ancient knowledge."

Wow, she was being really forthcoming. I relaxed a little. Hopefully she'd finally realized I wasn't a threat. This could be good for me long term, less of a chance I would be locked up for life.

"So," she said, looking at me pointedly. "Ayden and Eden stopped by and spoke to me about the trip you want to take. To Ealdoria."

I nodded. "To help get Ariyon back."

"I don't see why my nephew has to go," she muttered, pursing her lips. "But I will approve the trip so long as you are accompanied by a dozen Royal Guard. Anything to bring Ariyon back. He must be barely holding on down there." She wrung her hands together, and worry pinched her face. For the first time, I saw the aunt and not the queen.

I was relieved that Eden and Ayden had put up a united front and gotten her to agree. My bestie was formidable when she set her mind to something.

"He's okay," I told her. "He's tough, and I'm going to get him back and switch our powers. I promise."

She met my gaze then and nodded, her face sharpening. "That's actually what I wanted to talk to you about."

My stomach tightened as I braced myself. She'd danced around whatever reason it was she'd brought me here, and now I was finally going to find out. It felt like standing on the edge of a cliff and looking into the abyss below.

"I'll be honest, Fallon. I barely slept last night. I kept thinking about the cursed Bane girl who keeps saving my life when she doesn't have to."

I squirmed in my seat. "Any decent person would have done what I did."

She barked out a laugh, her loose blond curls shaking around her as she did. "Most wouldn't have fought the Grim on my behalf, I assure you," she said.

Silence stretched between us. Was she scared? Her fingers twitched slightly, and she swallowed hard before finally speaking.

"Some information has come to my attention recently that I feel would be better shared with you. That way, in the spirit of what Master Clarke is trying to do, we can work to head it off *together*."

I nodded, my concern for what she was about to tell me growing, yet I felt optimistic she wanted to work on it together. "I'd like to work together."

She blew air through her teeth and then sat next to me in the most casual manner I'd ever seen her. Leaning back against the couch, she peered over at me. "I have recently learned, through my council, that Marissa seeks to gain permanent bodies for herself and all of the Nightlings under her command."

I nodded, realizing just now that in all the drama of saving her life and then spending all night healing the wounded, I'd forgotten to tell her I knew that. "Ariyon said something similar, but he didn't really know what it meant. He said he wanted to talk to you about it. It isn't possible, right?"

The queen frowned. "That's what has recently come to light. It may be possible. With you."

I froze. "What do you mean?"

"As an heir to the Bane throne, you carry a special fae magic that connects you to your people, just as I am connected to my people. Because my mother was from the House of Light and Ether and my father from the House of War and Bone, my magic is connected to both houses, and every fae in The Gilded City from those houses."

I nodded. "So my magic is connected to every fae from the House of Ash and Shadow?"

"Yes, including *all* Nightlings. It's bloodline magic not commonly known about."

All Nightlings. Like Marissa. The fact that I was connected to the undead caused shivers to race up my spine.

"Okay…"

Solana squirmed in her seat and then looked over at me. "The Old Law states that each of the nine royal families would take turns ruling, one after the other."

I frowned. "But haven't the Maddens ruled forever?"

She cut me a glare, and I quieted.

"Well, yes, that's what has come to my attention, Fallon." She gave an exasperated sigh and continued. "Apparently, some several centuries ago, my ancestor Graysen Madden changed that law by royal decree. There was an uprising over it, which led to a war that he won. Then he conveniently edited all of this out of the history books."

My eyes widened at her admission. That was messed up. "And I'm the one with the dark history?" I gave her a little smile to let her know I was joking, and she returned it—thank the Light.

"So, now, what do I do with that information, knowing someone in the Madden history changed our oldest laws and covered it up?"

That felt like a heavy burden, and I was glad I didn't have to deal with it. "Maybe reinstate the original law? Finish out your reign, and when you pass, the next royal family in line gets the throne?"

She nodded, a crease forming between her eyes. "Therein lies the problem, Fallon. The next family in line to rule was yours."

I froze beside her. "*Oh.* I see."

The Banes? I *definitely* didn't want to be queen, not now, not in a hundred years. That kind of responsibility was my worst nightmare. Besides, I didn't have children or cousins or anyone else in line to rule. I was pretty sure you needed an heir to do that.

"You could skip me. I could sign something or forego my family's spot, and the throne could go to the next."

Her eyebrows shot up to her hairline. "You would do that? Give up the chance to rule an entire kingdom? To be the leader of the most powerful cities in our realm?"

I nodded, and she waved me off with a dainty hand.

"You're young. You might change your mind. Besides, it doesn't work like that. It would be Marissa's turn, not yours. She may be a Nightling, but technically she still lives even if it's in her own special undead way. She walks this realm and therefore could be queen."

I gasped at that. Marissa Bane, queen of The Gilded City? I could think of nothing more horrifying.

"I carry the monarch's power." Solana peeled down the high neck of her dress to show me a glowing red amulet at her throat. "It's an amplifier of sorts to my magic. The next person in line would get this amulet. If it went to Marissa, she might conceivably be able to amplify her power to breathe life into her people permanently. I don't know if she has that power, but my sources say that she is confident she can do it if made queen, which tells me she does."

I shivered at that. "What does that have to do with me?"

She sighed. "I went to The Academy with a particularly talented fae who could glimpse the future. She told of an upcoming Nightling war with the people of The Gilded City."

I remembered her saying something similar the first day I'd regained consciousness in that cell.

"You think Marissa is starting that war now? To try to become queen?"

Solana nodded. "I do. To get this." She tapped her chest. "So that she can give her people new bodies."

I frowned. "Why now? Why not ten years ago or five?"

Solana peered at me quizzically, as if wondering how much to tell me. "Because of you. She didn't have you, didn't know of your whereabouts until now, didn't even know if you were alive. Now she's emboldened."

"Why does it matter that I'm alive or that she knows where I am?"

Solana laced her hands over her knees. "Royal law states a monarch cannot rule without at least one blood heir, better if you have two."

She tapped the amulet again. "You place one drop of the reigning monarch's blood inside and another drop of the heir's. Only then does it activate. The nine original families encoded it with their blood eons ago. The magic inside would recognize Marissa as a Bane and then you. It would give her all the power of a queen and then some. I imagine this is how she will do it. She must have some type of magic that would give her people permanent bodies once the locket is activated."

Well, fae. Dread crept up my body from my feet to my chest, settling there like a heavy stone. That was not good but also made a lot of sense.

You belong with me. It was one of the first things Marissa said to me. She didn't want me. She wanted my blood, my heir status. I'd stupidly held out a bit of hope that she might actually want a relationship with me. Lost to the darkness or not, it was a nice thought that my own mother might want to get to know me.

My face must have betrayed my sadness because the queen reached out and patted my gloved hand. "That is the reason she cursed me to never have children and that my heir would die if I harmed you. She was ensuring that my line would die out, especially if I tried to take hers."

That was awful. It made my heart break to hear such a thing. Solana pulled her hand back and then looked down at her lap. "Fallon... It's also the reason I cursed you in her belly. To feel pain when touched. So that you could never fall in love, never have children."

I gasped, choking on the pure shock that rushed through me at her admission. Solana. It was Solana? Tears rushed to fill my eyes as my heart shattered, but the anger chased them away like a thief in the night.

"*You* did this to me?" I stood, and Yanric materialized in the room, a rush of shadows transforming to feathers and perching on my shoulder.

Solana didn't look up, just stared at her clasped hands, seemingly in shame.

"I was an innocent child!" I screamed, no longer caring if she liked me or I wasn't following protocol. I wanted to kill her.

"I've never truly hugged my own father. I...I can't believe you did this." I stumbled backward, still processing it all. All these years, I envisioned a monster had cursed me. An evil man with a cold heart who hated children. I'd assumed it was Ariyon's father and that he must have been a cruel king.

'*I will peck her heart out from her chest and feed it to the pigs in the stables,*' Yanric declared, and for the first time, I wanted to give him the okay to do such a thing.

"Look at me," I growled at her, knowing in that moment that if I had my magic, I would burn her alive. "You ruined my life. The least you can do is meet my eyes."

She took a shuddering breath then, tipping her chin up to meet my gaze, and it was like I had been socked in the stomach.

Silent tears streamed down her cheeks, flowing freely as her nostrils flared and she fought to keep composure. Her bottom lip shook as she seemingly forced down a sob. She stood, facing me.

"I thought you would be like her. Evil. Unforgivable. Lost to the darkness. I wanted to stop her from spreading her evil."

"I'm not evil!" I screamed, advancing on her. I was grateful I didn't have my power right then. I could have burned the entire realm to the ground with the rage I felt.

She swallowed hard but didn't back up. Instead, she tipped her chin high and awaited whatever I was about to dish out.

I said nothing. I couldn't speak, my words lost in a sea of pain and betrayal. "I'm supposed to bow to you? You're supposed to be my leader? My queen? My protector? You're my nightmare!" I declared.

Her bottom lip still shook, but she grit her teeth and held my gaze, blinking to shed the tears that kept coming. "Fallon." Her voice held a sorrow that I didn't think she was worthy of having. I was the one who had every right to be sad, not her! "Your mother is the reason I will never have children. Never know what it's like to be called mama. Never kiss the forehead of my newborn babe."

I crossed my arms. "And that's *my* fault? *Marissa* cursed you. Not me!"

She nodded, dropping her gaze and picking at her fingernails. "You're right. I'm sorry. You didn't deserve this. I don't regret a lot of things in life, but… I regret that, okay? If I could take it back, I would."

Her eyes misted over again, and I wondered how long she'd wanted to tell me this.

"I saved your life." My voice broke. "Twice. Now the woman who ruined my life is the one I am bound to follow?"

She nodded. "That's why I wanted to tell you. I wanted you to know everything, in the spirit of truth and working together. If you don't want to give your public vow now, I will understand.

I'll make an announcement about the attack, feed everyone, wish them a merry Winter Solstice, and send them home. You get Ariyon back, switch powers, and then you can stay in Bane Manor while I fight this war alone." She pursed her lips and crossed her arms, her tears finally drying as the strong queen I knew came back to the surface.

'I say we leave. We owe this ungrateful excuse for a fae nothing.'

"Stay in Bane Manor?" I laughed at Solana sarcastically. "As a prisoner!"

Her nostrils flared. "Fallon, your powers will eventually take you over! It's just a fact."

"Says the woman who cursed me to a lifetime of pain!"

She glared at me, and I suddenly felt like she was getting the motherhood experience right now and I was the rebellious teenager she had to deal with.

"Fine. You want to be a big girl? Make big-girl decisions? I think you're old enough to see this." She marched over to a bookshelf and yanked on a thick tome with purple leather binding.

With a slow and long creak, the bookshelf pulled back to reveal a secret room.

'Of course. Everyone has a hidden room around here,' Yanric observed.

I should leave, like Yanric had said, leave and never come back. But dammit I was curious, so I followed the queen wordlessly, still angry and processing the fact that I was sharing the same air with the person who had given me a lifetime filled with grief.

I expected a dark tunnel that led to a basement like Master Clarke's or something of that nature, but instead I was led into a nice-sized sitting room. It was brightly lit with four high-backed chairs circling a coffee table. On the center of the table was an oblong decorative wooden box. The queen sat in one of the chairs and indicated I do the same. I obliged her but made sure the disapproval was evident on my face with a glare.

"What do you want me to see?" I asked curtly.

She sighed. "My memories. Something I don't share with others lightly."

Her memories? How was I going to see those?

Reaching over, she unclasped the wooden box, and the lid sprang free to reveal a pair of beautiful delicate crowns. They were identical in every way. Both made up of gold swirls with turquoise gems that sparkled in the light.

I squirmed in my seat as she pulled one out and handed it to me. Then she peered at the top of my head. "You wear this one, and I will wear the other. This will allow you to see the memories I choose to share. You will also *feel* what I feel."

I gulped, placing the lightweight crown atop my head. "What are you going to show me?" Suddenly I wasn't sure I wanted to see anything.

"Just what kind of person Marissa truly is." She placed the crown on her head, and I was immediately sucked into a memory. My eyes were forced closed in that moment, but it felt like my body had been portaled to a different location.

My eyes snapped open in the memory, and I looked down at my hands and chest—I was Solana. The telltale glossy blond braid hung loosely over my shoulder.

"Princess!" a Royal Guard called from the doorway to the library inside the palace. "Marissa is at The Academy, and she's started a fire. I've advised the Royal Guard to ferry the king, queen, and princes to safety via the tunnels." He was clutching his arm to his chest, and soot marred his face.

Solana's head whipped in his direction as fear and anger simultaneously rushed through her. "Arrest her!" she bellowed.

"We're trying. She's powerful. Your assistance might be needed, my lady."

Solana growled, and I felt her power rise up inside her. In that moment, I had full knowledge of what she was capable of. Her brother was powerful, yes, and a good choice for king, but she was his equal in magic. She could lay spells over people and force them to tell the truth. She could do minor healing and make salves. But that was nothing compared to her warrior powers. Within her was a white light that seared. It was not like fire; it was hotter than that. Hot like the sun. She could blind you with it, explode your body into tiny particles. She could hit you with something akin to lightning and stop your heart. She was a ticking bomb. With her brother, the king, fleeing to hiding, she needed to bring Marissa down, lest the entire royal family fall to this madwoman.

Solana tipped her head high. The pride she took in being of service to her people welled within her. She would not let this menace inflict any more harm. Rushing out of her room at the palace, she leaped onto a waiting horse and rode fast and hard for The Academy.

Her stomach dropped when she saw the billowing smoke curling up to the sky like an omen of death. "No." Pure, unbridled rage welled within Solana, and I peered down to see a ring on her marriage finger.

She was betrothed.

Ethan Crawford was his name. He had been picked for her by her brother and sister-in-law, but even though it was arranged, she loved him. She'd loved him for the entire four years they studied together at The Academy, but she was too shy to say so. Now, they were betrothed with a wedding planned for next month, and she couldn't be happier.

Ethan Crawford… Blair Crawford's father? I found myself thinking. But I was sucked away from that thought and pushed back into the memory of the burning school. *Solana had arrived, and heart-stopping dread filled her when she saw nearly every building on campus raging with the purple flames of Undying Fire.*

"Marissa!" Solana bellowed, a shock wave of power snapping out of her as she searched for the Bane heir's energy signature among the campus. She hated Marissa, but not without cause. I was then slammed with an overwhelming montage of memories of every time Marissa had done something mean in Solana's presence—a bullying remark, a shove, tripping her, lighting the ends of her hair on fire. It was sickening to know that I was descended from such a creature.

"Your family will not take from me what is mine!" Marissa cried as something slammed into Solana's back.

One second she was standing, and the next, Solana was sprawled out on the grass. Immediately, she pulled up some kind of protective shield. Marissa loomed over her, her snake familiar wrapped loosely around her neck. Black smoke curled toward the sky as a heavily pregnant Marissa glared down at Solana in rage. Bile churned in my stomach as I saw there was no humanity in her gaze. The lights were on, but nobody was home. She'd been consumed by anger and hatred, and it was even sadder to see that she'd done that while pregnant with me, as if having a baby could keep someone from gravitating toward evil. *Her irises were half green, threaded through with black tendrils.*

"Marissa, the darkness is pulling you in! Stop this and I can help you," Solana said, trying to reason with her. I had access to all of Solana's thoughts and knew that she'd spoken with her brother and come up with a plan. In the event Marissa went dark, they would cage her, and if that didn't work, they would kill her.

"I don't need help. I need what your family stole from me," she seethed.

Solana genuinely didn't know what Marissa was talking about at the time, though here, in the present, I knew she was talking about the crown.

"You don't need help? You're burning the school down!" Solana *roared, getting to her feet and gesturing behind her.* *"With a child in your belly, no less! What kind of mother will you be, Marissa?"*

Solana had no idea who had impregnated Marissa, but she had her suspicions, all of which she kept from me in that moment. *Marissa's head reeled back as if she'd been slapped, and something flickered in her gaze. An inner horror, a knowing that she'd done something wrong. One hand went to her belly, and for a split second I saw humanity in her eyes, just before they iced over, making her look like she had been possessed.*

"What kind of mother will you make, Solana?" Marissa cocked her *head to the side, and the snake familiar at her neck began to slither down her arm, its scales glowing a soft yellow as some sort of magic built up in it.* *"With your* perfect *betrothed and your* perfect *royal family."*

No. I knew what was next, and I didn't want to hear it or see it.

Solana readied an attack, pulling on her magic as Marissa grinned.

"You know what? I think you won't be a mother at all. Ever. That's what I will do to the Madden line to punish you for what you stole form me. You, Solana Madden, will have no children." Marissa's *familiar shot off her arm and punched through Solana's protective shield, sinking its fangs into Solana's arm.*

"No!" Solana *cried, throwing up her hand to blast Marissa with magic, but it was too late. The curse had been delivered, in this case through poison her snake injected into Solana's bloodstream.*

Rage and fury ripped through Solana so hot, I felt sick. The one thing she wanted to be most was a mother, to hold a babe and kiss their little fingers and toes and sing them to sleep at night.

In a fit of rage, she pulled her own curse forward, a dark magic not normally used by her kind. But it was one she knew of from studying in the rare book section of the library at school.

"Then your child, Marissa Bane, will never be touched without feeling pain," Solana cried and released the curse. A blast of light shot out from Solana's palms, and everything went white, momentarily blinding Solana.

Marissa screamed, and Solana instantly felt regret for cursing her unborn child, an innocent party in all of this. But her anger at her own chance at children being taken away from her had driven her to darkness—just like the old fae who spent too much time around those in the House of Ash and Shadow. They all went dark too.

When Solana's vision returned, Marissa and her familiar were gone, and the school still burned around her. The sound of people pounding on locked doors and windows was a horror Solana would never forget. And now, I would never forget either. *She rushed forward with half a dozen Royal Guard and began to pry open doors that had been magically sealed, breaking windows, doing anything they could to free people.*

Young Solana, barely twenty-two, was sobbing as she pulled burned and unconscious people from various rooms, some clearly deceased. Citizens from all over the city arrived with hoses and water pails and tried to put out the fire. They heaped burned body upon burned body, each citizen muttering one name as a curse under their breath.

Marissa Bane.

I wanted out of the memory, but I felt Solana's hold on my

mind tighten. She wasn't done with me. I was pulled into another recollection. *It was at night. Solana was in her dressing robe, hair still damp from an earlier bath, when she heard a blood-curdling scream.*

Her sister-in-law, Rune. The queen.

Solana bolted out of bed, pulling on her power, and instinctively knew it was Marissa. Solana had known Marissa would be back one day. Months had passed since the fire, since Marissa cursed her with barrenness, since she'd ruined Solana's life. Not only had Marissa taken one hundred and seventeen Gilded Citizens to the Realm of Eternity, but she had also taken Solana's beloved Ethan away from her. Solana had had to be honest with him and tell him of her curse. She said a baby might not take hold, and they could still try after marriage, but he'd backed out of the agreement. He'd wanted to be a father since he was a young boy and didn't want to lose the chance. Now she had no prospects. No one wanted her and her barren, cursed womb. She understood. As heartbroken as she was, she didn't want to be the cause of someone else's despair. She promised herself if she ever saw Marissa again, she would kill her. She would finish this torment and save her people from sharing air with such a vile monster.

"Solana!" *Clarke ran down the hall, shirtless and in night pants. He'd been woken too. Her brother's best friend and the godparent to her nephews, Clarke had been sleeping at the palace so that he could go on an early morning hunting trip with Arkin.*

Oh Light. Her nephews. They'd better be safe.

They rounded the corner together and came upon heaps of dead guards, all burned or bitten by a snake.

"Marissa," *Solana growled and rushed forward, pulling her shield power to surround her and Clarke.*

They heard a crashing sound coming from the king's room and another scream. With one kick, Clarke busted down the door. The room glowed with Arkin's fireballs, and Solana and Clarke wasted no time rushing into the melee.

It was the twins' crying that first pulled her attention. She snapped her gaze to the corner of the room where the two cribs lay and pushed Clarke in that direction, hoping he got the message to get the children out. He nodded and bolted in that direction.

Marissa was in the center of the room trading magical blows with the king, and Solana was using all her might to stretch her protective shield so that it encompassed herself, Clarke, and now the two boys he plucked out of the crib. Ayden and Ariyon wailed, and Marissa directed her attention that way. Marissa pivoted to the sound of the children and raised her hands as if to strike out at them with her magic.

"No!" Solana cried, pulling even more power into her shields. Marissa tossed a purple-and-orange ball of Undying Fire right at Clarke, who held the twins, and my heart leaped into my throat as fear consumed Solana and me in tandem. The fireball splashed across the shield as if hitting glass. Solana wanted to kill Marissa right then, but she was using all her magic to protect the boys.

Clarke grunted as he used his telekinesis magic to open a secret bookcase at the back wall and carry the boys inside.

Marissa peered at Clarke as he tried to leave. There was so much hatred in her gaze, it confused me.

"This is all your fault," Marissa sneered at him.

Clarke looked like he'd been kicked in the stomach. "I tried to save you from yourself," he muttered.

Clarke's fault? I felt Solana's confusion as well, but Marissa was insane and not making sense, so she let it go.

Solana peered at Marissa's stomach then and noticed it was flat. "Where is the baby?" Solana asked, her maternal instinct welling up. Did she kill her baby? Solana wouldn't put it past her.

"If anyone alive today or their descendants kills my daughter, then the next Madden heir will drop dead!" Marissa spat in the king's direction, and her snake familiar struck. The king had positioned himself in front of the queen and had been preoccupied making sure that Clarke got the boys out. The snake hit him right in the chest, where his heart was.

No. Another curse.

Solana snapped then. But so did Queen Rune. They both ran at Marissa, magic filled in their palms and battle cries on their lips. But Ayden and Ariyon's mother never even had a chance. She had barely taken a few steps toward Marissa when my birth mother reached out and grabbed Rune by the throat, unleashing the destructive magic I'd once used on Solana's very own guard's blade. One second, Rune was there—the next, she was ash.

Shock and fury filled Solana, and she exploded, literally. White light formed in a concentrated beam and slammed into Marissa's chest, knocking her backward onto the floor. Her snake familiar fell limp to the ground, and Marissa's eyes rolled back in her head. In the center of my birth mother's chest was a hole the size of a melon, blood freely pouring out.

She was dead.

"Arkin!" Solana sobbed as she fell onto the bed where the king lay. A trail of poison-black veins grew up his neck to his eyes, white foam on his lips, no more life in his eyes.

"Rune!" Solana made her way to where the queen was just a pile of ash on the floor.

They were both dead, and Solana was losing her grip on reality, the horror of everything sinking in. She heaved huge lungsful of air in and out, but the panic wouldn't subside.

A guard rushed in with his blade drawn and stared in shock at the scene before him.

"Princess Solana. What…"

She was wailing, and I felt her grief into the very core of my being. Her brother who she loved deeply. She didn't have many friends growing up, and Avis and Arkin were all she had. Her best friends. Now he was gone. She couldn't accept it. She wouldn't. Propriety demanded that she be stone-faced and bark orders at the guard and take up position as the next reigning monarch, but she couldn't. All she could do was sob as the agony poured out of her.

"The twins?" The guard looked frantically around the room.

That shut the waterworks off immediately. Her nephews.

Solana flew into protective aunt mode.

"They escaped with Clarke through the tunnel." She rushed to the bookcase and threw it open. I felt her mind spiral out of control. Her brother and sister-in-law were dead. She couldn't be queen without an heir, and she was barren. The princes were the only thing keeping the Madden monarchy alive. She loved them so much, but she thought they wouldn't be safe here at the palace with her. If there was another attack, it was too easy to take the entire bloodline out, with all three of them living together. No, she would get a nanny and raise them outside the palace, and—

I was yanked from the memory as Solana pulled the crown off my head. Being so immersed in that horrific scene and then being torn away from it so suddenly caused me to gasp.

I reached up to feel that my cheeks were wet. The pain in my heart from feeling what Solana felt was so raw. It had been like I was there, like I *was* Solana.

The queen returned the crowns to the box quietly and then sat down on the chair next to me, folding her hands in her lap and staring at them.

I didn't know what to say.

Did Marissa's behavior excuse the queen for cursing me? No.

But could I now understand why Solana had done it? Yeah, I suppose I could.

Knowing that she was there when her brother and sister-in-law died, that she saw it all, softened my heart to her fully.

"You were only a few years older than me," I said finally, and Solana nodded.

I couldn't imagine seeing my dad or Eden murdered right in front of me. Or being cursed and not retaliating. The heaviness in my heart remained, and when I searched for the reason why, it dawned on me. Marissa *was* evil. She'd gone completely dark, not a shred of humanity left in her. She was drunk off her quest for power and dominance, and any hope I had—one I hadn't realized I was even harboring—that maybe she was misunderstood had evaporated.

"I understand now, Solana." I looked up, and she met my gaze. The pain in her eyes was something I understood now. Better than I wished I did. "I understand why you have been so harsh with me. Why you have created a prison to hold me. I even understand why you cursed me. I get it now."

She swallowed hard, fidgeting with her fingernails. "Nevertheless, I'm ashamed of the curse I laid on you. I was young and grieving and mad that my chance at being a mother had been taken from me. I'm sorry, Fallon. Truly."

It was a heartfelt apology, and while it wouldn't take my curse away, it did heal something inside me. It brought me closure. My entire life, I wondered how someone could do such a thing to a child. Now I understand.

I gave her a small smile. "I forgive you."

Her face went slack, her bottom lip quivering. It was as if

those three words had been something she hadn't realized she'd needed to hear.

She cleared her throat repeatedly and nodded a few times. "So, we're on the same team?" Solana asked.

I dipped my head to her. "Yes, team leader."

She raised one eyebrow, her lips curling into a smile. "Oh, I quite like the sound of that."

That caused us both to giggle.

Solana stood and faced me, smoothing the creases in her dress. "Are you ready to address our people?"

Our people. She said *our.*

Those two words made me feel like I finally belonged in The Gilded City.

"Yes, my queen."

15

FALLON

Queen Solana had invited the entire brigade from The Academy, including Ayden and the more advanced students. Even though I was basically an honorary member without my fighting powers, she allowed me to stand with them off to the side of a stage that had been erected. We were in the back garden of the castle grounds. A white silk tent had been raised over the stage, and hundreds of citizens fanned out along the lawn in tightly packed rows. The queen held a small voice projector to her lips, and her voice boomed out of speakers that sat along the edge of the grass.

"Citizens of The Gilded City!" she roared, and everyone stared up at her with their undivided attention. She wore very little makeup and no fancy dress. This time, she was in a black military suit as well, the flame emblem upon her chest no doubt honoring the fallen citizens. "A great injustice took place yesterday, and I failed to protect you from the attack of the Nightlings."

She hung her head low, and I heard a few murmurs rise up from the crowd. When Queen Solana lifted her head again, there was a spine-chilling fierceness in her gaze that made the hairs on the back of my neck stand straight up.

"But by the Light, I swear to you now that the next time the Nightlings come, we will be ready!" she cried, and the crowd rose up to meet that exclamation. "We will fight back!" she yelled, and the citizens of The Gilded City raised their fists. "I will not allow evil to penetrate the walls of this fine city again, not while I am still breathing."

The amassed peoples went wild cheering. It was like they were one living organism, and I found myself crying out with them, pumping my fist into the air.

"Now I know there are rumors going around about our new resident Fallon Bane, and people are wondering if she is the cause of these attacks," the queen said, and the entire crowd went dead silent. Slowly, each and every head turned to look in my direction. My heart hammered in my chest, my cheeks flushing and my palms going wet inside my gloves. This was it.

Solana raised her left hand. "I have questioned her myself with my magic, and I know it to be true that she is on our side."

A few people booed, and Eden slipped her hand into my gloved one as Ayden did the same on the other side.

'They're booing you? I'll rip their throats out,' Yanric called from the tree to my right.

"Oh, it's understandable that this would be hard to believe. So why don't you hear from Fallon herself." The queen then held the voice projector out in my direction, and a sudden wave of dizziness washed over me. I stumbled backward half a step, anxiety saturating my system. My father stepped out of the crowd then, worry etched all over his face. I dropped Eden's and Ayden's hands and stepped forward, trying to let him know I was okay, just the most nervous I had been in all my life. But he kept coming until he stood right before me.

"Need help?" He gave me his arm, and I offered him a small smile.

"I'm okay. Just got nervous," I whispered.

He nodded. "That's okay. Let them see that you're just like them. Nerves and all."

I hooked my covered arm into his and allowed him to lead me up the stage on wobbly legs. I wasn't prepared for this. They wouldn't believe a word I said anyway. It was well known by now that I started the fire at the school and stole Ariyon's powers. They...

'Breathe, Fallon. Just be yourself. Remind them that although Marissa may have gone dark, you have not. You will *not,'* Yanric reassured me.

He was right. I just had to do my best. Someone waved and caught my attention in that moment. I scanned the crowd and spotted Avis. She was beaming at me with a radiant smile and showing her support. It was what I needed to push myself to do this.

My father brought me to the top step and squeezed my hand in encouragement. I looked up at the waiting queen and gave her a small smile.

The people needed to believe me, to know that the words I was about to speak were true. I stood taller, a plan forming in my mind, and walked right up to Queen Solana. I gave her a deep bow and then took the voice projector from her. She began to back away, but I called for her to stop. She looked at me curiously.

I held the voice projector up to my mouth, like I'd seen her do, and spoke. "Queen Solana, even though it causes me tremendous pain, would you please use your power to compel me to only speak the truth so that I cannot lie?"

Gasps rang out through the crowd of people, and even Solana stilled. I'd told her before that I would take an oath while under her power, but I wasn't sure she believed I would actually do it or that I would give my entire speech under the influence of it.

"Are you sure?" Solana asked quietly.

I nodded, rolling the sleeve of my black brigade uniform up. Solana looked out upon her people and then back to me. Placing her hand to her mouth, she whispered, and a subtle golden glow formed around her hand for all to see. The crowd pressed forward, and I flicked my gaze to meet my father's. He looked like he was in agony.

'Yan, make my dad turn around,' I told my familiar. I didn't want him to see this. It would kill him. He hated seeing me hurt, even if it was only going to be for a few moments, until Ariyon's healing magic kicked in.

Yanric flew from the tree and perched on my father's shoulder, urging him to turn around. I looked at the queen and then dipped my chin.

She grasped my forearm, depositing the magical handprint, and I cried out in pain as I was brought to my knees. She quickly released me, muttering an apology and stepping backward to the corner. Gasps and cries of shock reached me from the crowd, but I barely heard them. I was too focused on the agony. Sharp and hot, it took my breath away, sliding up my back like a serpent.

Sucking in a few lungsful of air, I felt the healing magic awaken within me. The marks atop my hands were no doubt spinning under my gloves. That relaxed feeling came over me, making my anxiety flee and my tongue feel loose.

"Under this spell, it is impossible for me to lie," I told the crowd, and they stared at me with rapt fascination.

"Yes, I am Fallon Bane, birth daughter of Marissa Bane, heir to the House of Ash and Shadow."

Boos rose up from the crowd again, but I kept going.

"I am also Fallon Brookshire, daughter of Jeremy Brookshire, a magicless fae from Isariah, for most of my life. I'm a good person, a lover of huckleberry pie and my dad's famous sourdough pork sandwiches." I looked at him to find him beaming at me.

"Yes, I have a familiar." I pointed to Yanric who was still perched on my father's shoulder. "He's protective over me and my best friend. He likes belly rubs and the leftovers from my lunch."

'You're going to make me cry,' Yanric said.

The booing stopped.

"I was just as shocked as you were to hear about the evil deeds Marissa and my other ancestors did. But I assure you, I have had nothing to do with the Nightling attacks. I have never passed information to Marissa or any of her Nightlings about The Gilded City or any of its citizens."

Shocked murmurs arose from the crowd as they looked at each other and spoke among themselves.

"She can't lie," I heard one of them say.

I peered at Eden, my best friend, and was reminded of the first day she walked me into the East Side and what I'd said to her. I returned my attention to the crowd. "I'm asking you to give me a chance to let me show you that I am loyal to Queen Solana and you, the citizens of The Gilded City. Let me fight with you against this evil and proudly declare my allegiance to our queen!"

I turned to Solana and dropped to one knee, bowing my head

deeply. When I rose and peered up at her, Solana tipped her head back to me, smiling.

I faced the crowd once more. "And if I go dark, like many of you may still believe I will, if my powers overtake me like they did my mother, causing me to hurt good people like you…" I looked at Yanric, remembering what he said about doing dark with me. "Then you can kill me. I wouldn't want to live like that anyway."

My eyes flew wide with the brutally honest confession I hadn't meant to share. *Damn spell.*

People gasped at my statement, and the queen moved up to place a hand on my shoulder. "We're not going to let that happen. Not this time," she declared to me.

It started with my father—a slow clap as he beamed up at me with so much love and pride. Then Avis, Eden, Ayden, and the rest of the brigade. Then the entire city was clapping and looking up at me with respect.

My chest filled with pride at what I'd done, facing what seemed like an impossible task head-on. The queen dissolved her spell and took the voice projector from me.

"It doesn't feel right to celebrate Winter Solstice in the usual way," Queen Solana said through the voice projector. "I have canceled the light show. Instead, we'll share a meal in remembrance of those who lost their lives." She gestured offstage, and I followed that line of sight to see that three more silk tents had been erected. There were tables covered in food trays and attendants who stood at the ready to serve people.

Together, Queen Solana and I walked off the stage and over to a cordoned-off area where her Royal Guard were waiting.

"That was very brave of you, Fallon," she admitted.

I nodded. "Thank you." My body felt relaxed as I turned

to her. "Now, when can we leave to see the Ealdor Fae about Ariyon?"

She gave me half a smirk. "You don't even want to stay for food?"

I shook my head.

"I thought you might say that." She peered at one of her guards. "Nate, please ready the traveling crew for my nephew and his friends."

A guard with red hair and a matching red beard saluted her and stepped away. I thought for half a second of going back to Bane Manor to grab that crystal shell and bring it with me. It was, after all, a link to the Realm of Rebirth and therefore Ariyon, but I also feared it. Could they hear me on the other end when I spoke around it? What if it was planted there as a trick for me? Was it a dark artifact that would do something weird to my magic? I just didn't know, so for now, I was leaving it back.

Solana was still watching me with curiosity. "You know, you seem very invested in getting Ariyon back, which I'm grateful for, but I wonder if it's just to right your wrong or something more."

I bristled, worried that Solana may have picked up on my feelings for Ariyon. "I just want to get him out of there. Restore the power I took."

She nodded, looking relieved. "Good. Because I would hate to think there was anything romantic going on there." She laughed. "Especially since I've already betrothed him to Blair Crawford. They will marry upon graduation, and obviously I couldn't even consider joining our families in that way...not that it's even a possibility with your curse."

The ground felt like it had been pulled out from beneath me then. The breath whooshed out of my lungs as I struggled to comprehend what she was saying. "But they broke up."

Solana laughed. "Yes, on-off, on-off, that's their thing." There was a twinkle in her eyes as if to suggest that's just how lovesick teenagers were.

No.

I couldn't grasp what she was saying. "Married at graduation? But his life span…"

He told me he didn't want to make anyone a widow. Blair? He was betrothed to Blair? Did he know? Did she?

The queen nodded solemnly. "At least they will be able have a few heirs before he eventually passes."

Heirs. That's all she cared about? "Ayden will have heirs," I growled.

She stiffened. "The more the merrier, my dear. Especially since I am unable to have children." She pinned me with a glare, and I sighed.

We were back to our usual relationship.

Point taken. My mother took her fertility, so now she needed to keep her lineage going. I wondered what she would think if she knew her very own nephew was the only person in the realm who could touch me.

"Your Highness, we're ready." The guard, Nate, was back. "We expect one overnight and will be back the following day by sundown."

Solana nodded. "Go in peace, Fallon. And please get my nephew back."

I barely heard her. All that was on my mind was one name.

Blair. Blair. Blair.

I couldn't conceive of that witch marrying my man.

16

FALLON

Hayes, Ayden, Eden, and I had been traveling all night with over a dozen Royal Guard. We all rode in a carriage with a few days' worth of camping supplies, just in case. The guards flanked us on horseback in a protective formation. We'd gone east, and to a part of the realm I'd never traveled to before. I'd slept on and off, resting my head against the wooden lacquered wall of the carriage, as I didn't want to accidentally lean on anyone and risk being touched. Every bump woke me, which was often, and I couldn't stop thinking about Ariyon. My mind spun with the new information about Blair and Ariyon's betrothal, but I pushed it to the back. It didn't matter right now, and it wouldn't help me get Ariyon back. That's what I needed to put my full focus on right now. The only guy in the world who could kiss me was about to be taken out by some Nightling with a vendetta against his family. I recalled the conversation I'd overheard in the Bane Manor basement and shivered.

"We're here," Ayden announced. I looked down at the map in his hands and then peered up and out of the open window where he pointed.

I followed his line of sight to an empty meadow.

"Hmm, or we should be," he followed up.

Our carriage ground to a stop. The lead guard in charge, Nate, pulled his horse over to the window from where Ayden had been directing us and then looked at the open meadow.

There was a large weeping willow tree, as marked on the map, but no city where one should be.

One of the other guards cleared his throat. "Sir, I…sense something."

Nate flicked his head to his guard. "What is it? Speak up, Hansen."

The guard pulled his horse closer to us and projected his voice. "My magic is sensitive to shields and curses. I…sense something of that nature in the meadow," he said.

That was all it took for every single soldier present to pull their blades. The steel tips erupted with flames, and half the Royal Guard dismounted their horses in tandem and crept toward the meadow.

"Whoa," I said, looking at Ayden, who frowned.

"Which is it, Hansen? A shield or a curse?" Nate barked at his soldier.

He was looking from the map to the meadow and back at the guards fast approaching it. Suddenly, Ayden bolted into a standing position. "Stop!" he cried out, and the guards froze.

Ayden leaped from the carriage and hit the ground, and we all stumbled out after him. With large strides, he crossed the mossy forest floor and stood at the opening of the meadow.

"What is it, Prince Ayden?" Nate asked.

Ayden bent down and picked up a large rock. Reeling his arm back, he chucked the rock at the opening of the meadow, between two trees. It hit some type of a shield and burst into flames, pulverizing the rock into a pile of sand.

Oh fae.

"Retreat!" Nate yelled, and the guards huddled around Ayden in a tight formation, pushing him back to the carriage. As they did this, I watched in fascination as the air in the meadow opening shimmered and moved. One second, it was an empty meadow, and the next, it was like a mirage had fallen away and I was staring at a bustling city. A tall man in a cream robe stood in front of wrought-iron double gates.

"Ayden!" I hissed.

He turned and faced the man standing before the hidden city and balked. He moved to speak to the tall fae, but his guards stopped him.

Instead, Nate walked over and spoke with the man. I couldn't hear what they said, but as Nate walked back over to us, he was staring at me.

"They will speak with Fallon and Fallon only. No one else is allowed inside the city," he declared.

"No way!" Ayden roared, and Eden agreed.

I moved forward. "I'm going."

Ayden reached out and grasped my gloved hand. When I turned back to look at him, fear swam in his gaze, and he whispered, "Fallon, we know nothing about the Ealdor Fae and their magic. They are secretive and reclusive. You could be marching to your death."

I nodded. "If it will help get Ariyon back, then it's worth it."

He dropped my hand then, avoiding my gaze. I'd chosen his brother no matter the cost, and I hated that it still hurt him.

Yanric had been flying alongside us and staying out of the way, but now he landed on my shoulder.

'Surely they will not deprive you of your protector?' he asked.

I reached up and rubbed his black-feathered neck. *'We can try.'*

Hayes just gave me a head nod as I passed, and I took long strides over to where the tall fae patiently waited at the gates. He had long, brown hair tied into a thick braid that hung down his back. It was streaked through with silver.

As I approached, I noticed he looked older than I had originally thought. There were so many rumors about the Ealdor Fae, I lost count. Some claimed that they were immortal unless killed. Others said that they could regenerate and self-heal after an injury or that they didn't need food. Some rumors were comical, like they didn't poop, but I doubted that. The Ealdor Fae were a fantasy race of fae we talked about as kids, but now that I knew they were real, I wanted to learn whatever I could about them. Especially since I suspected and Clarke all but confirmed that Hipsie was one after she'd been arrested when the Royal Guards came for me.

"I'm Fallon Bane." I bowed to him, unsure of his station but wanting to show the proper respect.

"Please remove your gloves," the man said kindly, and chills raced down my spine.

'Not on your life, buddy!' Yanric spat.

The fae looked to Yanric, and my bird stiffened.

'He spoke back to me mentally,' Yanric said, sounding shocked. *Holy Fae.*

I looked at the man pleadingly. "I'm sorry, but I wear them because I'm cursed to feel pain when—"

"I know. I need to see your Maven marks to be sure you are the one," the fae told me, nodding.

Oh wow. He knew I carried Ariyon's marks. That was good. Maybe this guy was Emmeric. I pulled off my gloves and showed him the marks. He nodded, and then the gates opened behind him.

"Welcome to Ealdoria." He gave me a kind smile.

"Thanks." I returned it with a smile of my own.

'He knows when we speak to each other. Stay off comms. Rub your left ear if you need help,' Yanric said, somewhat paranoid.

I grinned, knowing the fae had probably heard that, and a hint of a smile played at his lips too.

'It's okay, Yan. I'm safe here.'

I don't know how I knew, but I just knew that this man had no ill intent toward me. Looking over my shoulder, I gave a cheerful wave to Ayden and the others waiting, hoping to keep them from worrying, and I followed the fae into one of the most beautiful villages I'd ever seen.

Dozens of little houses with moss-covered rooftops dotted the countryside as cobblestone walkways weaved in and out of the city. The market stalls were colorful tents made from crimson and yellow silk. Fae men and women worked in the fields of a farm, pulling corn off the stalk as goats ran circles around them. Children clacked sticks, pretending to be warriors, and rolled in the wildflowers. People here were happy and worked together, that much was clear.

"Are you Emmeric?" I finally got the nerve to ask the man beside me.

The fae chuckled. "No. I'm just a liaison of sorts. Emmeric is on our lead council."

I was relieved to hear that Emmeric was here.

I nodded. "And he knows I'm coming?"

The man looked sideways at me. "He does."

Not wanting to pry, I stayed quiet, taking in the wonderful village and waving to the children as they passed, laughing and trying to catch butterflies.

We approached a giant domed structure, and the man bowed lightly to me. "You will find what you seek inside. I will be waiting out here to escort you when you are finished."

"Okay," I said nervously, and I felt Yanric tighten his grip on my shoulder.

I didn't like walking into the unknown, but I had to do this for Ariyon.

I pushed the door open and stepped into a large space completely void of any furniture or decoration. It was a sizable meeting hall or ballroom of sorts, with wood floors and curved walls that led upward to a giant opening that allowed for sunlight to streak in at the center.

A single fae sat cross-legged in the center of the room on a small pillow. His eyes were closed, hands clasped in his lap, as he took in a deep breath at my approach.

'Is he praying?' Yanric asked.

'I have no idea,' I said.

Was he sleeping? I didn't want to disturb him.

When his eyes popped open, I gasped. They were a startling violet color.

"Hello, Fallon," he said, giving me a small smile.

"Hello. Emmeric?" I asked as a guess.

He nodded and patted the floor in front of him.

I took the signal and sat down, crossing my legs before him.

"Hello, Yanric." He tipped his head kindly to my familiar.

Yanric stiffened but bowed back.

"How do you know our names?" I asked.

He regarded me for a moment. "Can you keep a secret for me? Something that, if widely known, might endanger my life?"

Chills ran up my arms, and I nodded. "Of course." He seemed like a kind man, and I didn't want anything to happen to him.

"I can see snippets of the future before they come to pass," he said.

I felt my eyebrows raise in surprise.

'Whoa,' Yanric commented.

"I didn't know that was possible," I told him.

He gave me a small smile. "As a young child, I had a hard time understanding it myself. I would have visions and think they were daydreams, but then the things I saw would actually happen, and I knew I was seeing the future."

"Sounds like a lot of responsibility," I said.

His face went slack, and he looked far off, as if ruminating on something. "You have no idea."

'Ask him about Ariyon,' Yanric offered.

Right. The entire reason I was here.

"Have you seen anything about my friend Ariyon and how I can get him back from the Realm of Rebirth?"

He pursed his lips, nodding slowly. "I have. And more."

And more? What did that mean?

'I have a bad feeling about this,' Yanric said suddenly. *'I don't think you are going to like what this fae has to say.'*

Emmeric looked at my bird and nodded. "Your familiar is right. Not everything I tell you today will be pleasing."

'They can all read minds!' Yanric balked.

I laughed, and Emmeric smiled.

"Only when you project it so loudly," he told Yanric.

"I can handle bad news. I just need to know how to get Ariyon out of there."

Emmeric inclined his head to the side. "Very well. I will give you the information you seek."

I waited for what seemed like an entire minute as he stared at me, possibly assessing some unseen future.

"There is only one way that Ariyon and you make it out of the Realm of Rebirth alive, with both of your bodies."

I leaned forward, and so did Yanric, gripping the fabric on my shoulder tightly. "How?" I didn't want to miss a word of this. In fact, I should have brought something to write with so I could take notes.

"You, Fallon Bane, were born with two chances at life: your fae one and your Nightling one. You must cross over into the Realm of Eternity, switch powers back with Ariyon, and give up your opportunity at rebirth, give up your Nightling life."

I scoffed. "That's all? Done! I don't want to be a Nightling anyway."

His face grew somber. "Before you decide, you should know a few things."

I swallowed hard. The moment Yanric feared felt like it was coming.

"One, when you give up your Nightling life, your ability to control the dark magic you carry will be lost."

I gasped. *No.* He saw that? Did that mean I would go dark? If so, how quickly? My heart began a frantic war drum beat against my chest as my breathing came out in quick bursts. The edge of a panic attack loomed over me as I fought for composure.

"And two, by this time next year…you will be dead and unable to be reborn because you will have forfeited that second life to save Ariyon."

I folded in on myself, the crushing weight of depression sinking in on me. A sob formed in my throat as the shock of his words crashed into me one by one.

Dead by nineteen? No. It wasn't enough time. Eden, my dad, Ayden, Ariyon. A year wasn't enough time to be with those I loved. He had to be wrong. His gift wasn't perfect, right? Yan snuggled into my neck, and I reached up with a shaky hand and stroked his feathers as my heart threatened to stop beating.

"Are you sure?" I asked, panic seizing me in its grip as I fought for composure.

"I have never seen something that has not come to pass. That being said, I do not see everything. Just snippets in time, like a series of pictures."

I met his violet gaze. "If you have seen it, then you already know I will choose to save Ariyon and give up my chance at a second life," I told him.

He nodded. "I do know that."

Yanric nuzzled my neck again, and I sighed. So it was true, my death within a year's time. "How do I die?"

Emmeric beamed at me, pride, much like a father would have for his child, in his gaze. "Saving the people of The Gilded City. I saw you die a hero, Fallon."

A lightness grew in my chest, chasing away the depression like a bad dream. If there was a chance to save all those people I cared about, then death was a small thing in the grand scheme. Truth be told, I wasn't afraid of death so much as I was afraid of going dark and hurting those I loved.

"I think I'm okay with that," I told him.

I'm assuming I die a hero too? Do they chant our names in the street afterward or what?' Yanric wanted to know.

Emmeric and I both burst into laughter.

As weird as it felt, knowing when you were going to die was kind of freeing. I was going to make the most of the time I had left and know that when I did cross over, I was doing so a hero, saving those who I loved.

"So how do I do it?" I asked him. "How exactly do I save Ariyon?"

Emmeric folded his hands. "You need to travel to the Realm of Eternity on a dying body. Only bring your soul," he said, and I winced. I literally just did that with Solana. I guess I would need to wait for someone else to be mortally injured. Not ideal, but okay.

"And then?"

"You ask to see Ariyon. The Grim will allow it. Once you get to him, you need to quickly switch powers. It will weaken you considerably at first, but then you will be stronger than ever before. Ariyon has been using your magic to stay alive in his fights, and he's unlocked more power than you are used to."

That was slightly terrifying.

"How do I switch our powers back?"

He frowned. "You don't know how to do that yet?"

I shook my head.

He shrugged. "You'll figure it out. I saw you do it."

I'll figure it out? That was all he was giving me?

"Oh-kay. So, once I follow a body down there, see Ariyon, and switch us back, how do I get the Grim to take my Nightling life?"

He nodded. "Before you ask the Grim to see Ariyon, you ask for an audience with the Quorum. Such a request cannot be denied from a Maven."

The Quorum? "Okay, and when I meet with them?"

"This is very important, Fallon. You ask to meet with the Quorum, *then* you see Ariyon and switch powers, and *only then* do you actually meet with the Quorum, at which time you will no longer technically be a Maven."

It sounded like I was tricking them, which I didn't care about really. I'd do whatever it took.

"Okay, and when I stand before the Quorum?" I had no idea who they were.

"I assume you say you are willing to give up your chance at rebirth to send both you and Ariyon's body back home."

"You assume?" I raised an eyebrow.

He shrugged. "I didn't see that part, but I know you give up your chance at rebirth to save him, and I did see you and Ariyon back at The Academy afterward."

I sighed in relief. That's literally all I wanted.

"Are you sure I go dark? I mean, it sounds like I save everyone. So how does that work out? I can't go dark and be a hero, can I?"

His face fell a little. "I only see snippets in time, but... I'm certain you go dark at some point."

The heaviness was back. Dying within a year, I was okay with. But going dark? Hearing voices, lighting things on fire with my mind, hurting those I loved—I didn't want that. I hoped he was wrong about this, that this would be the one time his visions failed him.

Again, Yanric nuzzled my neck to let me know that either way, we were in this together.

I slipped my gloves over my hands and held them out to the Ealdor Fae. When he took them, I squeezed. "I'm so very grateful to you, Emmeric. I was feeling very lost on how to fix this, and..."

I trailed off, remembering what Ariyon had said about Emmeric. "Ariyon said you came to him in a dream and gave him your name. Is there some link you have to him? I mean, why of all people in the realm are you having visions of him and me?"

He smiled sweetly at me, his eyes crinkling at the edges. "Ariyon reminds me of my son."

I frowned. "What do you mean?"

He looked over at a window and the light streaming through it, as if reliving some memory. "My son was a Maven healer, so I have a special affinity for those who carry the burden of great healing."

Was. He said *was.* "An Ealdor Maven healer? He must have been very powerful."

Emmeric nodded. "Lived twice as long as they said he would." His smile turned into a frown. "The only thing worse than burying your child is knowing you will live forever without them."

Grief welled up in my chest at his words. So it was true. Ealdors lived forever unless killed. Immortals. Except when they weren't, like in the case of his son. I still wasn't sure if being a Maven healer was a blessing or a curse.

We sat there for a few minutes in companionable silence, and then he looked at me with a small smile. "You are very brave, Fallon. Only a small percentage of the people whose futures I glimpse can withstand knowing about them in advance."

He unfurled his legs and stood, so I followed his lead.

"It was a pleasure to meet you, and I really appreciate you helping me figure this out. Ariyon appreciates it too, I'm sure," I told him.

He walked me to the door and opened it for me. The sun

had set, and I knew Ayden and the others would be worried if I didn't get back soon.

"The pleasure was all mine."

After saying goodbye, I met the fae outside who stood in wait. He tipped his head to me and without a word began to walk me back to the gate.

The information that Emmeric had given me settled heavily in my chest. Knowing I would save Ariyon and die a hero were good things. But not having a normal lifetime to spend with my loved ones wasn't something I could easily process.

'Maybe we can find a way around it,' Yanric said. *'Maybe he didn't see the whole picture.'*

'He said I died, with no second life to come back with. That's pretty much a whole picture.'

Yanric was silent after that.

'Yan, this is our secret to bear. You can't tell anyone. Not my father, not Eden, no one. There's no point in stealing their happiness if it's inevitable.'

For the first time, I saw tears well in Yanric's little black beady eyes.

'Okay, Fallon. Our secret,' he confirmed.

I nodded. We would let our loved ones live whatever time we had left together in happiness. It was a heavy secret to carry, but one I would for everyone's sake. Even if it crushed me, even if this weight that suddenly sat on my heart never left. The last thing I needed after being the cursed girl my whole life was people looking at me with pity because I had an expiration date drawing near.

I saw Ayden pacing the front gate with Eden. I waved to them, but it didn't look like they could see me.

"Did you put the shield back up?" I asked.

He nodded. "Many fae would seek to capture an Ealdor and exploit their magic."

Oh. That was awful. When we reached the gate, the man turned to me and pulled out a small vial with a golden cap. Inside was a shimmering purple fluid. "This is a rare gift from Ealdor Emmeric. He spent weeks making it in anticipation of your arrival."

My eyebrows shot up. He knew I was coming for weeks? Possibly before I even discovered my power and went to The Gilded City. The thought was unnerving.

"What is it?" I took the vial and looked it over more closely.

The man gave me a little smile. "For about five minutes, it will suspend your curse, allowing you to touch and hug those you love without pain."

A sob formed in my throat as I clutched the vial tighter.

"He only wished he was able to make one that was more permanent."

I nodded, clutching the vial to my chest and treasuring it. "It's perfect."

I stowed it away safely in my pocket and bid him farewell. The gates opened as the shield parted, and I stepped through them. Ayden and Eden immediately rushed up to me.

"Are you okay?"

"What happened?"

I nodded. "I'm fine. I got the help I needed. I know how to save Ariyon."

Ayden beamed. "That's great news!"

We set up camp outside the gates. We were all exhausted and needed some proper rest before beginning the travel home.

After lighting a fire, Eden snuggled close to me, careful not to touch me but leaning against my clothed arm and leg.

"You've been unusually quiet. What happened in there?" she asked.

I forced a smile on my face. "Nothing. I'm just tired."

She nodded. "You're a bad liar, Fallon, but that's okay. I still love you."

Ayden and Hayes entertained us that night with stories about their childhood, and when I finally fell asleep, my thoughts were a jumbled mess.

Ariyon was betrothed to Blair.

I was going to die.

And I still had to figure out how to switch our powers back.

17

ARIYON

HAVING PAX HERE WITH ME HAD BOOSTED MY MORALE. WE'D become fast friends, talking every day through the window, giving each other fighting tips, and giving Maze and the others the middle finger every chance we got. Pax had a unique outlook on life as someone from the House of Ash. He said he never asked to be born with magic, so he wouldn't mind being reborn without it. He was a good guy who had died before he'd been lost to the darkness of his magic and had no desire to return to it. I respected him for that.

"So, what's your plan after you win and get reborn?" I asked him one morning. I'd been hoping Fallon would have come for me by now, but I wondered if time was different here. My hair had grown longer, and it felt like I'd been here an eternity, yet the nights of sleep didn't add up to it. I tried not to think about it because it freaked me out too much if I did.

Pax replied after pondering a bit. "Get reborn in the Outer

Stretch and live life as a magicless nomad. I've always wanted to travel. The Yellow Mountains, the hot springs of Galeesh, The Gilded City."

I grinned. "You go there and tell them Ariyon Madden said to treat you like royalty."

Pax barked out in laughter then, grinning ear to ear. "You know I might just do that."

Now I was smiling. It was a nice thought. "And you'll never... You'll always stay magicless?"

Pax nodded. "I've heard the pull to feed and regain your magic is strong in the first month, but then it eventually goes away entirely. I'll just need to stay strong until then. I don't want to come back here. Ever."

That we agreed on.

"Well, if Fallon can get me out of here, I'll be in The Gilded City. You can always come visit and I can help you with whatever you need, man," I told him.

Pax made a fist and held it up to the bars, and I bumped it.

"If Fallon doesn't come, for whatever reason, ask for me in the Outer Stretch. We can be magicless together," he said.

It was a sobering possibility, one I had to prepare myself for. Living without magic. No healing, no protection other than a sword or my fists. No fire or destruction magic. All the parts of Fallon's magic that I had hated when I first met her had kept me alive down here. I'd gotten used to having them, to being feared. I felt invincible. Could I live without them? If it meant the alternative was drinking fae blood and blipping in and out of this realm forever, then yeah...I could.

"All right," I told him seriously. Maybe I would. I wouldn't want to face my aunt or Fallon or any of my friends at school with no magic. My entire life I'd been revered almost as a god. The most powerful healer of my generation and an heir to the most influential throne in the realm. For me to then be turned magicless… Well, it was laughable.

"Pretty boy. Dung for brains. Get up. You got a fight," Maze growled from the hallway.

I stiffened. "Both of us?"

I had a dark fleeting thought that they might pit us against each other at one point, but I hadn't let the thought go any further. It would be too cruel. He was my friend.

"Yes, both of you. Get up," he said.

"Against each other?" Pax's voice had lost all emotion—he sounded as dead inside as I felt in this moment.

Maze grinned, but it didn't reach his eyes. "It's a double fight. You're a team."

Relief spread through me, and Pax grinned. "Oh, now *that* sounds fun."

Pax and I were ruthless together, and he reminded me of Ayden. We fought back-to-back and won. I trusted him. Now, we were being hauled back to our cells, bloody but not broken. We grinned at each other as we were tossed in, wincing from pain but still high off the glory of the fight. Fallon's powers were insane! They were evil and I'd hated them because they were what killed my parents, but there was also a beauty to that much magic. Pax dominated by shielding and sending out force-field blasts. I had mastered Fallon's destruction magic. One sustained touch and I could turn a grown fae to ash. I felt bad afterward, but it was kill or be killed, so I was doing what I had to in order to survive. Before Maze shut the door, he rapped on my bars with his knuckles. "Sleep tight. Tomorrow, you fight each other. Winner gets reborn."

I heard Pax's sharp intake of breath in the cell next to me. My own breath shuddered in my chest. I was speechless. They wouldn't. They couldn't be so cruel, could they? They'd seen us bond, fight together.

If I fought someone I considered to be a friend and killed him, what did that make me? A monster. Something I wasn't willing to become for any reward. If I forfeited, they could throw me into the Bottomless Pit, and my soul and body would cease to exist forever. Or they could keep me down here, as a slave like Maze. I'd mop the blood off the floors and ferry souls in and out of fights for eternity. That was a worse fate than the Bottomless Pit in my opinion, but I wasn't willing to kill a friend to save myself, so if that's what happened, then so be it.

Tomorrow I would forfeit, and Pax would be reborn magicless. I hoped he lived a long and happy life and ended up in the Realm of Eternity. Maybe he could take a message to my parents for me.

Neither of us said a word after that, and I didn't sleep, not even for a second.

18

FALLON

WE'D BEEN BACK AT SCHOOL FOR TWO DAYS NOW. NOTHING IN The Gilded City was the same after the latest Nightling attack. Guards roamed the streets tenfold, and we had drills on what to do in the event of another attack. The basement of each building was magically reinforced with protections and shields in the event it needed to be used as a safe shelter.

Large parts of The Gilded City's perimeter were being shielded to a certain degree, but the fae could only expend so much magic, and the city was too large to encompass entirely.

I'd given Queen Solana a breakdown of what I had to do to get Ariyon back, but without compromising Emmeric's secret ability of foresight. All she knew was that I needed to ride down on the next dying body and that she needed to have faith that I knew what to do from there. I admitted to her that this was hidden knowledge among the Ealdor Fae that I could not share. She didn't like being left in the dark on that but had nodded, trusting me. Now I was grappling with my own panic about not knowing exactly how to switch powers back with Ariyon once I eventually made it down there. The only ray of hope I had was that Emmeric seemed confident that the information would reach me in time.

"It's so weird that I'm just waiting for someone to be mortally injured so that I can save Ariyon," I told Eden in the library.

She nodded, scanning a book about the dark powers of House of Ash and Shadow. "I won't lie. I've had some morbid thoughts about harming someone so that you get can down there sooner."

Yanric nodded. *'I approve.'*

The door to the library burst open just then, and I looked up to see Queen Solana. Her face was ashen, and her hands shook slightly. The Royal Guard behind her appeared stricken as well.

"What's wrong?" I didn't curtsy or even give her a proper hello. I just rushed forward and waited for her to drop some horrible, heavy news on me.

She swallowed hard and tipped her chin high, clearly making an effort to remain composed. Her eyes misted with tears, but she blinked them back. "A man on my staff has been poisoned and is on death's door. If you want to save Ariyon, now is your chance."

"Yes!" Eden shouted and jumped up, causing us all to turn and look at her. She winced. "I mean, I'm so sorry to hear that, but yay for bringing Ariyon home," she amended quietly, and then gave a deep bow.

I turned to the queen, who was already heading out the library door, and ran to follow her. Yanric flew to my shoulder and assessed Solana. *'She's too coldhearted to be so upset over just any man on her staff.'*

'Be nice,' I warned him.

'*What I mean is, I think he might be her lover.*'

Oh. That would explain her shaken appearance.

When we reached the courtyard, Ember was already waiting for me, along with the queen's horse and two of her guardsmen.

"How did he get poisoned?" I asked.

She wiped at her eyes. "During lunch, with food that was meant for me. I'm sure it was Marissa," she snarled.

So they were having lunch together? Might be a lover, for sure, or a food taster. Or both. Marissa sure knew how to hold a grudge; constantly trying to take out Solana was getting old. What would she gain? Did she really think the people of The Gilded City would bend a knee and worship her if she became queen? No way. Solana was stern, but she was beloved by her people. Her family had served for generations, and Marissa wasn't going to be able to waltz in and just take that.

We were silent as we rode to the palace. My mind splintered off in a dozen different directions. Was I ready to save Ariyon? I still didn't know how to switch our powers. Every late-night studying session and the trip to meet Emmeric had built up to this moment, and now I feared I would screw it all up. My palms sweated inside my gloves as I fought for strength I wasn't sure I had right now. It wasn't just losing the queen's nephew that I feared. It was losing the only guy I'd ever love, the only person in the realm who could touch me without pain.

The Grim's words came back to me in that moment, and they made me smile.

Ariyon is your balance. That you found him in your lifetime is incredible.

The Light had to be on our side, didn't it?

'*Yan, I need that info on how to switch our powers back,*' I told my familiar with renewed hope.

'Let me worry about that,' Yanric stated beside me.

I nodded, my heart fluttering in my chest as I tried to remember everything Emmeric had said.

Switch powers, ask to meet with the Quorum, then give up my chance at a Nightling rebirth. No, not that order: ask to meet with the Quorum, then switch powers, then give up my Nightling life.

I got this.

We all rushed at a hurried pace through the street and right up to the front palace doors. The queen dismounted and ran inside, and I followed her, pulling off my gloves. I wasn't 100 percent sure I had to physically touch him to be brought down into the Realm of Eternity with him. But I had touched Solana and Ariyon, and I didn't want to screw this up, so I was going to recreate the scenario. A little pain was nothing if it got Ariyon back.

The Royal Guard was scattered throughout the house, watching every door and entrance to the building. It was clear something had gone down, and now security had been tightened.

The queen stopped in the opening to the dining room, and I heard her swallow a whimper. Following her gaze, I gasped. A handsome man about forty years old lay on the ground. He was twitching and foaming at the mouth. His black hair was streaked through with a few grays, and his large muscular build suggested he'd been one of the bigger guards.

I grasped Solana's covered elbow and forced her to face me. Silent tears fell down her cheeks.

"Do you love him?" I asked blankly.

Her bottom lip quivered at my question. She blinked rapidly, her chest heaving before she nodded once.

I peered at my familiar. *'Change of plans. We save the guy, then get Ariyon back.'*

'Whoa, whoa, whoa. That doesn't sound smart. You could get killed. We barely beat the Grim last time.'

'Emmeric said I die saving The Gilded City, not the queen's lover,' I reminded him, walking over to the man's thrashing body.

'Oh, so now we can be reckless with anything that doesn't line up with what the Ealdor Fae said?'

'Pretty much.' I knelt and took a steadying breath. *'I can't let the queen's lover die, not if there is a chance I can save him,'* I told Yanric, peering back at Solana to see her flattened against the wall and avoiding my gaze. She looked traumatized, like she wanted to mourn but also had to keep her composure and be a leader, and instead, she was just stuck.

"I'm going to save him too," I told her, and her gaze whipped to mine as she peeled herself off the wall and walked toward me. Hope bloomed in her gaze as tears leaked out of the corners, and her hands came up to grasp her chest.

'Oh great, promise her something you aren't sure we can deliver,' Yanric announced.

Damn right. I wasn't going to waste Ariyon's powers. If he were here, he would do the same. I may only be a temporary Maven healer, but I was still a Maven.

'Ready?' I asked my familiar.

'Not really, no.'

With that, I sprung to action. Reaching out, I grasped the man's bare arms, and for once in my life, I welcomed the pain that laced along my spine.

19

ARIYON

Maze could come for us any minute, and I sat, bleary-eyed from a night without sleep, and peered through the window bars. Pax sat at the edge of his bed with his head down. He stared at his hands as if lost in thought.

"I'm going to forfeit," I said, my voice raspy.

Pax's head shot up. "No," he growled.

I nodded. "I've decided. It's done. I'm going to forfeit, and you can be reborn and live a nice, long magicless life traveling." I gave him a small smile.

He shook his head. "You don't understand, Ariyon. The final fight can't be won by forfeit. One of us has to…"

A strangled sound ripped from my throat, and Pax turned his head away as if he could no longer look at me. It felt like I'd been gutted like a fish, my insides ripped out and thrown away. All night, I'd lay there and come to terms with my decision to forfeit, and now he was saying we would be forced to fight to the end—one of us forced to kill the other.

Footsteps sounded down the hall, and panic seized me.

No.

No way, I couldn't.

Pax stood and walked over to the barred window as I stared up at him in panic and leaned forward. "It's okay, Ariyon. I won't fight you. Just make it quick, okay?"

I shook my head vigorously. "No. No, I won't do that!"

The footsteps were closer.

Pax gave me a sad smile. "You have an entire kingdom waiting for you, bro. I don't have anyone."

Breathing became hard. It felt like I was sucking air through a straw, unable to get enough air. No. This wasn't happening. I wouldn't do it.

Maze and Hawk both arrived, and I felt myself go numb. I didn't want to go through with this. It was too hard, too much. I was a healer. I helped save lives. I didn't kill innocents. Those other guys I fought in the arena were evil, but Pax was good. He was a good person born into a bad family, like Fallon.

"I won't," I growled as Hawk opened my cell and dangled the cuffs at his side.

"It's okay," Pax said, his voice defeated, as if he was already gone in his mind.

My mind raced trying to think up a scenario in which I didn't have to fight my friend, but by the time Maze and Hawk brought us into the fighting ring surrounded by screaming crowds, I had thought of nothing. I recognized a few off-duty guards and some Nightlings who had attacked Ayden at my party, but I didn't care about that right now. All I could think about was the fact that I was going to have to fight someone I cared about and respected. A cold emptiness bloomed in my chest. I would have to succumb to my fate.

20

FALLON

I LANDED ON THE GRASS IN THE REALM OF ETERNITY AND barely acknowledged the body of the queen's lover at my feet. Instead, I peered across at the Grim. He leaned casually against a boulder, reading a book.

"Grim!" I called out, and he smiled lightly, looking up at me expectantly. "I challenge you for this man's soul."

The Grim set his book down and rolled out his shoulders before taking a few steps closer. His eyes ran down the length of my arms and stopped at the tops of my hands. "I see you still carry the power of a Maven healer, and so I grant your request, but I must remind you. Last time, I was going easy on you. This time, I most certainly will not. Some souls are destined to cross over at the appointed time."

Panic seized me, but I couldn't give up—I couldn't do that to Solana, not after everything she had lost in her life. Her brother, her betrothed, her ability to have children; I couldn't let her lover be taken too.

I sucked in a calm breath and heard Master Hart's voice in my head, something he had said in one of his lectures. *A Maven healer is the only way to avoid certain death. But not every Maven healer will save every soul they intend to. Some souls, the Grim won't let go of.*

I hoped that this wasn't one of the souls the Grim didn't want to let go of, because I really didn't want to go back and see the queen heartbroken, my promise to her broken.

He tossed me a sword and I caught it, hefting the weight of the blade in my hand as Yanric took to the air.

'You must be ruthless, Fallon Bane. Go for his eyes, his throat, anything you can gouge out,' Yanric told me.

I winced, holding the sword aloft. *'I don't want to kill him.'*

'You can't kill him! He is the Fae of Death!'

With that, the Grim came for me faster than ever before, and by the time I knew what had happened, a cut had formed on my upper arm, blood blooming to the surface.

Bastard!

With a battle cry, I charged forward, faking right but then moving left at the last instant. He didn't fall for it. He stepped to the left, crouched, and swung for my legs with his sword.

Jump!' Yanric coached. I did but too late. The sword crashed into my ankle, and I cried out, falling to the ground.

'I'll kill him,' Yanric seethed, and dive-bombed from the sky.

I could feel the murderous thoughts coming from my familiar, but all I could think of were two things.

Save the queen's lover. Save Ariyon.

The Grim looked up, anticipating Yanric's attack, and I used the distraction to kick at his knee as hard as I could. My foot made contact, and I pushed with every ounce of strength I had.

With a growl, the Grim went down. First his butt hit the hard-packed dirt, and then his back followed, his sword dropping as he tried to catch himself. I didn't let up. Leaping on to top of him, I drove my sword right into his chest, hoping it wasn't possible to actually kill him.

Instead of blood pouring from his wound, *light* did. Bright, buttery shafts of light splintered from his chest and hit me in the eyes, causing me to cry out in surprise. The Grim reached up to grasp my upper arms, seemingly to throw me off him, but Yanric was too quick for that. My familiar landed on his forehead and pecked at the tip of his nose, coming away with a small chunk. More light shot from the opening Yanric had made, and the Grim merely stared up at me, his skin already stitching back together to cover the holes we'd made in him. My sword magically pushed its way out of his chest, and I rolled off him, bleeding and breathless.

That was three, right? Kicking the knee, the sword, and Yanric. That was three!

The Grim announced, "Well done, Fallon Bane. I will grant your request and return this soul to his body."

"Thank you," I breathed.

He nodded. "I want you to know that the intensity at which you fight for those you care about is well noted."

What did that mean? Was that a compliment?

I swallowed hard, looking back at the queen's lover just in time to hear him gasp and sit upright, his presence here fading away to nothing, and I knew he'd just rejoined his body.

Now for the reason I was really here. I recited the steps Emmeric had given me in my head before I spoke.

"Grim, I would like to speak to the Quorum regarding Ariyon. And I need to see Ariyon one last time beforehand," I told him.

'Yan, how do I switch our powers? You said you would handle it.'

'Right. BRB.' Yanric poofed into black smoke.

The keeper of death peered at me with a stern expression, and my heart fluttered wildly in my chest. What if he said no? What if—

A smile broke out on his face, and he nodded as if he'd known I was going to do it. "As a Maven healer, your request for a meeting with the Quorum is granted. You have five minutes with Ariyon before the Quorum will be ready to meet you both."

"Five—" I was jerked off my feet then and flying through the air. One second, I was standing before the Grim, and the next I was transported to…a giant room full of screaming fae. I frowned, trying to make sense of what was going on around me. The fae pushed against each other, chanting something as they crowded around a roped-off mat.

I spun, doing a full 360, and saw Ariyon enter the room with another fae beside him.

My mouth popped open at Ariyon's chiseled, shirtless form. He was covered in yellowing bruises and small scars, and his hair was inches longer than I remembered and slicked back. The fae beside him was about our age, with inky-black hair and covered with tattoos. They were being paraded to the roped-off mat, which I now realized was a fighting ring. Both guys looked downcast at the floor.

'Yan!' I called out to my familiar. According to Emmeric, I had to switch powers with Ariyon first, and only then could I offer to give my Nightling life away to the Quorum.

I had no idea what I was doing, but I was in a room full of some very questionable looking fae, and I wasn't about to just walk up to Ariyon until I knew exactly how to switch our powers.

Yanric didn't answer, and so I slunk into the corner of the room and watched from afar. When my birth mother strode into the space, my knees went weak. She walked behind Ariyon with her head high as she spoke to another woman beside her. Seeing Marissa, with her black hair and pointy chin, always jarred me. We looked so much alike.

If I grabbed Ariyon right now, how would this work? Could they hurt me? But I couldn't sit by and let Ariyon fight, not when I had a Quorum meeting in a few minutes to fix this whole mess.

Ariyon and the tatted-up guy dipped below the ropes and entered the fighting ring, and the amassed crowd of about a hundred fae went wild with whoops and cheers. I peered around looking for an exit, but this appeared to be some type of large jail with a network of hallways and cell doors.

The woman next to my birth mother clapped her hands once, and the crowd went silent. Marissa stood next to her, grinning, as she stared at Ariyon like he was her next meal.

What the fae was she looking at him like that for? It made sweat break out on my palms—even more than it already was. She'd already killed him once. What did she possibly have in store for him now? I hated her.

"The winner of this fight will be deemed one of the strongest among us and therefore will be granted rebirth!" the woman called out, and the crowd went wild again.

My stomach sank. This was it, the final fight.

Meanwhile, Ariyon was looking at the tattooed guy and shaking his head. Tattooed guy only nodded back in defiance.

Were they friends? What was going on here?

"The loser," she went on, "will be tossed into the Bottomless Pit, vanishing forever."

Bile rose up into my throat at that. We were nearly out of time. I jumped a little when Yanric appeared right in front of my face, first as a ball of shadows and then as my feathered friend. *'I got it!'* he said, just as the fight bell rang.

"Ariyon!" I screamed at the top of my lungs and beelined for him.

Ariyon's head snapped in my direction, and he grinned. "I forfeit!" he bellowed, as the crowd fell into shocked silence and then screamed a chorus of boos.

"You can't forfeit!" the woman who had spoken previously announced, and she turned in my direction at the same time as Marissa.

"Fallon!" Marissa bellowed across the space.

Everything happened so fast then. Ariyon leaped from the ropes and hit the ground running toward me, just as Marissa and two big-looking dudes rushed at me as well.

'Blood. It takes a blood transfer. Ariyon was bleeding the night you switched powers. Eden thinks you may have had a cut on your hand too. She said that the power to switch back always stays with the spell caster, so even without your other powers, you should still be able to.'

Thank the Light for Eden and her brilliant mind.

Ariyon reached me first, but just barely. I wanted to hug him, to kiss him, to explain everything, but there was no time. Marissa and her men were right behind him.

Ariyon spun, taking a protective stance in front of me, and held out his hands. The air crackled with electricity, and then a powerful blast of energy left his palms and slammed into Marissa and her goons, throwing them several feet back.

Whoa. Was that *my* magic? I'd never done anything like that before. It reminded me of Ayden's shock wave, but it was also some type of a defensive shield. I had no time to dwell on it because Marissa was already preparing her retaliation.

"Trust me!" I shouted to Ariyon as I swiped my finger over the cut the Grim had made on my arm before it could heal more. Red, thick blood coated my finger, and I reached up to a dried scab on Ariyon's neck. Marissa threw some type of magic at us, but Ariyon shielded the blow, grunting as the force of Marissa's magic slammed into him. I felt pretty helpless as a healer, but he seemed to know what he was doing, so I tried to relax and focus.

'This is gross,' I told Yanric as I pulled the scab on his neck apart to reopen the cut. Ariyon hissed, and I shoved my blood-tipped finger onto his cut, mixing our blood together.

'Now imagine the powers flowing from you to him and then from him to you, like in a stream. You might see them in your mind's eye as colors, Eden said,' Yan instructed, and then flew into the fray as Marissa and her thugs launched a barrage of assaults at the shield Ariyon had erected over us.

Stream, colors. Got it.

Against every instinct I had, despite all the danger around me, I closed my eyes and envisioned my current Maven healing magic as a yellow, buttery light flowing into Ariyon's body like water.

"I feel that!" Ariyon said, and relief crashed into me, but then I lost focus and the image I'd conjured in my mind blipped out. All of a sudden, Ariyon slammed into me, taking me to the ground. I cried out in pain as he fell on my barely healing ankle, sending a sharp stab of agony up my leg.

With a growl, he popped up quickly, and I gasped when I saw that the top of his left hand held the Maven healing marks and the other did not. I peered down at my hands and sure enough, the right held the marks, but my left did not.

Okay. We are halfway there.

'Quick! His powers are back and are healing the cut!' Yanric bellowed and dove down into Marissa's hair, as Ariyon shot an arrow made of shadows right at her stomach.

Holy Fae.

I wanted to ask him how he was doing all of this, but I needed to focus. I really wished I'd tried to figure out this portal thing with Eden. That would have come in really handy right now. If that was in fact how I got Ariyon's body into the Realm of Eternity, it would be so much easier to exit us both out of here that way.

Closing my eyes again, I brought up the image in my mind of the buttery, yellow light, flowing like a river into Ariyon, and then suddenly, a purple, glowing water rushed from him and straight into me. It hit my chest with such force, I gasped as the weight of it settled over me. A sickening feeling slithered through my body then, and I felt a darkness cinch my heart before I quickly pushed it away. I was reminded of what Emmeric said about going dark.

I am not going dark! Not an option. No thank you, I mentally screamed.

"Fallon, I can't protect us anymore," Ariyon breathed, and my eyes snapped open.

He was staring at the backs of his hands, which both held Maven marks. Marissa was five feet in front of us, wearing a scowl. He was the healer again, which meant I was the only one who could protect us.

"You belong with me, Fallon. I'll let him go if you just—"

I didn't even let her speak because now that I had my power back, coupled with the rage she ignited in me, I held up my palms and let go of everything I'd been holding in. Purple fire exploded out of my hands with such force, it blew Ariyon and me backward a few inches. A ten-foot-wide wall of flames had been conjured in front of us, causing everyone in the room to shout in alarm.

'*Read my letter,*' Marissa whispered into my mind, and fear flushed through me.

There was a pull, and then Ariyon, Yanric, and I were yanked from the Realm of Rebirth and went flying through a dark tunnel.

"Fallon!" Ariyon's panicked screams surrounded me in the darkness.

"I'm okay!" I told him, my body spinning and twisting in such complete blackness I couldn't even see the shape of my own limbs in the void.

It felt like we'd tumbled around in the pure blackness for eternity when finally, we were spit out into...

Water?

My body was plunged into warm liquid, and I barely had time to close my mouth before my head was submerged. Kicking my legs, I popped back up to see Yanric and Ariyon splashing beside me as we treaded crystal-blue water. I had to shield my eyes against the bright glow coming from somewhere in front of me, much too bright after being encased in such darkness.

We were in some kind of grotto, with stone walls all around us and an open top that showed a sliver of blue sky. The bright light was coming from right in front of us, but it was slowly dimming. I treaded the water carefully, trying to calm my heart down as Ariyon swam up next to me with a wet and pissed-off Yanric on his shoulder.

'*I cannot swim,*' my familiar declared angrily.

Ariyon reached out and tugged at my hips, pulling me closer

until I was resting against him, both of us slowly kicking our legs to stay above water.

"You came for me." He leaned his forehead against mine, and in that moment, it was all worth it. All the nights I stayed up scouring books for any information that might get Ariyon back, trekking to Ealdoria to see Emmeric, fighting the Grim. It was all worth it the second Ariyon's skin touched mine and I didn't feel pain. Since the day I'd first met him, first looked into his silver eyes, I'd felt a magnetic attraction to him. He was my normal, the only man in the realm to give me what had been denied to me since birth.

"Fallon Bane!" Multiple voices boomed at the same time, and I pulled away from Ariyon, snapping my head up to peer at the light.

I gasped as the light dimmed to a manageable level. Standing there on a large boulder in the middle of the pool that we were floating in was…a creature. A creature with four heads, one of which was of a fae man, one that of a lion, one a raven, and one a woman. Their body was one being, feathered in parts, fur on others, with multiple arms, legs, and paws and even a pair of wings.

This was the Quorum?

I swallowed hard, knowing I was in the presence of great power. Invisible waves of energy radiated off their form, like heat from the ground on a searing-hot day.

"Thank you for agreeing to see me." I wanted to show respect since I knew this creature had Ariyon's and my fates in their hands.

"We agreed to see a Maven healer," the heads all spoke at once, which was terrifying.

I swallowed hard. I had technically tricked them into seeing me. "I am a Maven healer and whatever else you want me to be. I can be anything. My power is such that I can switch abilities with anyone."

"House of Ash and Shadow," the female head growled.

"Against creation," the lion said.

"Yes. Not natural," the male fae agreed.

The raven just crowed loudly, causing Yanric to shiver slightly from his place on Ariyon's shoulder.

I swallowed hard, trying not to let what they were saying affect me. I had no idea what they were talking about.

Against creation?

"It's not her fault," Ariyon called out beside me, "that she was created this way. It was my family's doing. Wasn't it?"

What?

I glanced at Ariyon like he'd lost his mind, and then the light flickered in the grotto.

I peered up at the Quorum to see the lion head regarding Ariyon curiously. "A Madden who knows the true history. Interesting indeed."

The creature shifted its weight so that the woman's head was facing us. "It matters not. Why have you called this meeting?"

Okay, this was getting confusing.

I swallowed hard. "I think I accidentally used a portal to bring Ariyon's body here when I saved his life. I know bringing a mortal body into the Realm of Eternity is against the rules, and so I'm begging you to let him go home. You can take whatever you want from me. Let me bear the consequences of my mistake. I am even willing to give my life."

"No!" Ariyon yelled, and then I was yanked up out of the

water and suspended midair. My stomach lurched as panic shot through me. I had been lifted out of the water by an unseen force, water dripping off my limbs as I floated directly above the Quorum.

Ariyon and Yanric were screaming, but I couldn't hear anything; their mouths were moving, but nothing was coming out. I peered down at the creature and watched in fascination and horror as they peeled their bodies apart, no longer sharing one form. The fae man and woman were naked as they walked up into the air to meet me head-on, as if ascending an invisible staircase. The lion swished his long tail, and the six-foot-tall raven took flight to land behind me. I was surrounded.

"Fallon Bane, you would give your life to return Ariyon Madden back to the land of the living?" the woman asked.

Ariyon flailed in the water madly, but I couldn't hear a sound. I could only see him struggling. He was trying to get my attention, shaking his head vigorously to get me to say no. I looked away from him to the woman who had spoken.

"I would," I said without hesitation.

The lion tipped his head back and roared, a haunting sound that caused a scream of surprise to rip from my throat.

The raven peered at the fae man, and its eyes flashed silver. "Take her second life. Let her keep this one. There is still good she can do with this body."

The fae man nodded. "Very well. Ariyon Madden will return to the land of the living. You, Fallon Bane, will be restored as well, but when you die, that is the end. No rebirth, no chance to live forever in the Realm of Eternity."

I frowned. "Well, that was never an option for me anyway, right? Those from the House of Ash and Shadow don't go there."

They all shared a look then, and one by one, they nodded.

"Because you need to know what you are giving up, I am going to impart information into your mind. You will know the true history of your kind, all at once."

My chest heaved as I anticipated a feeling similar to when I'd shared Solana's memories with her; it was overwhelming, but this was also just history. What did that mean? What "true" history did I not know? Were some people of the House of Ash and Shadow allowed into the Realm of Eternity?

"This might hurt a little," the man said.

The fae simply pointed at me, and a massive headache formed in my skull. I gasped as a wealth of information was dumped into my brain as if I'd just read a hundred books.

In the beginning, there were only two houses. The third was created by fae. My people were experimented on and given dark powers they were never meant to have: unnatural fire, destructive magic, curses, and plagues. A tear rolled down my cheek as I processed everything. The experiment had unintended consequences, and my ancestors started to go mad. To control the damage done, the other royal families voted to slaughter them. When they died, they were taken to a new place, the Realm of Rebirth, and given a chance at a new life, one without magic. Except, that new magicless life didn't appeal to most of them. They couldn't live without power, and they grew thirsty for it. So they learned how to get around the system. They fed on blood of living fae with magic and siphoned power from them, creating what they are today, Nightlings. Abominations in the eyes of creation.

A single tear slipped down my cheek.

I now knew about the Bottomless Pit and how the souls who

chose to become Nightlings by feeding on blood were tossed there upon death and basically wiped out of existence. It's the place I would go when I died, having never proven that I could live a magicless life and withstand the urge to steal power from another and use dark magic.

My chest heaved as I processed this supernatural dumping of so much knowledge at once. I glanced down at Ariyon, who was still screaming and trying to get my attention.

That's what he meant when he said it was his family's fault I was this way. The Maddens were the leaders of this dark idea, the ones who led the experiments on my ancestors. How funny that my people were the victims at first and yet eventually became the perpetrators of violence.

But just as I thought it, the knowledge of why became available to me: the Banes and others who were subjects of the experiments had volunteered. They wanted more power, and they didn't care how they got it. They'd given consent and now had to live with the consequences.

I gave Ariyon and Yanric a small smile to let them know I was okay, and then I looked up to face the Quorum.

"I understand. Thank you," I told them. "I'm okay with losing my second life. Just let Ariyon go home."

The fae woman seemed slightly surprised by my answer but nodded curtly. Then she stepped forward. "Very well, Fallon Bane. Your request is granted."

Ariyon was sucked into the water then, and Yanric flew up into the air to avoid it. I screamed as the Quorum let go of whatever power was holding me in the air and I plunged into the water, taking in a huge mouthful and then trying to cough it out. My lungs burned as the water entered my mouth, suffocating me.

Yanric dove into the water, pecking at my hair and fingers trying to pull me up, but blackness danced at the edges of my vision as my body jerked.

I looked around the water frantically but couldn't find Ariyon. And then it hit me.

I'm dying. They are taking the second life from me right now. They're killing it.

If I had another fifty years to live, I wouldn't have minded ending everything after and not getting to live forever, even in the beautiful afterlife that I had read about in books that the Realm of Eternity offered. But knowing I would die before a year would pass caused an ache to form in my chest.

A feeling of emptiness suddenly smacked into my stomach, as if an unseen force was pulling the second life from my body. A gloomy, sickening sensation replaced it, like there was suddenly more room inside my body and my dark magic was expanding to fill the space. In that fleeting moment, I heard Emmeric saying my dark powers would overtake me once I gave up my second life. That premonition felt true in that moment, but I didn't have any time to wallow in the thought—the blackness took me, enveloping every part of my soul, until there was nothing left.

21

FALLON

My eyes snapped open, and I gasped for air, rolling onto my side and coughing out a mouthful of water.

"Fallon," Ariyon breathed, rubbing small circles on my arms. My throat and lungs burned like I'd ingested fire.

"You can touch her?" Solana's voice cut through my confusion, and Ariyon's hands froze on my exposed upper arms. "Since when?" she asked, a trace of accusation in her tone.

I sat up slowly, taking stock of the room around me. Ariyon and I were covered in water, as was Yanric, who hopped over to be near me. Solana and her Royal Guard lover were standing above us in the same dining room I'd saved his life in. He looked worried but unharmed.

"Since now," I lied, after Ariyon was quiet for too long. "Must be a side effect of us changing powers."

Her eyes narrowed, but she nodded, softening a little. "I can't thank you enough for saving them both, Fallon." She bowed lightly to me, which was unheard of for a queen. Pride unfurled in my chest at her humble acknowledgment.

I nodded, giving her a weak smile and a head bow of my own.

With Ariyon's help, I got to my feet, swaying a little. The cut on my arm was healing, and I realized it was because Ariyon was feeding me magic.

"Hey." I pulled away from him and shot him a glare.

He reached out and took my arm in his hands again, his gaze smoldering as if daring me to tell him to stop.

'Let him heal you. You just gave up your shot at eternity for him,' Yanric advised.

Well, when he put it that way…

'Go tell Eden, Hayes, and Ayden that Ariyon is back,' I said to Yanric, and he flew from my shoulder, turning to smoke before fading through a wall.

The queen looked at Ariyon's hands on my arm, and her eyes narrowed again. "Fallon, I'm sure your father is worried about you. And I'd like some family time alone with my nephew after this ordeal. I'm sure Blair and Ayden are eager to see him too."

Blair. My heart sank at the mention of her name. Solana was not so subtly reminding me that Ariyon was betrothed, and I shouldn't pursue whatever this was between us. Unfortunately for me, this was deep, irrevocable love.

I glanced at Ariyon, trying to keep the hurt off my face, and gently peeled my now-healed arm from his grasp. "Glad you're back. Sorry it took so long."

"Fallon—" he started.

"We can catch up later. You should be with your family now. Everyone has been so worried." I walked a few steps away from him and stood before Solana, giving her a deep curtsy, which she returned with a nod of her head.

"I won't forget what you did," she said and motioned to the man beside her, the lover whose name I didn't even know.

I swallowed hard and nodded, giving her a forced smile.

Blair. He is betrothed to Blair.

I wanted to celebrate that Ariyon was safe, that I'd finally managed to bring him back alive. And though I was so happy that was true, I couldn't rejoice because the reminder that he would marry someone else was soul crushing. I just wanted to be alone.

I left the room and followed the guard to the entrance of the castle. He gave me a curt nod as I took off down the front steps, through the garden, and toward the thick trees. I couldn't help but let the grief take hold inside me.

Never in a million years did I think I would find a guy that could kiss me and touch me and then I would have to watch him be married off to another. Not that I'd actually see it happen— I'd be long dead by the time they finished school and married. Maybe that was for the best. Ariyon would have Blair to comfort him after I died saving the city.

"Fallon!" Ariyon shouted as I reached the forest path that would lead back to town, where I was hoping to find Eden and cry myself to sleep.

I stiffened when I heard him call but kept walking. I didn't want to see him right now. I didn't want to have the inevitable conversation about his duty and Blair and the fact that no matter how much it felt like fate had created us for each other, we'd never actually be able to be together.

Solana wouldn't allow it, and neither would the citizens of

The Gilded City. Besides, I only had a short amount of time to live anyway. Best to just live out the next several months honing my skills to save everyone before I died.

"Fallon Brookshire!" Ariyon bellowed, and my heart pinched at his use of my father's last name. He pulled on my shoulder and I spun, just as his lips crashed onto mine. I gasped and he swallowed the sound, using the opening to slide his tongue into my mouth and stroke it against mine. A whimper formed in my throat, and he pushed me backward until I was flush up against a tree.

Desire bloomed inside my chest, causing heat to travel between my legs. My heart fluttered as he moaned against my lips. Fingers trembling, I reached up to stroke the chiseled lines of his jaw. This kiss was hungry, desperate, as if I was oxygen and he had been drowning. It was a kiss that spoke of promises and a love waiting to bloom.

His fingers pulled at my hips greedily as our bodies pressed together, and I could feel his rapid heartbeat match mine. When he finally tore away from me, there was a wild look in his molten-silver gaze.

"I'm in love with you, Fallon. Deep, mad, scary love," he exclaimed boldly.

A grin swept across my face—but then the memory of Solana telling me about his betrothal to Blair entered my mind.

"I love you too, Ariyon." I did—he was my first love, something I never thought I would have. "But your aunt said you are supposed to marry Blair and have children before you…"

He shook his head defiantly. "She's been saying that since I was six years old. Not going to happen, and I tell her that—often. Ayden will marry and have children. I won't. I won't willingly make a widow and orphans of anyone."

Relief rushed through my body at his words. Even though what he said was sad on so many levels, it was what I needed to hear. I swallowed hard, thinking of the fact that I had a dark secret of my own, that I would in fact be the one to make him the equivalent of a widower when I died within a year.

"I'm so glad you're back." I pulled him back to me, wrapping my arms around him as our bodies crushed together in a tight embrace. His smell enveloped me; it wasn't anything I could place, like sandalwood or mint. It was just Ariyon.

"I almost went insane down there, Fal," he breathed against my neck. "I hope my friend Pax got out." He pulled back.

"That tattooed guy you were about to fight?" I asked.

He nodded. "Since I forfeited, I figure they made him fight someone else, and if he won… They should let him be reborn."

Now that I had the knowledge of what all that meant, I knew that Pax would be reborn magicless and be given the choice to become a Nightling and eventually have his soul erased in the Bottomless Pit or remain without magic and live in the Realm of Eternity when he passed. An easy choice for me if I still had it. "Do you think he'll stay magicless?"

Ariyon looked surprised. "You know about that?"

I nodded. "The Quorum gave me a giant supernatural information dump." I tapped my head.

He nodded. "He said he wants to, but that the first month is hard. I don't really know what that entails." Ariyon looked lost in his thoughts, his brows drawing together with concern for his friend.

There was so much to talk about, and I wanted to shower and change clothes.

"I'm going to go home and change. You go visit with your

aunt. Yanric is getting word to Eden and the others. Let's all meet at your house in like two hours?"

Ariyon pulled me closer to him. "Forget my aunt. I don't want to let you out of my sight ever again. I can walk you home and wait outside. Marissa is looking for you, Fallon. She wants something from you," he asserted.

I knew what she wanted from me, a drop of blood for the necklace she was seemingly trying to steal from Solana so that she could take the throne. Ariyon yanked me toward the West Side, but I pulled him to a stop, facing the direction of Bane Manor, which was on the East Side.

"I live in Bane Manor now. Your aunt invited me into the brigade, and I swore allegiance to her in front of the entire city."

His eyebrows shot up, and he ran a hand through his hair. "Well, damn, we do need to catch up."

Leaning forward, I placed a kiss on his lips. "I'll meet you at your house in two hours. Please go sit with your aunt for a while and calm her nerves? She's really missed you."

He frowned. "Okay, but take Ember."

I rolled my eyes. "Fine."

After we walked back to the palace, Ariyon led me to the stables and got me situated on Ember. I rode home, my head buzzing with everything that had just happened.

It was the culmination of some of the most stressful weeks of my life. But Ariyon was back now, and I was beyond relieved.

When I got home, my dad was there. He had gotten word, probably through Yanric, that I'd gone to the Realm of Eternity and saved Ariyon. He wasn't happy about it. He spoke to me for at least an hour about making good choices and staying safe. I assured him at least twenty times that I was okay and wouldn't be returning to the Realm of Eternity anytime soon now that our powers had been switched back. He finally relented and allowed me to shower, change, and head for the twins' house.

I rode Ember down the streets, and as I passed a fae couple, they bowed to me and held their fists over their hearts in a sign of respect.

Huh.

The next passerby was a woman with a small child, both carrying wildflowers in from a meadow.

"Mommy, she saved the prince!" the girl announced. She ran after Ember, throwing her flowers my way, but they were too far for me to catch and fluttered to the ground.

I waved at her in shock, just as Yanric landed on my shoulder.

'The queen is giving you the Order of the Flame,' Yanric announced.

'The what of the what?' I peered over at him.

'For extreme acts of bravery, you will be awarded The Gilded City's highest medal of honor.' There was pride in his voice.

I swallowed hard, looking over at my familiar.

'Queen Solana said that?'

She was so hot and cold that I had a hard time reading her. Did she like me or just tolerate me?

'She decreed it. Posted it outside the palace on the messenger board. Now everyone in this city knows.'

It was a good feeling, one I'd chased after since the day I got here. A lightness spread throughout my chest, and I smiled, carrying myself a little taller.

'I think by saving her lover boy, you really showed her she could trust you,' Yanric added.

I laughed at that. *'But not me saving her life two times?'*

It was weird to get all the waves and bows of respect on the ride over to Ariyon's, but it was definitely better than the glares I'd gotten when I first arrived here.

The second I pulled Ember up to the opening that led to Ariyon's stables, Eden tore out of the back door of the house and ran toward me.

"You did it!" she cried, wearing a giant grin. "Well, technically *we* did because I'm the one who figured out how to switch the powers."

I beamed at my bestie and reached for her hand, squeezing hard. "I literally could not have done it without you."

Yanric squawked.

"And Yanric," I added.

Ariyon stepped out of the house next and crossed the yard to pull Ember's reins, leading her in the direction he wanted us to go, before reaching up and clutching my waist. As if I weighed nothing, he lifted me off the horse and planted me on my feet in front of him. Leaning forward, he pressed a kiss to my lips.

"Aww," Eden gushed. "Lovers reunited."

Ariyon grinned, slinging an arm around my shoulders casually and tucking me into his side as if it were the most normal thing in the world.

My heart fluttered wildly at the contact, something I'd ached for but was not yet used to.

Ayden and Hayes stepped out of the house and greeted us. Ayden's gaze went to Ariyon's arm around my shoulders, and he smiled. It was small but genuine, as if he was coming to terms with the fact that I was with the right brother, the one who could give me everything I needed. I hoped so. I really wanted Ayden to stay in my life, but I couldn't deny that Ariyon was the one I was meant for.

"Bro, you got chiseled in jail," Hayes said as he approached Ariyon, and we all laughed.

We moved the little party inside, where we played Nightling Chess, ate takeout food, and told stories until it was nearly curfew. Ariyon insisted I ride Ember until he could get me my own horse. So I took Eden home and then headed to mine after. Once I arrived back at Bane Manor, I sent word back with Yanric that I had reached home safely, as Ariyon had insisted I do.

'He'd better give me a snack for all this flying,' Yanric said and then took off.

I smiled saying good night to my dad as I got ready for bed. A few minutes later, I was tucked under the covers and staring at the decorated bedroom ceiling with a grin on my face.

I got Ariyon back, and he said he loved me. Nothing could ruin this feeling. *Nothing.*

Except for the night full of tormenting dreams, during which I barely slept.

22

FALLON

I AWOKE GROGGY THE NEXT DAY, SITTING UP IN BED AND TRYING
not to think of the horrible dreams. Blood, ghosts, me running
after Ariyon in the forest only to see him making out with Blair
against the trees.

I shook my head. *What an awful night.* I never had nightmares, or dreams for that matter. Usually, once my head hit the
pillow, I was out, and when I woke up, I remembered nothing.

When I got downstairs to the large kitchen in Bane Manor,
Yanric and my dad were sitting at the table eating, while our new
cleaning lady wiped down the counters.

"Morning." She smiled cheerfully at me. Her name was
Daniella, and she was super sweet. It turned out that the fae
hired by the queen to service Bane Manor were from the West
Side and really needed the jobs. They were higher paying than
anything they could get otherwise, so we'd kept them on. It was
funny because my dad still cleaned up after himself, so Daniella

would just follow behind him and wipe a perfectly clean counter down again. We all sort of had an understanding that we were keeping them employed as a favor, not because we couldn't answer our own door or pick up our own mess. My father even insisted Daniella sit down and eat a hot lunch while she was here.

There was a knock at the door. I stood to get it but saw Benjamin, our new butler and a thirty-something father of two, rush to get it first. A moment later, he reentered the room with Ariyon.

"Prince Ariyon Madden is here for Fallon, sir." He addressed my dad like he was a king or something, and it made me grin every time.

My dad chuckled. "Okay, thanks. Come on in, son."

My heart nearly flipped over in my chest as I watched Ariyon approach, wearing a shirt that barely fit his more muscular form. Whatever had happened to him down there had done good things for his appearance. His blond hair was shoulder-length and pulled into a man-bun at the nape of his neck, and his arms were bigger than Ayden's now.

"Hey." Ariyon waved at me and then faced my father nervously. "I know it's early, but I was hoping I could have breakfast with you guys and talk to you, sir?"

Apprehension bloomed in my gut. Why did he want to talk to my dad?

"Of course." My dad looked a little surprised but gestured to an empty seat. "It's a much nicer breakfast than the one I served you in Isariah." My father pointed to the fresh fruits, scrambled eggs, and honeyed ham.

Ariyon smiled, taking a seat. "That's what I wanted to talk to you about, sir. I never really apologized for running off that day and for being rude to you. I really care about your daughter, and I was hoping we could get to know each other better."

A lump formed in my throat. He came over to apologize and get to know my dad better? Swoon.

'*You should marry him and have his babies,*' Yanric observed, just as I took a sip of water.

I coughed in shock, almost spitting it all over the table but managing to make it back into the glass as both men stared at me.

"Yanric said something funny," I wheezed, and glared at my bird.

"You don't need to apologize, son. I understand now that it was a shock to learn that Fallon was the daughter of the woman who killed your parents."

Ariyon reached over, squeezed my bare hand, and then looked at my dad. "Thanks for understanding. So, tell me about your life growing up. What did your parents do? Did you always live in Isariah?"

My dad nodded and began to tell stories as I sat back with a smile and watched the two men I loved most in this world get to know each other. This was the best thing ever, and yet... I hadn't felt like myself since waking up this morning after a night full of tormenting dreams. It was like a dark cloud had settled over me, and I couldn't shake the sadness that was trying to creep into my heart and take up residence there.

'*It's been a crazy few weeks. Give yourself a break,*' Yanric offered.

I nodded, reaching out to give my bird a little neck scratch and then a taste of breadcrumbs. Breakfast went quickly. When Ariyon and I stepped outside to go to school, I gasped at the white stallion tied up at the stalls. He had a long blanket wrapped over him with the queen's royal flame emblem embroidered on the back-right corner.

"His name is Ranger. He's gentle but strong. One of my aunt's best battle horses. He's yours," Ariyon said.

"She...she's okay giving me this?" I couldn't fathom owning a horse by myself, let alone one this beautiful.

Ariyon nodded. "The least she can do after you saved Bastian and me."

Bastian. So the lover had a name.

We rode to school side by side, Ariyon on Ember and me on Ranger. It felt surreal, going to school with my *boyfriend*, being in love. It was something I'd always wanted. But I couldn't shake that uneasy feeling I'd had since I woke up. I was just in a bad mood and hoped a good night's sleep would shake me out of it.

After dropping our horses off at the stables, I pulled Ariyon in the direction of his studio. I wanted to show him something before class. When we ducked into the small garden courtyard where he'd once given me the painting of red roses, he grinned, stroking his thumb over my palm.

"I missed this place," he said as I led him inside.

I imagined he did. It was filled with so much of his talent and creativity, but it also seemed to be a place where he went to blow off steam.

Flicking on the light, I pulled him to the back wall, the place that held the white tally marks for all the days he'd taken off his life.

He looked up at it, his eyes squinting at the half-dozen bright-yellow tally marks directly under his white ones at the top.

"What are they?" he asked in awe. I was glad he didn't sound angry. I had touched his art, and I didn't want him to be mad about it.

I turned to him, peering into his seemingly endless gray-blue eyes. "When I had your healing gift, I really got to experience what it was like to be you, what it was like to feel others' pain and to know that you could help them. I knew what it was like to save a life or mend a wound and how that pales in comparison to the time it takes away from your life."

His sharp intake of breath caused chills to break out on my arms. "The yellow marks are from people you have healed?" Again, there was awe in his tone.

I nodded. "You might be consumed with the fact that you're literally giving away parts of your life, but I was enthralled with the lives I was saving." I still had to add Solana's lover and Ariyon to the tally.

His face fell for a moment, and he looked gutted, like I killed his pet or something.

"Oh no, Ariyon, I'm sorry. Did I...did I say something wrong?"

He shook his head, reached out, and ran his fingers over my cheek and then down my neck. "My entire life I've had this gift, and I'd only ever focused on what it was taking from me. You had it for less than a month and you saw the beauty in it. You focused on what it was giving others."

He pulled me closer to him, leaning his forehead on mine and pressing his entire body against me. It fit perfectly against mine, and I inhaled, smiling. His scent was intoxicating.

This right here, this kind of full-body contact, was something I didn't think I'd ever get used to. It was great to not have a spike of fear rush through me at close contact with another person, to feel normal in all the ways a teenage girl should—any person should.

I tilted my chin up just as he looked down at my lips and

then leaned forward to capture my mouth. Our lips met in a slow, tantalizing kiss that sent waves of pleasure throughout my body. There was that magnetic pull between us, as if fate was trying to bring us even closer together. His hands gripped the back of my neck, tongue softly stroking mine, and a heady rush of happiness flooded through me. But it was quickly chased away, dampened by the black cloud that felt like it was following me. It was as if I was feeling emotions at 50 percent, somehow diminished.

He pulled back, and I gave him a sheepish smile as he grabbed the sides of my cheeks gently. "We should get to class, or I'll never want to leave."

I was breathless. I wanted to tell him we should ditch class and make out in here all day, but I knew his teachers and friends were eager to see him after so long. And I didn't fully feel myself today, if I was being honest.

With that, we walked to class together, only for me to realize that I was no longer a healer. Master Clarke was waiting for me outside Pyrotechnics class with a copy of my old schedule. The only addition was that once a week after class, I had brigade weight training with everyone else who had been invited. My tutoring had also been dropped down to once a week, as my reading had improved tremendously.

"I'm proud of you," Master Clarke said, squeezing my shoulder before he left.

His words were sweet and should have made me feel good, but again I couldn't shake the melancholy that clung to me, pulling me into a sort of numb sadness.

'You okay?' Yanric asked.

'I'm fine. I just need better sleep. Meet me at lunch?'

He flew off, and I slipped into class just as the bell rang.

The rest of the day flew by quickly. Ariyon sat with me at lunch, holding hands, stroking my cheek, running his fingers through my hair. He touched me every chance he got, and I felt so seen, so loved, so normal. He asked me a couple times if I was feeling okay. I think it was obvious that I was off, but I told him and Eden I hadn't slept well.

Now I was on my way to Avis's with Hayes. We were going to have a meeting before my shift about the "ice cream" shop on the West Side that would double as a second student healing clinic for The Academy.

When we stepped inside the apothecary shop, Mable was there. Avis greeted us with a smile, but when she looked at me, her face fell. "Feeling okay today, Fallon?"

My stomach tied into knots. She knew. She could see energy, so of course she would know I was feeling off.

I shrugged. "Barely slept. It's been a wild few days."

Mable frowned. "Understandable, dear."

We moved on from that, but Avis was still sneaking wary glances at me, which was making me nervous.

Avis hung up the Closed sign, and we all went into the kitchen in her house to sit around the dining table for our meeting.

"As you have noticed, I have invited Mable to our little project." Avis smiled at Eden's mom.

Mable beamed back at her.

"No offense, but why? She's not a healer," Hayes asked.

Avis nodded. "Because she just donated her parents' house on the West Side to be the location of our ice cream apothecary shop."

I gasped. "Mable, that's so kind of you."

Mable offered a small smile. "Eden will have to live with me forever now."

We all chuckled at that and then got into logistics. Mable knew a vendor who supplied the Hummingbird Inn with treats and who could make our ice cream. Word around town would spread that if you bought ice cream, you would get a healing or tincture for free.

"You think the queen will shut us down if she finds out what we are really doing?" Hayes asked.

Avis took a sip of her tea and then pursed her lips. "I hope not. It's a by-the-book way to offer healing to those who need it most."

"Or she could just change the law," I growled.

Everyone looked at me, and Avis cleared her throat. "We will deal with any roadblocks to this special project as they come up."

The rest of the meeting went well. We decided to be open three days a week to start. We'd all take shifts to help meet the need, and we could start going in next week and setting up shelving and stocking the store. I was no longer able to do hands-on healings, but I'd worked at Avis's long enough to know what tinctures would help people for certain ailments. It was exciting, a passion project close to my heart, and yet when the meeting came to an end, I couldn't find myself feeling happy about it. I just felt…*blah*.

I needed sleep. We all stood to go our separate ways, Mable to the West Side, Hayes to the East Side, and me to start cleaning up the store, when Avis grasped my gloved hand. "Stay and talk with me for a minute?"

Hayes and Mable left, and I chewed on my lip as I looked up at her. "What?" I asked defensively.

Avis swallowed hard and then sat next to me. "You've changed," she said flatly, and tears welled in my eyes.

"What do you mean?" I played stupid, but the truth was, I didn't know which change she was talking about: the nightmares, losing my second chance at life, the fact that I was going to die within a year? Take your pick, there was a lot to choose from.

She frowned, her own eyes misting over. "Oh, Fallon, honey, what happened to you down there?"

The tone of her voice ripped my heart right open. She sounded…disappointed in me. Like I'd failed her. What, I had to be perfect all the time? I couldn't be grumpy or tired? I found myself glaring at her and then shook myself. What was wrong with me? This was Avis, the sweetest woman I knew, and yet I could still feel the anger rising up within me.

"Nothing, okay? I saved Ariyon, and I didn't sleep well. Leave me alone!" I stood so hard that the chair scooted backward and fell over.

Avis's mouth popped open in shock. "No," she growled.

"What?" I asked her again, defiance in my tone.

She stepped closer to me, giving me a firm glare. "I will *not* leave you alone, Fallon. Something has changed in your energy field, and we are going to fix it before it becomes permanent."

Her words sent chills down my spine.

Yanric poofed into the room and landed on my shoulder. *'I think whatever happened with the Quorum has got us in a funk. I feel it too, like a darkness trying to pull me under. Let her help us.'*

I sucked in a breath and nodded. It was all I could do because in that moment, I was terrified. Was I going dark? Surely this wasn't what it felt like, right? Emmeric had said he'd seen me go dark, but I had hoped it wasn't true. I more easily believed my life would end than I'd ever go dark, but now I wasn't sure.

Over the next hour, Avis fed me different herbs and tinctures:

Sad-Be-Gone, Grief-Mend, Mind-Enhance, Clarity-of-Thought.
Nothing worked. Nothing made the foreboding feeling go away.

She feverishly ground herbs in a mortar, whispering over them, rubbing them in her palms, and finally made a paste that she handed to me. "Rub this on your arm. It should make you laugh uncontrollably if you are suffering from depression."

I swallowed hard, trepidation worming through me. Taking the yellowish-brown ball of goo, I began to spread it on my forearm.

Yanric peered at me expectantly, and even I was waiting for a bout of laughter to strike me…but nothing happened.

Avis swallowed hard, nodding. "Okay…well, I just need to research some more, and we will try again tomorrow."

Defeat hit me like a sack of bricks, but instead of wanting to cry about it, I just felt numb.

It was time to go home anyway. My dad would be waiting. "Don't bother. Thanks though," I muttered and grabbed my bag, slinging it over my shoulder.

"Fallon!" Avis called after me.

I spun to look at her, and she gave me a small smile. "Don't give up hope."

I couldn't bring myself to smile back, so I just left, letting the door close behind me. The darkness crept a little further into my heart, like the cold on a freezing night.

Yanric and I were silent the entire ride home. Ranger was a good horse. He kept a steady pace and didn't jostle me too much. More fae came out to the road to bow to me or hold their fists over their chests as a salute, but I didn't feel like waving back at them. I felt like all the happiness was being siphoned out of me.

'Yan, I'm scared,' I told my familiar.

He'd been silent since we left Avis's shop, and now he hopped closer to my neck and nuzzled it.

'Me too. But we're in this together.'

That wasn't much comfort. It actually made me feel worse. I didn't want to bring him down with me if I was going dark. No matter how much I tried to think of happy things, my body wasn't responding. For the first time in my life, there was no joy in my being.

And it terrified me.

23

FALLON

THE NEXT MORNING, ARIYON RETURNED TO EAT BREAKFAST with us. I hadn't slept again, tossing and turning with nightmares, this time of Marissa feeding from my neck and my eyes going black as I screamed and lost my mind.

Ariyon was looking at me oddly, like he knew something was wrong, but said nothing as he exchanged pleasantries with my dad.

After we ate, we stepped outside to get on our horses, but Ariyon stopped me.

"What's wrong?" His voice was laced with concern.

"Why does everyone keep asking me that!" I snapped at him, and his brow furrowed.

Guilt rushed through me, and I reached for his chest, pulling myself to him as his hands came around my waist. "I'm sorry. I'm not sleeping well since you got back…"

He sighed. "Do you want to talk about it? You gave up your

chance at a second life, Fallon. You shouldn't have done that for me. That might have led to some weird consequences in your body."

He has no idea.

I nodded, pulling away from him. "Whatever I did, it was worth it."

He looked gutted, sagging against the barn door. "No, Fallon. If you get hurt, nothing is worth it." Reaching up, he pulled a black, glossy strand of hair away from my cheek, and my eyes filled with tears. He froze, his face falling.

I should tell him—tell him I think that I'm going dark. Someone needed to know so they could keep an eye on me and lock me up when needed.

"What is it that has you so sad?" Ariyon swiped a tear from my cheek.

"Blair," I blurted out, the lie coming easily to me. "Your betrothal to her. It's…unsettling."

"We are *not* betrothed. My aunt and Blair's dad try to plan these things behind our backs, but I haven't signed anything, and she doesn't have a ring."

I nodded. "So, she knows you won't be marrying her?"

He gave me a long look. "I mean, I dumped her for you, so I would hope she got the message."

I shrugged and then stepped into the stall. I didn't want to talk about this anymore.

"You don't believe me?" he called out.

"Let's just get to school," I offered and got on Ranger.

We were quiet the entire ride, and I couldn't stop feeling like I wasn't myself, like I couldn't control my emotions, and it scared me. Ariyon was everything I wanted, and he was so sweet to come to eat breakfast with my dad and me. Why was I picking fights with him?

When we got to school, we dismounted, and he slipped his fingers into mine. Instead of going to our first classes, he walked right to the courtyard and called Blair over.

My eyes flew wide. "What are you doing?" I hissed.

He looked at me with blazing silver eyes. "Proving to you how much I care about you and only you."

My knees went weak at the declaration, and then Blair was upon us. She stood there with her arms crossed and a stink-faced glare. Blair's skirt was so short that I was worried if the wind picked up, we'd see what color underwear she had on. Maybe I was just jealous; her long, lean legs were beautiful, and I was never allowed to show mine for fear of being touched. Blair's gaze went to our interlocked fingers, and she appeared surprised. No one else knew we could touch, but it seemed Ariyon didn't care about keeping that secret anymore.

"What's up?" she asked Ariyon, her tone suspicious.

Ariyon cleared his throat. "You know how my aunt and your dad are always saying one day we will marry and how they would love for us to have kids before I—"

"Yeah…" Blair cut him off, standing straighter and dropping her arms to her sides.

"That will never happen. I will never marry. I don't want children, and I love Fallon."

My mouth popped open, and I could see the moment Blair's heart was smashed into a thousand pieces. Her eyes filled with unshed tears, and it was clear that she thought that possibility might have been in her future.

"I'm sorry if that hurts your feelings, Blair," Ariyon added, seemingly surprised by her reaction as well.

"Oh, screw you both!" she snapped, spinning on her heels and stomping off.

Ariyon turned to me then, leaning forward to plant a kiss on my lips. "Happy?"

I wanted to say yes. I wanted to say that was the sweetest thing anyone had ever done for me, but… I felt like I was walking against a strong river current, fighting to make my way upstream.

But I nodded, giving him a weak smile.

The second I stepped into class, Mrs. Bardot clapped her hands. "Don't get too comfortable! We are having a practical lesson today on the field."

I stopped myself from placing my backpack on the desk beside Ayden, and we all made our way outside.

"I can't believe my aunt is giving you the Order of the Flame. Did you get it yet?" Ayden eyed my bag as if I were hiding it in there.

I chuckled as Eden stepped up beside us. "No, not yet. What is it, anyway?" I asked Ayden.

"It's a gold pin, but not just that. It's like the most badass medal any citizen outside the Royal Guard can get," he answered.

I nodded, not really caring too much about the medal.

"Guess all that ass-kissing paid off," Blair snarled as she passed us.

Anger flared inside me, but I tamped it down.

"Ignore her." Eden waved Blair off as the bully ran to catch up with some of her friends. "She's just jealous."

True, and certainly more so because of what Ariyon had said to her this morning.

Mrs. Bardot spent the next few minutes instructing us on how to toss fireballs at a moving target. The moving target in this case was a metal dummy covered in armor, which was charred black from all the hits it had taken. His nickname was Sir Burns-a-Lot, and he was on a pulley system that allowed some of my fellow classmates to tug a thin metal chain that moved him along the track. He would go back and forth across the training field as we threw fireballs at his chest. Or attempted to.

Mrs. Bardot had assigned two students the task of putting out unwanted fires that may spring up from a fireball missing its target. They held spray canisters full of water at the ready.

Eden and Ayden were some of the first students to go and executed the task perfectly, hitting the target in the chest every time he passed. Blair was next and missed one, but it crashed into the rocks behind Sir Burns-a-Lot and didn't start a fire. Then it was my turn, and to my surprise, when my name was called, quite a few students clapped for me.

I guess saving Ariyon and getting awarded this medal really had won the people over in my favor.

"Now, I know it's been a while since you used your fire powers," Mrs. Bardot commented. "So just do the best that you can."

I nodded. She was right. Up until a few days ago, I was working with Ariyon's power to heal people. It felt a lot more special than fire and all the powers from House of Ash and Shadow, but I was encouraged by Emmeric's vision of me saving everyone. If I was a hero, it meant I did something really amazing to save everyone, and I needed my House of Ash powers for that.

Pulling off my gloves, I set them to the side and grinned

when I saw that Ariyon had just shown up. Sitting on the grass with his brother, he gave me a wink.

As if I wasn't already nervous enough, this added to my anxiety, but it was sweet he'd shown up to support me.

Rubbing my palms together, I felt for my power. It was thrumming under the surface of my skin. It was as if it had grown in Ariyon's body and then transferred back to me stronger than ever before.

With a mere thought, a perfectly round orange-and-purple fireball formed in my hand.

"Yeah, go, Fallon!" Ariyon whooped, and I internally swooned. There was nothing quite like being cheered on by your boyfriend.

Sir Burns-a-Lot rolled across the tracks, and I tossed the fireball at him, but I was too slow, and it crashed onto the metal track about a foot beside him.

"Maybe the queen should take her medal back," Blair snipped, and a few of her friends snickered.

Anger flared to life inside me, and two fireballs formed on my palms. I shot her a glare over my shoulder and then turned back to the test dummy as it raced past me again.

I reeled my palms back to throw—

"Watch out!" Blair called, distracting me just as I was about to throw. I faltered, ducking as if something was going to hit me, and both flame balls fell to the grass, more than six feet away from Sir Burns-a-Lot.

Blair and her goons burst into laughter, and a red-hot rage I'd never experienced before rushed through me, making my heart beat wildly and the blood rush to my ears.

"Shut up, Blair!" I screamed as I spun on her.

Purple flames erupted on the ends of Blair's hair, and chaos broke out on the field.

I staggered backward in shock as Blair screamed bloody murder. Her hair turned into a full-on fireball as the two students holding the water canisters rushed forward and sprayed her liberally from head to toe.

No.

There's no way I did that. No way. I didn't throw out my arms or anything! I hadn't meant to...

The flames were purple, a strange male voice spoke into my mind.

I yelped, grabbing my face. I was hearing voices?

I glanced toward Ariyon, Ayden, and Eden for comfort but was only met with three horrified gazes.

'I'm going dark,' I told Yanric. The shock and truth of it hit me so deeply, I felt bile rise in my throat.

He appeared out of shadows and solidified on my shoulder. *'I'm here. You're not alone,'* he said. What he didn't do was argue with my statement.

I'd made Blair's hair catch fire out of anger.

I did that.

I looked at her in horror, covered in water from the fire extinguishers. Her hair was a mass of little molten nubs, and she was crying. Her neck looked blistered and burned. Ariyon approached her, the wheels on his hands already spinning to heal her, and I wanted to crawl out of my skin.

I could have killed her. Bile crept up my throat.

"Fallon?" The teacher held her hands out to me, speaking in low, calm tones as if I would light the entire class ablaze at any moment.

She's scared of me.

I turned and took off running then, away from the class and

back toward the school. I wanted to get out of there, to get away from the faces looking at me like I was a monster.

Because I am.

'Take a deep breath. You haven't used your powers in a long time, and Blair was being a royal hag,' Yanric said.

'Don't talk to me.' I reached up and shooed him off my shoulder as silent tears streamed down my face. He screeched as he was forced to flap his wings and fly a few feet away from me.

It happened. Just as everyone said it would. Just as Emmeric predicted. I was going dark, and I'd be damned if I was going to let my friends get hurt along the way, Yanric included.

I was heaving for oxygen by the time I reached the stables. Within seconds, I had mounted Ranger and was galloping through the city toward Bane Manor.

Solana had remodeled the house to also work as a prison, to contain me if I ever went dark. One letter to the queen telling her to lock it down, and I would be shut in there for the rest of my life. But the problem was, my father was in there with me. I knew he would never leave me, and I would never forgive myself if I hurt a single hair on his head. No. I had to be smart about this. I had to run away, far away, where no one I cared about would ever find me. Because even if I locked my dad out, Ariyon would come for me. He'd never let me spend my life imprisoned, and I couldn't risk hurting him either.

I raced home, grateful my father was at work and that there was no Royal Guard waiting for me. They didn't keep watch while I was at school, and the queen seemed to have loosened up ever since I returned with Ariyon.

When I stepped inside, I passed the kitchen and found Daniella baking something. I told her I hadn't been feeling well and was going to sleep it off in my room and to turn anyone away who came by. She wished me well, and I snuck into my father's bedroom and lifted the mattress off the frame. The two runaway bags were tucked perfectly beside each other. It would kill my father to know I left him behind, but there was no reality in which I would ever risk hurting him.

Yanric poofed beside me, and I looked at him, my heart breaking for what was happening. *'I'm sorry, Yan, but I'm hearing voices that aren't my own. I'm not able to feel happiness. I'm having nightmares, and I just lit Blair's hair on fire. This isn't just lack of sleep.'*

He nodded solemnly. *'We're going dark.'*

I burst into tears, reaching down to heft one of the bags over my shoulder. I couldn't believe this was happening. Walking over to the nightstand, I picked up a pencil and a piece of paper, wiping at my eyes feverishly.

A few tears dripped onto the paper as I brushed them off my cheeks and blinked rapidly to clear them.

Dear Father,

You might hear about something I did at school today, and I want you to know I didn't do it on purpose. Maybe it's worse that I didn't. I have all the signs of going dark. Nightmares, hearing voices, a lack of happiness around things I used to love, power that I cannot control. I'm so sorry to leave you like this. I know it will break your heart, but I can't stay and risk you getting hurt. Please know that out of everything in my life, I loved you the most, the man who took a chance on the cursed girl in the basket. I think I stayed sane this long because of you.

I will always carry your kindness within me, even if I can no longer feel it.

Love always and forever,
Fallon

P.S. Please give the other note to Ariyon.

Then I wrote a second note to Ariyon, unable to stop the tears from spilling out onto the page.

Ariyon,

Where do I begin? How about with the first time you touched me, and it didn't cause me pain? You gave me hope. I loved that someone could touch me without triggering my curse. It made me feel normal, something I had longed for my entire life. Then I got to know you, and no matter how much I tried to fight it, I fell for you. You try to act tough, but you have the biggest heart of anyone I know. I'm sorry it had to end like this. I truly didn't think I was capable of going dark. Even now, when I search inside myself, there aren't hatred and anger there like I thought there would be if I went dark. There's a void, a numbness. I can't feel anything. I don't know which is worse.

Please tell Blair I am so sorry and that I didn't mean to hurt her. Give Eden and Ayden my apologies and love. And know that you gave me more joy in our short time together than in all my life before you. You made all my dreams come true.

I'm going to go where I can't hurt anyone anymore.

Love,
Fallon

By the time I had finished both letters, I had no more tears left to cry and no more feelings left inside me. I was a hollow shell, lost at sea, drowning as if tied to an anchor that was pulling me into the deepest depths of the ocean.

I left the letters on my father's bed and, with Yanric perched on my shoulder, made my way to my room. I grabbed a few more things I knew I would want and shoved them into the bag. As I was about to leave, I stopped at the half-open drawer on my nightstand. At first, it was the bottled tincture that Emmeric gave me that caught my attention, the one that would suspend my curse for a few moments. Then I saw the folded note beside it, and I collapsed onto my bed.

It was time—time to read whatever Marissa had left me. She left it at my feet the night of the dance, right before she killed Ariyon. She told me to come find her, that there was more I needed to know or something of that sort. Reaching inside the drawer, I pulled out the note and opened it. As expected, a small map fell out onto my lap. I had wondered if it would be a map because of what she had said about finding her. I studied it. There was a red circle on the eastern part of the realm, between Willow Groove and Sterling Reach.

Turning away from the map, I flattened the letter, smoothing the creases of the vanilla-colored parchment. Marissa's handwriting was neater than I thought it would be. Steeling myself, Yanric looking over my shoulder, I began to read.

Fallon,

Your entire history is a lie. The Bane family, once respectable members of the House of War and Bone, were experimented on with dark magic. Our natural magic was corrupted, and they turned us into what we are now, the House of Ash and Shadow, the most powerful magical beings in the entire realm. When we displayed these newfound, awe-inspiring powers, they began to regret their mistake and tried to purge us from existence. They took our homes, our money, and our status, all because they feared our power. They took our chance at the crown, something owed to us by birthright.

I paused, looking over at Yanric. *'I know all of this. I don't care.'* Marissa wanted revenge and the crown. I understood that, but I didn't want those things. What was done was done, and there was no changing that.

Yanric went eerily still then, eyes widening. *'Keep reading,'* he said.

My eyes flicked back to the page.

I expected them all to turn against me once I came into my power, but not him, not Clarke. I loved your father. He was the only fae I ever gave my trust to, and he betrayed me.

I gasped, my hands shaking as I read the words *Clarke* and *your father* in the same sentence.

No. No way. It couldn't be. But even as I tried to convince myself of that, memories of Clarke and how much he tried to help me and keep me alive every time the queen tried to hurt me sprang forth in my mind. With my heart pounding in my throat, I read the rest.

You, Fallon, were the only good thing to come out of that short-lived relationship, and on the day I birthed you, I thought I would trust him one last time. I sent a messenger to fetch Clarke so that he could meet you. I thought that a father would want to see his own daughter, cursed or not. When he arrived, he tricked me. He stole you and left you at the gates of that magicless town to live alone all these years, without proper training for your power. Had I known you were in Isariah this entire time, I would have come for you sooner.

I've enclosed a map that leads to our city. Please don't share it with anyone. I would hate to have to hurt your friends or anyone else who comes poking around here uninvited. Come find me. I can show you how to truly use your magic.

Marissa

Clarke. Clarke stole me from Marissa and left me at the gates of Isariah? Shock flooded my system, but it was almost immediately flushed out by anger, and in that moment, it felt so good to feel anything at all that I latched on to it.

He left a defenseless, cursed child at the gates of a magicless town and then never checked on me!

The bastard. The rotten, cold-hearted bastard!

Fire sprouted from the tops of my hands, and I yelped, dropping the letter. I shook my hands to make them go out before they burned something. I needed to get out of here. Grabbing the letter and map, I folded them and shoved them in my pocket. Hefting the bag and with Yanric still on my shoulder, I snuck down the staircase and tiptoed past the kitchen, where Daniella was humming softly to herself as she baked what smelled of apple pie. Benjamin was nowhere to be found, thankfully, so I slipped out the front door and walked over to where I'd left Ranger tied up.

After tying the pack on his back, I hefted a leg over the horse and rode out the front gates quickly. I knew that Mrs. Bardot would sound the alarm about what happened to Blair. The queen would send Royal Guards here to lock me down, and my father would insist on continuing to live with me. I had to get out of the city as soon as possible.

I pulled up the hood of my traveling cloak and asked Yanric to fly above me so he wouldn't attract more attention; I was the only one who rode around town with a bird on my shoulder. The main gates to The Gilded City were open in the daytime, though I had never tried to leave. I had seen guards regularly talking to people as they came or left. Maybe they were asking for ID, maybe they were just telling them to have a nice trip. Either way, I was about to find out. I'd fight my way out if I had to, but I didn't want to draw attention. I just wanted to be far away from everyone I loved when I went fully dark.

I'm ready to create a distraction if needed,' Yanric said from somewhere above me.

I nodded under my hood as I sidled my horse into the short exit line, next to a man in a cart full of supplies that seemed to be for trading. There were furs, tapestries, and some hand-painted crafts.

The guards up ahead spoke to a woman who was on foot, and I was close enough to hear.

"Where are you headed?" one of the guards asked her.

She held up her basket. "To go wild apple picking. They make the best cider."

The guard nodded. "Indeed, they do. Return before curfew

or the gates will be closed."

She nodded and walked out the opening.

Okay, so she didn't need papers or ID, just a good excuse.

Peering at the man who sat beside me, I dug into my pocket and pulled out three coppers. It was a decent amount of money, part of what I had brought to stay at an inn, but I was okay sleeping under the stars so long as I made it out of here.

"Psst." I caught his attention. "Say I am traveling with you, and these three coppers are yours. I'm going to see my boyfriend in Isariah," I lied.

I reached out my gloved hand to him as he turned to look at me.

His brows drew together suspiciously, but when he saw the coppers in my hand, he took them without a word.

When it was our turn, the guard walked over to look in the back of the man's cart before coming to speak to him. I sat beside him on Ranger with my head low. I'd pulled off the flame-emblem saddle blanket he usually wore that signified him as a royal war horse.

'Ready for diversion if needed,' Yanric said again, and my gaze flicked up to the sky to see him circling above.

'Just wait,' I told him.

This might work. This had to work.

"Where you headed?" the guard with blond hair asked.

The man riding the cart pointed to me. "Me and my companion are going to Moons Reach to attend the traders' festival."

The guard directed his gaze at me, and I nodded, giving a tight smile, hoping only the bottom half of my face was visible. He stared at me for an uncomfortable amount of time. My heart hammered in my chest as I felt my power rise without my pulling for it.

"I hope you make lots of coin. Safe travels," the guard said, and he stepped out of the way.

I released a shaky breath and kicked Ranger hard, and he took off at a quick trot. He rushed through the gates, and the man with the cart trailed behind me.

"Thank you!" I tossed the words over my shoulder at the man as I broke into a gallop, careening toward the thick, dense forest, off the well-worn path that led south. I would ride alone, in the woods and out of the way of people.

Yanric swooped from the sky and came to rest on my shoulder as I slowed Ranger to a slow trot. I had no idea where I was going. I couldn't go to Isariah; my father was right in it being the first place they would look, and everyone I loved there was at risk of being hurt. I needed to be as far away from people as possible. The trees were so thick, poor Ranger had to weave in and out of them as I led him southeast without a solid idea of where to go. Maybe it was best to ride until dark, make camp for the night, and figure it out in the morning.

'We could go to Marissa's little Nightling city in the map that she left,' Yanric offered.

I scowled. 'Are you insane? She's still evil, even if they lied to her. She still did awful things.'

Yanric nodded. 'But what if those things were accidents, like with Blair? What if she really can help you control your power like she said in the letter? Besides, if we are around a bunch of Nightlings, it won't matter if anyone gets hurt.'

He made a fair point, but I still didn't 100 percent believe the letter. Master Clarke was my father? That was impossible!

I'd spent hours with him. He had said Marissa was evil from the moment he met her. He wouldn't have fallen in love with her, bedded her. Would he have?

'Marissa said she would teach me how to use my power, not control it,' I corrected Yanric, and he went silent.

"Fallon!" a familiar voice shouted through the trees, and I pulled Ranger to a stop, my eyes going wide.

As if I conjured him by mere thought, Master Clarke rode up beside me. He was panting, hair a mess, and peering at me with a wild gaze.

"I know about what happened with Blair. We can work on this together. Please don't run away like Marissa did," he begged.

I glared at him, chest heaving as I tried to control myself.

"Are you my father?" I blurted out, unable to find an eloquent way of asking such a thing.

He nodded, and the look of guilt that washed over his features sent a tidal wave of anger rushing through me. I had to bite the inside of my cheek to keep from killing him where he stood. Ranger whined, shifting a little as if he felt my anger and was ready to bolt.

"Are you kidding me!" I roared. "All those times we spoke, you never found a good moment to tell me that you were the one who fell in love with Marissa? That you bedded her and are my real father?"

Real father felt like an insult to my actual father, the one who raised me and would never lie to me, but I wasn't very good with words right now.

He swallowed hard, reaching out his hands. "Let's sit and talk, Fallon. I will explain everything." He gestured to a flat rock, but I just scowled at him, ignoring his request as I stayed mounted on my horse.

"You liar! You said she was evil from the moment you met her, no remorse, no friends—"

"She was!" he yelled back, cutting me off. "She was, and I thought I could fix her. I thought if I flirted with her a little or made her feel loved, then she might turn good and see reason." His face sagged with the admission, and I shook my head, my stomach turning sour.

"You tricked her? You made her think you liked her, slept with her, and then dumped her? That's sick."

He shook his head. "No. That wasn't how it happened, Fallon. She...seduced me. I never meant to...let it go that far." He stopped speaking and stared at his hands. "I made a mistake, okay? I was trying to save her from herself. I didn't know she would fall in love with me after only one date. It was a sick, sadistic, jealous love where if I didn't do as she liked, she would hurt people."

I knew the words he was saying required an emotional response from me and that maybe I should even feel empathetic toward him, but I couldn't. Inside me was just a cavern of numbness mixed with swirls of wrath.

"So, after I was born, Marissa asked you to come see me, and you stole me from her? You are the one that put me at the gates of Isariah? An innocent child?" I demanded. This was quite possibly the most important part to me, the one I cared about most.

Tears filled his eyes now, and he peered up at me, nodding. "Yes, because the second Solana found out Marissa had a baby, she wanted you found and killed. I did it to save you, Fallon. I waited in the woods all night until your father, Jeremy, came and picked you up. I—"

I screamed then, loud, haunting, and right in his face. Hot, burning fire ripped along my spine as the numbness retreated and was replaced with an unyielding fury. This wasn't me—I didn't get mad like this. It was as if the magic was taking over my body and acting without my will, just like Solana and the others said it would.

A stream of purple fire ripped through the trees then, catching half a dozen of them alight. At the sight of my uncontainable power, I was overwhelmed and burst into sobs.

"Leave now," I told him, crying uncontrollably, no longer able to reign in my emotions or power. "I'm going dark. You were right. Everyone was right."

More fire ripped through the woods, and I realized it was too late. I couldn't stop it. I couldn't keep the anger and magic from spewing out of me.

Instead of looking fearful, Clarke simply nodded, reached out, and grasped his hands lightly around my exposed throat.

My eyes bugged as my curse ignited, and pain shot up my spine to take up residence inside my entire body. Clarke's telekinetic power wrapped around my arms and pinned them to my sides, leaving me helpless. I jerked with a spasm, but he held on tighter. His face was full of compassion, sorrow, but not anger. I was so confused about what was going on. Why would he do this?

But I couldn't care. I was lost in my own abyss of uncontrollable emotions.

Rage. Numbness. Pain. Darkness.

Yanric dove for him, but Clarke used his power to pin my bird midair. Unseen bands of telekinetic energy kept Yanric flapping there, unable to move.

Blackness danced at the edges of my vision. He wasn't letting go, but he wasn't trying to strangle me either. I could still breathe.

"Why?" I croaked, tears running down my cheeks and over his fingers that held me.

"When you get angry, your magic is uncontrollable. I'm going to hold you until you pass out so you don't burn down the entire woods. And then when you wake, we will work out a plan to control this. I will *not* let you go dark, Fallon Bane. On my honor," Clarke declared, patiently holding on to my skin as the pain threatened to eat me alive.

Light, help me, I prayed.

Tears spilled from the corners of my eyes, and for a split second, a shred of light splintered into my soul, and I nodded.

Then the darkness took me.

ACKNOWLEDGMENTS

A huge thank-you to the entire team at Bloom Books (especially Christa and Gretchen) for their hard work on this series. Also, to my agents Flavia and Meire at Bookcase Literary for your steadfast handholding, you're the best. To my husband and children who always have to share me with my wild imagination, I love you all endlessly. And lastly, to my amazing readers who allow me to call what I do a "job," though it's never felt that way.

ABOUT THE AUTHOR

Leia Stone is the *USA Today* bestselling author of multiple bestselling series including Matefinder, Wolf Girl, Fallen Academy, and Kings of Avalier. She's sold over three million books and her Fallen Academy series has been optioned for film. Her novels have been translated into five languages and she even dabbles in script writing. Leia writes urban fantasy and paranormal romance with sassy kick-butt heroines and irresistible love interests. She lives in Spokane, Washington, with her husband and two children.

Instagram: @leiastoneauthor
TikTok: @leiastone
Facebook: leia.stone

See yourself *in* Bloom

every story is a
celebration.

Visit **bloombooks.com**
for more information about

LEIA STONE

and more of your favorite authors!

 bloombooks   @read_bloom   read_bloom

Bloom *books*